A Bad
Reputation

Books by Jane Tesh

The Grace Street Mysteries
Stolen Hearts
Mixed Signals
Now You See It

The Madeline Maclin Mysteries
A Case of Imagination
A Hard Bargain
A Little Learning
A Bad Reputation

A Bad Reputation

Reputation

A Madeline Maclin Mystery

Jane Tesh

Poisoned Pen Press

Poisoned Pen Press
6962 E. First Ave., Ste. 103
Scottsdale, AZ 85251
www.poisonedpenpress.com
info@poisonedpenpress.com

Printed in the United States of America

To my dearest friend, Mark Gillespie,
who has quite a reputation, but not a bad one.

Willow, where we met together.
Willow, when our love was new.
Willow, if he once should be returning,
Pray tell him I am weeping too.

From *The Ballad of Baby Doe*
by Douglas Moore and John Latouche

Chapter One

You could say that winning a beauty pageant and solving a murder have some similarities. In a pageant, you're competing to beat the other contestants. In a murder investigation, you're competing against a killer to bring him or her to justice. You work hard to achieve a goal, and in the end, you've got a crown or a criminal.

Emotionally, however, when someone is killed, you have to deal with something far more serious than a rival queen or a broken zipper. Seeing a dead body, even if it's someone you don't know, is disturbing no matter how many times it happens. And this has happened more times than it should. Like right now. A body stretched out at my feet in the evening light…

It wasn't supposed to be like this.

When my husband, Jerry Fairweather, inherited his eccentric Uncle Val's old house in the small town of Celosia, North Carolina, and we moved from the much larger city of Parkland, I'd taken a big leap of faith, followed my dream, and opened a private investigation service. I thought I'd be finding lost objects, or at worst, trailing unfaithful spouses. And I did have cases like that, looking for lost umbrellas, tracking down overdue library books, and hunting through attics to solve elaborate riddles. But Celosia, like most small towns, was full of secrets and family feuds and long-held grudges. Really long.

Now, most police departments don't want amateur sleuths getting in the way, but I was fortunate to make friends with Chief Gus Brenner. He appreciates the fact that I'm able to see things from an outsider's perspective, and as long as I share my findings, he's willing to let me poke around. I don't have access to his crime lab or his network of contacts, but I have my own resources. I tend to find little things that are overlooked—things that, at first, don't appear to be clues.

But Jerry was still figuring out what to do with his life and needed plenty of things to keep him occupied. Gus' daughter, Nell Brenner, our resident handywoman, didn't want him helping her with home repairs because he was always tripping over ladders and tracking paint everywhere. He'd worked for a while as a salesclerk at Georgia's Books, but Georgia didn't need him except on the occasional weekend. I was concerned that all this inactivity would lead to a rebound into his shadier world of fake séances and cons. In fact, I knew it would.

Jerry and I met in college and had been best friends for years before he realized that he was in love with me. We had worked through most of our emotional baggage—mine from being hauled around to Little Miss pageants from the time I could sit up, and his from a mistaken belief that he'd been responsible for the fire that killed his parents. I'd solved that mystery, so he had closure, and my success as a private investigator had proven to me that I was more than a pretty face in an overly sequined gown. Thanks to Jerry's insistence, I'd taken up painting again, something I'd always loved and needed to rediscover.

However…Jerry comes from a very wealthy family and never had to work. Add that to his past feelings of unworthiness, a mischievous nature, and an open, trustworthy face, and you have the perfect con man. For about three years after we graduated, I lost track of him, hearing from him only occasionally. What he did during that time has kept coming back to haunt us.

He also had a great deal of musical talent. I kept trying to steer him toward jobs that took advantage of that. I may have given up all the pageant nonsense, but I was still competitive. I was going to reform him if it killed us both.

Jerry and I have problems and differences to sort out, but our little troubles can't compare with the labyrinth of tangled relationships and emotions I uncovered in my new hometown. That web soon led me here, into another betrayal and murder.

Chapter Two

"Camp Lakenwood! Camp Lakenwood!
Each day is bright and new!
Camp Lakenwood! Camp Lakenwood!
There's fun for me and you!"

I groaned and buried my head under my pillow. "Jerry, for heaven's sake."

As was his custom, my husband had gotten up bright and early this Monday morning and decided to serenade me, not with his usual attempt at an aria, but with Camp Lakenwood's theme song. He'd already showered and dressed and was toweling his light brown hair.

"You have to sing it at the top of your voice to really make it work," he said.

"Not every morning."

Last month, I'd helped Nathan Fenton solve his uncle's riddle and win enough money to buy and renovate Camp Lakenwood. Nathan had asked Jerry to help out, and since Jerry has always been in touch with his inner child, this was an ideal job for him. I couldn't wait to see him in his camp t-shirt and shorts. However, the camp wouldn't be open until next June. This was October.

Jerry tossed the towel in the general direction of the bathroom. "Waffles for breakfast?"

I had hoped for a few more minutes of sleep, but this was not going to happen. "Okay."

Jerry bounded down the stairs, still singing.

"Camp Lakenwood, Camp Lakenwood,
Where waffles grow on trees!
Camp Lakenwood, Camp Lakenwood,
There's syrup in the breeze!"

By the time I staggered down to breakfast, he had orange juice, melted butter, and warm syrup on the table and was mixing his trademark batter. The kitchen stretched wide across the back of the house and hadn't needed a lot of repair. Jerry's Uncle Val had surprisingly modern appliances, all in good working order. We decided not to replace the old-fashioned square white wooden table with four matching hand-carved chairs to add a little retro charm. The chairs with curved backs were solid and sturdy, so I bought blue-and-white striped cushions to soften the look. Nell had pulled up the ancient curling linoleum and put down a shiny white floor decorated with blue willow leaves. I'd replaced the faded white curtains with new ruffly ones that reminded me of the freshly starched lace in my grandmother's windows. The view outside the kitchen windows showed a field bursting with a colorful mix of wildflowers, and trees bright with red and yellow autumn leaves. The field, like the meadow in front of the house, stretched to a wooded area that belonged to the farm next door, and occasionally we'd see deer at the edge of the wood or rabbits bounding in the tall grass. The whole space was calm and peaceful—a changing scene I'd grown to love.

When we'd first moved to the old house, I hadn't been impressed. It was a huge, two-story rambling structure, basically an old gray farmhouse, with a flat front and a wraparound porch. Quite frankly, it looked seriously haunted. It needed a lot of work, but Nell was up to the challenge, saying she'd always wanted to get her hands on the Eberlin House. The kitchen, living room, and two of the five bedrooms were now done, plus two of the three bathrooms. I'd created my art studio, and Jerry had designed and filled his music room. I was especially pleased with the living room, once a gray stuffy room crowded with heavy-footed dark furniture. The space had been transformed into a relaxing refuge in light blue, with a curved white sectional sofa sprinkled with cushions in shades of aqua and midnight, glass end tables, a glass square for a coffee table, an entertainment center along one wall, and a rebuilt carved mantel. My best painting, *Blue Moon Garden*, commanded center stage above the fireplace.

Thanks to all the renovations, the house was now our home. Celosia—the town name came from a little feathery flower—was becoming home, too, with a surprising number of cases for me to investigate.

Celosia-proper had about eight thousand residents, but if you counted the outlying areas, the few suburbs and farms, the number was closer to ten thousand. Not a huge population, really, when compared to the two hundred and fifty thousand who lived in the nearby city of Parkland, but I was amazed by the things that went on in our small town. It didn't take much to set people off. I'd even solved a murder involving Miss Celosia Pageant contestants.

"How many waffles do you want, Mac?"

"Just one, thanks." My stomach felt a little queasy. I wondered if I was coming down with something.

Jerry poured the batter into the waffle iron. "Anything happening at Madeline Maclin Investigations today?"

"Things are pretty slow."

"No lost dogs or cheatin' husbands?"

"Nope. Not yet. Did you check on our tires?" Our Mazda needed two new tires, and Jerry had promised to call around for the best deal.

"Fred's Garage has some we can afford."

"Okay, we can get that done this week."

He brought me a cup of coffee and said, "I thought I might call some friends today and see what's going on."

"What kind of friends and what kind of goings-on?" Jerry likes to wear flashy ties, and today's choice was a tie decorated with green dollar bills. I wasn't sure I liked the significance of that.

"Oh, I don't know…the usual."

At one time, "the usual" meant scamming people out of their hard-earned cash. I sincerely hoped Jerry wasn't backsliding. He'd promised he was through with the illegal part of his life, but his so-called friends had a way of pulling him under.

"Please tell me you are not involved in something shady."

"Nothing shady. I just like to keep up with what's new."

"New, as in the latest tricks?" I sipped the coffee, wondering why it didn't taste as good as it usually did. "See, here is where we are radically different. I have absolutely no interest in what's going on in the pageant world. Can the allure of Con World be that strong?"

"It's a nice place to visit, but I no longer live there."

"Yes, but you keep getting postcards saying 'Wish you were here.'"

He checked the waffle. "I haven't heard from anyone in a while."

"Sometimes they just show up, like Rick." Rick, one of Jerry's ex-partners in crime, had invaded Celosia not long ago to take full advantage of the Mantis Man mania, even dressing up as the legendary creature and causing all kinds of havoc—that is, until he became a murder suspect.

"Ah, but once you cleared him, he became a model citizen."

"Until he moved on to the next unsuspecting town."

"My friends know better than to mess with you." Jerry opened the waffle iron to check again just as his cell phone rang. He answered. "Hello? Oh, hello, Evan."

Evan James was the director of the Celosia Community Theater. Please let there be a job for Jerry, I prayed. A music job. He'd played for the theater's production of *The Music Man* and really enjoyed it. Plus those long rehearsals took up a lot of his time.

"Sure," Jerry said, "but I thought Larissa was doing that." He listened awhile and then said, "Yeah, I'll have a look at it. No problem. Okay, see you." He hung up. "Evan says Larissa

Norton is sick and can't play for *Oklahoma*. He wants to know if I'd do it."

Thank you, Lord. "Sounds like fun."

"And it's a paying gig."

"Even better."

"So I won't have time to con anyone today."

He said this lightly, but I didn't want him to think I didn't trust him. "You know I love you, even when you are in the middle of some idiotic scheme."

"And I know that my track record isn't the best, so you have every right to be suspicious. Can you drop me off at the theater on your way to work?"

"You bet."

He lifted the lid of the waffle iron. The waffle met with his approval because he pried it free and plopped it on a plate. "Here you go."

All of a sudden, waffles did not sound appealing. "I don't think I want one, after all."

"You sure?"

"I'm not very hungry this morning. I hope I'm not getting the flu."

"Would you rather have scrambled eggs?"

Ugh. I must have made a convincing face.

"Okay, just coffee," Jerry said. "I can always eat another waffle."

My stomach rumbled, so I knew I was hungry. I loved waffles, but what I really wanted was some ice cream. "Do we have any ice cream?"

"I don't think so."

"Some Chunky Monkey would taste good."

"For breakfast? I mean, I'm all for it, but you usually want the standards. Hold on." He turned from his cooking, his gray eyes wide. "Do you want a pickle with that?"

"A pickle? No. Why would I want a—" I suddenly knew where he was going with this. "Oh, no. I am not pregnant."

"Are you sure?"

"I'm more than sure. It's probably just a stomach virus."

"Virus Fairweather. It's an odd name, but then again, this is the South."

I had to grin. "Stop it. We've discussed this. We are not having a baby."

"Okay."

He wanted children. Bill, my first husband, had wanted children, too, and now thanks to his second wife, had a whole pack of them, but with Bill it had been a matter of proving his manhood. Jerry had far better reasons for wanting to be a father: He wanted to make up for his interrupted childhood. I simply wasn't ready, and didn't know if I ever would be, although lately I'd found myself leaning a little more toward the idea. It was not something I spent a lot of time thinking about. Actually, I spent a lot of time trying *not* to think about it. I wasn't sure what was holding me back. It certainly wasn't Jerry, who looked at me with a mixture of humor and concern.

"How about a banana?" he asked. "That's as close to Chunky Monkey as I can get."

Actually, a banana sounded good. "Thanks." What I really meant was thanks for dropping the subject, and he knew it.

As promised, and with a great sense of relief, I took Jerry by the theater. Celosia's community theater is in the Samuel Baker Auditorium, a substantial brick building a wealthy man had donated to the city years ago. Crouched in the midst of ancient oak trees, the building resembles an old high school, but inside, the auditorium is a modern, spacious room with walls in muted shades of gray and four hundred comfortable seats with red cushions. Jerry went in through the double glass doors at the front, pausing to give me a good-bye wave.

Then I drove the short distance to my office on Main Street. Most of Celosia's main street looks the same as it did in the late 1930s: the banks and churches made of granite blocks, the storefronts mostly brick. Trees surrounded by small gardens stand on each corner. The street lamps date back to the 1880s, and the ornate brass clock by the post office always chimes the wrong time. My office is in one of the brick buildings at the end of the street next to a parking lot. Pamela Finch was waiting outside my door. I hoped she had a case for me, but she was excited about something else.

"Madeline, I knew you'd want to hear about this. Wendall Clarke is coming back to town, and he wants to open an art gallery! Isn't that exciting? I told him you'd be glad to help."

"Hold on, hold on," I said. "Help with what?"

Pamela Finch was tall and thin with light wispy hair. Her hair was just as excited as she was. "Well, with setting it up and running it and all that. Since you're an artist, I figured you'd want to."

"I'm sure Mr. Clarke can handle things on his own." I unlocked my door and invited Pamela to come into my office and sit down. My office is small, but it's all mine and has a pleasant view of the swing set in the yard next door. The walls are paneled in golden pine, and the carpet is new, an odd beige color I wouldn't have chosen, but it was neutral enough not to clash with anything. The dark-brown desk and olive swivel chair had belonged to the former occupant—again, not very stylish, but new and serviceable. I'd brightened up a tall bookcase by the window with books, photographs of Jerry and me in colorful frames, some topaz and emerald glass fish I'd bought in Bermuda when we were there for our wedding, a paperweight filled with pink and blue flowers, a frog my grandmother had made of multicolor patchwork fabric, and two of my smaller paintings. One was of the Queen Anne's lace in our meadow. The other was an abstract in swirls of brown, yellow, and turquoise that Jerry had titled *Fudge Ripple Gone Horribly Wrong*.

I sat down behind the desk, wondering why Pamela thought I'd like to run a gallery. When I rediscovered my love of painting, I enjoyed spending whatever time I could in my studio, a remodeled upstairs parlor at our house, but I wasn't interested in the business side of the art world and certainly didn't feel qualified.

Pamela took a seat in the green and beige client armchair, another legacy, and chatted on about Wendall Clarke, Celosia High School's former star football player and editor of the yearbook. He'd gone to Parkland to pursue an art degree, majored in art and business, and made a fortune when one of his designs was chosen for a perfume bottle that sold well on a shopping network. "But he's always wanted to have a gallery."

"Why not have one in Parkland?"

"I don't know, but I'm absolutely thrilled. I so hope he'll put some of my work in his gallery."

This was news. "I didn't know you were an artist. What do you do?"

"I paint wildflowers, mostly. I'd love for you to see! Come over any time. I live on Beech Street."

"Well, I'm very happy for Wendall and hope his gallery succeeds," I said. "Was there something else I could do for you?"

"Oh, yes. I almost forgot! I've lost a very important letter. I think I know where it is, but it's going to take forever to sort through all the papers in my shop to find it. Do you do things like that?"

At this point, I was willing to take any job. "I'd be happy to. When would you like me to start?"

"Right away."

Pamela Finch owned a little dress shop on Main Street. "Why don't I come by this afternoon?"

"That would be fine." I told her my fee, and she wrote me a check. "And at three o'clock, we're having a reception for Wendall at First Baptist. You have to come meet him."

"If my schedule permits..." That was a laugh. My schedule permitted just about anything. But I had to admit I was curious about Wendall Clarke.

My issue with breakfast must have been a fluke, because by eleven o'clock I was seriously hungry for a cheeseburger and fries. I called Jerry and asked if he was ready for lunch.

"I am always ready for lunch."

He was waiting for me in front of the theater. He got into the car and showed me the large book of music.

"So you're going to do it?"

"I'll be practicing for the rest of my life, but yes. It's a pretty tough score."

I glanced through the pages crammed with masses of notes. Jerry liked to joke that he lived in the musical shadow of his older brother, Des, a concert pianist, but I think Jerry is equally talented. "Looks like a challenge," I said.

"I may have to do a little modifying. Oh, I'm officially musical director. Evan wants me to round up some more musicians for the orchestra. I have a list of names to call."

This sounded more and more like a really good, safe, involved job. "How about a cheeseburger to celebrate?"

"With or without pickles?"

I punched his arm. "Don't start."

Our favorite place to eat in Celosia is a little diner called Deely's Burger World, always a popular hangout, first as an ice cream parlor and then as the quaint restaurant it is today. The diner still has its original gray-and-white Formica countertops, silver stools with red cushions that had been replaced many times, and wallpaper with faded designs of ancient slogans for Coca-Cola. We were way ahead of the noon rush and chose a booth near the front. As more people streamed in, I caught bits of discussion about Camp Lakenwood, auditions for *Oklahoma*, and the proposed gallery. True to form, people were already arguing about who would be the best leads in the show, and fussing over what the gallery would cost.

The talk that struck us was news about Deely's closing.

"Had you heard anything about the restaurant closing?" I asked Jerry.

"No. I'd hate for that to happen. Let's ask Annie."

When Annie stopped by our table to take our order, I said, "What's this about Deely closing the place? That's just a local Celosian rumor, right?"

"It's an old story going around. Deely's been threatening to retire for years. He's waiting for one of his sons to take over, and that could be a while because they'd sooner die than flip burgers. I'm pretty sure I've got job security."

"That's a relief," Jerry said. "I couldn't go on without my cheeseburgers."

"Coming right up."

I told Jerry about Pamela Finch. "She's lost an important letter. I'm going to stop by her store this afternoon and help her look for it. She was much more interested in a fellow named Wendall Clarke who wants to open an art gallery in town. She thought I'd want in on the action."

"Do you?"

"Not really. But I do want to meet him. There's a reception for him today at three."

Annie brought our order, and we enjoyed happy moments in cheeseburger heaven. Then she returned to ask if we wanted more fries.

"Of course," Jerry said.

"Oh, and Jerry, I wanted to ask you something else. I'm trying to decide between these two guys, and I know you can get in touch with the dead. I want to check in with my Aunt Gloria, because she'd give me good dating advice. Are you still holding those séances at your house? Can I get in on the next one?"

Even though he really wanted to say yes to both questions, he managed to say, "Sorry. I'm out of the séance business."

"Couldn't you do just one more?"

"I'm sure you can get good dating advice from someone more qualified."

"Nobody's more qualified than Aunt Gloria. She was married six times. How about holding one here after hours? I'll ask Deely if it's okay."

"Sure." He folded, and I kicked him under the table.

"Ow! Mac, the deal was no more séances at the house."

"Annie, Jerry can't really talk to the dead."

She wasn't discouraged. "But the dead might talk to him." A little bell chimed from the kitchen. "Fries coming up."

As she walked away, I gave my husband the eye. "The dead are not going to talk to you."

"One more little séance. I won't charge her for it."

"You're driving me crazy. What can I do to make you stop this?" The minute I said this, I knew I'd made a mistake.

"Well, now that you mention it, perhaps a little deal could be made."

Uh, oh. "What do you mean?"

He reached across the table to take my hand. "Will you consider—just consider—the possibility of us becoming parents?"

I sucked in a deep breath. "You know how I feel about this."

"Just consider it. Think about it."

Here's what I thought. "We're barely making enough money for the two of us. If you hadn't accepted your brother's generous birthday gift, we couldn't pay Nell for all the repairs."

Jerry was notorious for refusing any of his family's fortune. Somehow his younger brother, Tucker, had convinced him to take some money for the house. "That's true. And I would accept another generous gift for a new little Fairweather. But let me take back what I said about a deal. I don't want you to think this is like our last bargain."

In our last deal, Jerry had agreed to find a job if I agreed to take up my artwork again. This had been a slightly one-sided bargain because the jobs he'd found had fallen through.

"We're getting along great right now, but maybe we could make some plans for the future. You've got your agency, and I'm going to find a real job, I promise."

"I know you will. Look." I gave his hand a squeeze. "I don't want you to think I'm trying to manage your life."

He grinned. "Well, you are."

"Well, you're letting me."

"Maybe I like strong women."

"Hush."

"Strong controlling women who want to rule the world."

I tightened my grip. "When I'm queen, you'd better look out."

"I thought you were already queen, Miss Parkland."

Jerry's about the only one who can get away with calling me Miss Parkland. "Yes, during my reign I learned many important lessons about controlling the masses. You should fear my wrath."

"That's okay," he said. "I know how to stage a coup."

Annie plopped another basket of fries on the table. "There you go, Jerry. Deely says it's okay to have the séance here, but he'd rather you do it in the back room. We can do it after he closes tonight if you like."

He hadn't taken his gaze from me. "It's up to Mac."

"You promise..." I said, "you swear on your weighted dice and marked cards that this is absolutely the last séance ever?"

He smiled the smile that had charmed me from the very first moment I met him. "I promise."

Chapter Three

As much as I would've liked to have spent the rest of the day with Jerry, I had a job to do. I gave him a ride back home so he could start learning the *Oklahoma* music while I returned to town. On the way I thought about what he'd said. I didn't mind being referred to as a strong woman, but did I really want to rule the world? After spending my younger years under my ambitious mother's thumb and following her rules for pageant success, I liked being in charge of my own little world, running my agency the way I wanted, setting my hours, having the freedom to do as I pleased. Of course, as Miss Parkland, I had ample opportunities to speak my mind, but I was always working with other people's schedules. Now I appreciated the luxury of being in control. Maybe the real reason I was reluctant to have a baby was that it would upset my neatly ordered life.

Something to think about.

Flair For Fashion, Pamela Finch's dress shop, was located on a charming stretch of Main Street. It was one of several artsy little boutiques with rich green awnings and large planters filled with fall chrysanthemums—antique gold and crisp yellow—accompanied by pansies in watercolor shades Monet would have loved: blue, lavender, white, and velvety purple. Since Celosia was only thirty minutes from Parkland, these businesses did very well, especially the novelty candle shop and the local crafts store with its array of homemade jams, jellies, honey, and quilts. Flair

For Fashion was an upscale establishment, the kind my mother would love, offering overpriced clothes, jewelry, and purses. The windows displayed sleek outfits on faceless mannequins admiring themselves in fancy oval mirrors.

Pamela met me at the door. "Thanks for coming, Madeline. Let me show you the problem."

Stepping inside was like walking into a movie star's oversized closet, all shiny floor and lighted mirrors. The jewelry was sorted by color on small tables draped with silky cloths, and the purses hung from curly gold hooks. As I passed by, I glanced at a few price tags and wondered who in Celosia could afford these things. Dresses and scarves were hung on matching hangers padded with contrasting colors. Another mannequin stood with arms on hips, its outfit a tight leather skirt and cream-colored silk blouse. It looked oddly defiant, as if to say: Buy this if you dare!

Pamela was dressed in similar style: a snug green leather skirt and matching sweater. Her metallic bronze high heels clicked on the gleaming floor as she led me to the back of the store and opened the door of a room packed with bulging file boxes and untidy stacks of paper. "See what I mean? I know that letter's in here somewhere."

The room looked like a real closet—a hoarder's closet. I wasn't sure where to start. "Have you checked any of these file boxes or stacks?"

"I've been through that one," she said, pointing to a gray three-drawer file cabinet. "I've been trying to do a little every day, but the phone's always ringing, and I have customers to take care of. It's just overwhelming."

"Okay, what am I looking for?"

"It's a one-page letter from Daniel Richards. He used to own this building, and now his son, Daniel Junior, is the owner. In the letter, Daniel Senior gives me permission to make whatever changes I'd like, including expanding the shop at the back. His son won't let me do anything unless I produce this letter."

"All right." I took another look at the daunting stacks. "You're sure it's in here?"

"I can't think of any reason why that letter would be in my house, but I've searched thoroughly, just in case. It has to be in here."

"Do you have any help in the store?"

"That's another problem. I am so short-handed right now. The woman who usually helps me out is having a baby and will be gone for at least half a year. When she was here, we could take turns watching the store, but now it's just me."

I spent the next hour going through every piece of paper in one of the filing cabinets. It was slow work because Pamela had saved every receipt, every order, every packing slip, and every piece of correspondence she'd ever received.

Pamela apologized for the extra stacks. "There's a lot of Art Guild information, too, Madeline. Copies of our bylaws, minutes of our meetings, program booklets, things like that. Bea Ricter used to be our secretary, and now I am, so she gave all that stuff to me. It should all be in one filing cabinet, but there may be some stray papers in some of the stacks."

"I'll separate anything that looks like it belongs to the Guild."

When I took a break, I noticed several pictures of flowers on the walls of the shop and asked Pamela if the paintings were hers.

Her cheeks went pink. "Oh, do you like them? They're nothing compared to your work."

I'd seen hundreds, maybe thousands of paintings like these, typical, orderly still lifes of flowers in vases, flowers in pots on windowsills, flowers drooping on trellises. Nothing badly painted, but nothing remarkable either. Not like the vibrant flowers spilling out on the sidewalks, but Pamela had some talent.

"They're very good, Pamela. I like your color choices, and you have a very soft way of shading."

She let out a relieved breath. "Thank you. I work very hard on them."

"Have you had lessons, or does this just come to you naturally?"

"I've taken lots of lessons at the community college. The teachers there say I have a real flair for flowers."

"Yes, you do. Have you tried painting other things?"

"No, just flowers."

Derivative and safe. "Well, you have some fine paintings here."

"Thank you, Madeline. That means a lot coming from you. I do collages, too, but those are at home. I'd love for you to see them some time."

At three o'clock, Pamela put a sign on the door saying the store was closed for the afternoon. "One of the perks of being the owner," she winked, and we went to the fellowship hall at First Baptist Church.

First Baptist was the largest church in town, a massive cathedral of granite blocks. The fellowship hall was equally impressive, a gymnasium-size room with gold walls and plush gold carpet. No folding tables and metal chairs here. Polished wooden tables covered with gold embroidered tablecloths and matching straight-back chairs were arranged around the room, and a longer table filled with refreshments stood along one wall, sparkling with crystal and silver dishes. This was the first fellowship hall I'd ever seen with chandeliers.

As big as the room was, Wendall Clarke filled it. He was a large man with strong features and an impressive moustache, a commanding figure all in black with a black-fringed scarf around his neck. He had his arm around a young and extremely pretty blonde woman whose beautifully tailored suit and silky blouse could've come from Flair For Fashion.

"Good heavens," Pamela said. "I don't believe it."

"What?"

"Tell you later."

Wendall Clarke came toward us, his voice booming. "Ms. Maclin, such a pleasure to meet you! I saw your work at the Weyland. I adore *Blue Moon Garden*."

"Thank you very much."

"This is my wife, Flora, but everyone calls her Baby."

Whoops. I had thought the young woman was his daughter. I shook hands with Flora, who seemed shy. "Pleasure to meet you. I'm Madeline."

She nodded and smiled but didn't say anything.

Wendall turned to Pamela. "Is this Pamela Finch? How are you? It's been quite a while, hasn't it?"

Pamela's reply was polite but guarded. "Hello, Wendall."

"Have you met my wife, Flora? Baby, this is one of my old school friends, Pamela Finch."

Pamela didn't smile or shake hands. "How do you do?"

Again, the young woman just smiled.

Wendall Clarke gave the scarf a theatrical toss over his shoulder. "I suppose you've heard all about my little project. I am so excited by the prospect of bringing this facet of culture to Celosia. If there had been a gallery like this in town when I was growing up, I wouldn't have taken so long to find my true calling. I hope to inspire generations of children to love art."

"That sounds like a worthy cause, Mr. Clarke," I said.

"Oh, call me Wendall, please. It would be a real honor to have you on board, Ms. Maclin. I promise your duties will not be extreme."

"Let me think about it."

"Splendid! I'd really appreciate it." He gave his wife's shoulders a little squeeze.

"Come along, dear. I want you to meet everyone."

Her eyes got big. "Are you sure?"

"Of course! Don't worry. They'll love you."

Flora did not look convinced. I didn't have long to wonder about her reluctance.

Most of the people at the reception gave Wendall Clarke and Flora less than welcoming glances.

"What did you want to tell me?" I turned to Pamela, although I had figured most of it out.

"That's Wendall's trophy wife. Everyone knows he left his first wife for her."

"She seems really sweet, though. Did she actively pursue him?"

"Oh, yes. She left her husband for him."

"Spreading local gossip, Pamela?" came a harsh voice.

I recognized Larissa Norton. "Larissa" sounds like a lovely waif-like creature that dances in the forest, but this Larissa was a tall dark-haired woman with a firm chin and a highly annoyed expression.

I held out my hand. "I don't believe we've met. I'm Madeline Maclin Fairweather."

She eyed me with a dark unfriendly stare and did not shake my hand. "Yes, I know. Are you acquainted with Wendall Clarke?"

"We've just met."

Larissa Norton transferred her glare to Wendall. "He has some nerve coming back to Celosia and bringing that woman with him, expecting everyone to be thrilled with his plans. Clarke comes swanning into town, and everyone falls over themselves to do his bidding. I can't believe it. Celosia doesn't need an art gallery. That's sheer foolishness. It'll go under in a week, maybe less. And don't give me that sad face, Pamela. You haven't a chance in hell of showing any of your pitiful pictures in Clarke's gallery or anyone's gallery, for that matter."

Pamela flinched at this cruel remark. "I'm going to ask him anyway."

Larissa gave a derisive snort and left. Pamela watched her go and shook her head. "I'm not surprised she's so upset."

"Is she that much opposed to an art gallery in town?"

"It's not that. She's Wendall's ex-wife."

"Oh." That could sting a little.

"He became fabulously wealthy, dumped her for a younger woman, and now rolls into town with all sorts of big plans. She'll be opposed to anything he proposes."

"Understandable."

"I'd never tell her how delighted I am about the gallery," Pamela said. "I've always dreamed of having my own art show. I don't see why Wendall wouldn't help me."

"I'm sure he will. He'll need pictures for his gallery."

"As long as he doesn't put Bea Ricter's pictures in."

"Why is that?"

"Oh, she thinks she has talent. It's really sad. She does these primitive things, you know, like painting on old pieces of rotted wood. I'm surprised you haven't met her."

I found it ironic that Pamela would talk down a fellow artist after Larissa's cutting comments about her own work. "Jerry and I haven't been in Celosia very long."

"Oh, Madeline, I've just realized why Larissa was so abrupt with you. She really wanted the job at the theater."

"What job? Do you mean playing for *Oklahoma*? I thought she was sick and couldn't do it."

"She probably said that so Evan would beg her."

That explained Larissa's unfriendly stare. "Is that the sort of thing she'd do?"

"Oh, yes. I hope Jerry does such a good job that Evan hires him for all the shows. It's about time Larissa learned she can't get everything she wants."

Watching Larissa's face as Wendall paraded Flora around the room, I thought, no, she didn't get everything. I could understand her resentment, but in fact, very few of the people at the reception had welcoming expressions for Wendall and his new bride.

"Has Wendall done something else to alienate people besides marrying Flora?" I asked Pamela.

"He was always somewhat of a braggart and a show-off, always talking about how he couldn't wait to leave this pitiful little hick town and make his mark on the world. Now that he's actually done it, his attitude is going to be hard to take. Oh, there's Bea. I'll introduce you."

Bea Ricter was a small round woman, her graying hair cut in an unflattering bowl style. She was wearing a plain, dull-colored jumper over a blouse decorated with brown flowers, green striped socks, and worn red sneakers looking as if she'd just come in from weeding her vegetable garden. All that was missing was a torn straw hat.

Pamela introduced us. "Bea, have you met Madeline Maclin? Madeline, this is Bea Ricter."

Bea's handshake was firm. "Yes, I know who she is. You need to join the Celosia Art Guild, Madeline. I'm sure someone's invited you."

Pamela looked at me in surprise. "You mean you're not a member? I thought you were."

I'd actually been approached by another member of the Art Guild, but I didn't want to get involved with what appeared to be a social club. "Thanks for asking, but I'm afraid I don't have time. My agency keeps me busy."

Bea Ricter made a face. "Oh, nonsense. There can't be that much call for a detective in Celosia. We meet every month at the library. Tuesdays at ten. You should join. It's very important that we artists stick together."

Was there a polite way to refuse? "Thanks. I'll think about it."

"I'll expect to see you there. Now that Wendall Clarke is planning this gallery for us, we have to make certain it's run properly. We can't have just anybody's work in there. Some people do nothing but junk."

Pamela gave me a look as if to say, *see what I mean?* "That's up to Wendall to decide, I guess."

"Why should it be up to Wendall?"

"Well, his design was chosen for Elegant Dreams Perfume."

This was a sore point with Bea, who made a dismissive snort. "For some tacky shopping network. I'm talking about real, honest-to-goodness, taken-from-nature-and-the-earth art, not some sissy design." She eyed Clarke as if he were a dog she'd found digging holes in her garden. "Is he going to show your stuff, Pamela?"

"I haven't asked, but I'm sure he will. I would hope he'd include everyone in the Guild."

"I'd better have a word with him," Bea said.

Pamela and I watched with some apprehension as Bea crossed the room to Clarke. She poked his shoulder and started a fierce dialogue. We couldn't hear everything they said, but at one point Bea's voice carried well enough.

"You should be ashamed of yourself, Wendall Clarke! You need to do the right thing, and you know what I'm talking about."

Pamela gulped. "Oh, my goodness. I can't believe she said that."

Wendall Clarke didn't appear offended for himself or for his new wife. His voice was calm but firm, and he made certain he was heard. "Why don't we discuss that later? I'm sure we can come to some agreement." He patted her shoulder. "Come on, now. No hard feelings, eh?"

Apparently, there were some very hard feelings. They talked a little while longer, and then we heard Wendall say, "That's not going to happen."

Bea grumbled back to us. "He's got some nerve!"

"What did he say?" Pamela asked.

Bea, distracted by her argument with Wendall, muttered under her breath about how Wendall was going to be sorry.

"Wendall Clarke's never been sorry a day in his life," Pamela said, "and he's not going to be sorry if the gallery goes well. What did he say about including the Art Guild's work? Is that what he meant by 'That's not going to happen'?"

"He's the same arrogant jerk he always was."

"Or did he mean we shouldn't worry because he's not leaving anyone out?"

"Thinks I wouldn't forget what he's done."

"But the gallery—"

Bea rounded on Pamela. "Just shut up about the gallery."

"Well, excuse me."

Bea frowned and didn't say anything else, but she glared at Wendall and Flora the rest of the afternoon. Now I was curious about what Bea might do to make Wendall sorry, and what he meant by "That's not going to happen." Knowing my fellow Celosians and their tangled relationships, *something* was going to happen.

Chapter Four

Back in my office, I called the theater to speak to Evan. I asked him if Larissa Norton wanted to be musical director for the show.

"She told me she didn't want to do it," he said. "She said her health wasn't good and she wanted some time off. Actually, she left us in the lurch. If Jerry hadn't been available, I'm not sure who we could've called."

"You're absolutely sure she doesn't want the job?"

"Yes. And just between you and me, Madeline, I am very relieved. Larissa is a wonderful musician, but she can be extremely difficult to work with. At least with Jerry, I know we won't have to put up with screaming fits and hurt feelings. And he plays just as well as Larissa, maybe better."

"I don't think he's conducted an orchestra before."

"I'm sure he can handle that. The people I asked him to call have all had experience playing for musicals. They'll love him. He worked with several of them on *Music Man*. I don't think there will be any problems."

It always worries me when someone says that.

"Thanks, Evan. What happened to *How to Succeed in Business*? I thought that was the next show." *The Music Man* director had been certain Jerry had a lock on the lead role in *How to Succeed* as the conniving young man who schemed his way to the top. The director hadn't known this would have been perfect typecasting.

"We found out Parkland and Abbingdon both planned to do that show, so we changed our plans. People love *Oklahoma*. I think we could do it every year. Will we see you at tryouts tomorrow night? You'd make a convincing Laurie, or even Ado Annie."

My days on stage were over, thank goodness. "Only to drop off Jerry."

After I hung up, I had a phone call from someone I hadn't heard from in years, an old pageant pal, a veteran of the pageant wars.

"Madeline! It's a voice from the past, Miss Little Valley Princess Supreme!"

I recognized Billamena Tyson's voice right away. After all, how many times had I heard her bellow "Tomorrow" from *Annie* for her talent? "Billamena." Isn't that name sad? Her mother had wanted something original. "Billie, where in the world have you been hiding? It must be ten years since I saw you last."

"It took me that long to pry my mother off my arm! I had to beat her over the head with my tiara to make her let go." Billie's raucous laugh made me hold the phone away from my ear. She'd been a large, aggressive little girl whose mother, like mine, had insisted she be in pageants. Billie had enjoyed the experience as much as I did.

"At least you and your mother are close. Mine hardly speaks to me."

"I wish mine didn't! Do you know she's still after me to be Mrs. America? I have purposely put on fifty pounds to save myself. But I hear you've truly broken the mold and become an investigator! How exciting!"

"Thanks. And what are you up to these days?"

"Nothing so bold. I married a great guy, second marriage for both of us, no kids yet, and I work as a secretary at an insurance firm. But I didn't call to talk about the good old days of way too much makeup on our poor little baby faces. I hear you married Jerry Fairweather."

"Yes, I did."

"Congratulations! And is he still doing those little games of his?"

I thought of the scheduled séance at Deely's and tried not to sigh. "Unfortunately, yes."

"Oh, but that's good news, Madeline, because I need his help."

What could she possibly need Jerry's help for? I was afraid to ask. "Do you need to speak to the dearly departed?"

"What?"

"Jerry holds fake séances—did hold fake séances. His very last one is tonight if you want to get in on it."

"No, not that. My husband and I were conned, and I want Jerry to find the people who did it. Or maybe you could find them! Let me hire you."

"I'd be happy to let you hire me, Billie, but I'd need to have all the details. Where are you? Can we meet somewhere?"

"I live on the other side of Parkland on Pumpkin Lane. Do you know where that is?"

My mother's neighborhood. "Yes, I do."

"How about tomorrow evening around six?"

"All right. I'll bring Jerry along as creative consultant."

"Wonderful, thanks! I'll dust off my many Ultimate Grand Supreme crowns so you'll be jealous!"

When I got home, Denisha Simpson was waiting on the front porch. Denisha, a self-possessed little black girl, and her best friend, Austin, an energetic little white boy, had adopted Jerry as their older brother and were often at the house, usually around mealtimes.

"Well, hello, Denisha."

"Hi, Madeline. Jerry's practicing the piano for *Oklahoma*."

From the front parlor window, I could hear a pretty good attempt at the title song. "Are you trying out for it?"

"I don't know if there are any kids in it, but yeah, I might."

"What about Austin? He might like to be a cowboy."

"No. He thinks it's silly. And he's the reason I'm here today. I need to ask you something."

"Sure. Have a seat."

Denisha sat down in one of the rocking chairs. Her dark brown eyes were serious. "You know that Austin and I are going to Camp Lakenwood this summer."

"Yes, I hope you enjoy it."

"I'm much more excited than Austin. He thought camp would be boring without TV and video games. This was before he found out Kennedy was going, too."

"Kennedy?"

"Kennedy Marshall. She's in our class. All the boys like her, and I know why."

I knew the girl Denisha was talking about. I'd often wondered what possessed her parents to name their daughter after a president partly known for his assassination. I expected Denisha to comment on Kennedy's flowing blond hair and shiny pink perfection. I was ready with the Everyone is Beautiful in Her Own Special Way speech.

"She's got that new Wow System," Denisha said. "It's like Wii, only better. Austin's into that."

"Oh."

"He's been over at her house every afternoon. He doesn't want to ride bikes or play in the creek or nothing." She sighed. "I tell you, I'm at my wit's end."

I tried not to smile. I'd heard Denisha's aunt use that expression many times when dealing with her niece. "I think the newness will soon wear off," I suggested.

Denisha dug into the pocket of her shorts. "I want to hire you, Madeline."

"What would you like me to do?"

She unfolded three dollar bills. "Find out if Kennedy is Austin's girlfriend."

"Couldn't you just ask him?"

"I don't want him to think I care."

"I see."

Denisha gave me a very grown up look. "You know what it's like, Madeline. You and Jerry were best friends before you got married, and when he was hanging around with another girl, you weren't very happy about it."

"That's because she was not the right one for him."

"Exactly. And Kennedy Marshall is not the right one for Austin, only he's too dumb to see it, just like Jerry was."

I had to chuckle. "You've made your point."

She indicated the dollar bills. "Is that enough?"

"More than enough."

"Thanks, Madeline. When can I expect results?"

"I'll get on it right away."

Denisha stood and shook my hand. "Thank you." She went down the porch steps, picked up her bike, and rode away.

Jerry came to the door. "All clear? Looked like some serious girl talk."

"Come on out." He propped himself on the porch rail. "Denisha has hired me to find out if Austin and Kennedy Marshall are an item," I said.

"Kennedy Marshall? Male or female?"

"A female classmate. A very pretty blonde classmate with the latest video game system."

"Uh, oh."

"The pretty blondes are on the move today." I explained about Wendall Clarke, Flora, and Larissa Norton.

"That's eerie. It sounds exactly like what I've been listening to lately, *The Ballad of Baby Doe*."

"Okay, I don't know that one."

Jerry has a fondness for opera, and it's odd sometimes how the stories reflect what's going on with my cases. "It's based on a true story. Horace Tabor made a fortune back in the 1800s in silver mines. He left his wife to marry a beautiful woman nicknamed Baby Doe. The opera's about the relationships of those three people."

"I'm guessing the ex-wife wasn't very happy with Horace."

"She has some particularly scathing songs to sing. She refused to divorce Horace, so it was quite a scandal when he took up with another woman. In the opera, everybody shuns them, the silver mine fails, Tabor goes crazy—"

"And everybody dies."

"Yep. Beverly Sills was the composer's favorite Baby Doe. You've got to hear this aria."

The downstairs parlor used to be where Jerry held his séances. He surprised me by hiring Nell to paint the walls bright yellow, and then he parked a gleaming golden-brown baby grand piano in one corner. He went inside his music room to root through his CDs. After a while, a beautiful soprano voice soared to impossibly high notes. Jerry came back to the porch. "What do you think?"

"I think that's gorgeous."

"It's called 'The Willow Song.' That's what Baby Doe is singing when Tabor first sees her. Love at first sight for both of them, although Baby Doe knows he's the richest man in Colorado, so I think she was a bit of a schemer."

"This is too strange," I said. "Wendall calls Flora 'Baby.'"

Jerry laughed. "Baby Flo! Perfect."

"What exactly happens in this opera? Does anyone get murdered? I want to be ready."

"No. There's a lot of singing about gold becoming more popular than silver, and Tabor backs the wrong man for president, so there's a lot of singing about that, too. At the end of the opera, Tabor is broke and ill. He spends a long time having a breakdown and dies in Baby Doe's arms. The real Baby Doe froze to death in her cabin at the silver mine."

"These stories are always so cheerful. What about the ex-wife?"

"Her name is Augusta, and when Tabor loses everything, she sings about wanting to help him because she still loves him, but she doesn't go back to him."

"I seriously doubt Larissa wants to go back to Wendall. She won the gold medal in the If Looks Could Kill competition today. She even had one for me."

"You? What did you do?"

"I'm married to the man who took her theater job. Evan says she often pulls this trick so he'll beg her to stay."

"Too bad. It's my job now," he said. "I like *Oklahoma*. It's not as stirring as *Ballad of Baby Doe*, but at least everyone comes out of it alive—no, wait, everyone except Jud, but he's a complete villain. No one's really evil in *Baby Doe*."

The music had changed from Beverly Sills' glorious soprano to a strident female voice singing her demands and wanting to know what Horace Tabor had been up to. I didn't even know this opera and I felt sorry for him.

"When are *Oklahoma* rehearsals?"

"Tryouts are tomorrow night, and rehearsals will be every weeknight from seven until nine or ten."

That should cut down on Jerry's scheming time. "What about the Christmas cantata?"

"'The Glory of Christmas' is in the bag. I called the church this morning to tell them I'd do it."

"Can you do both productions?"

"Sure. You know how Wednesdays are around here."

I had been surprised to find out that Wednesday nights in Celosia most people went to church, usually for choir practice, but also for family night dinners and Bible study groups. "So Evan will let you off on Wednesday night?"

"Up until the last two weeks. *Oklahoma* opens the end of November, and the cantata's not until December fourteenth."

I felt a sense of relief. Two things to keep him occupied. No, wait, I'd almost forgotten about Billie. "There's something else you can do," I said. "My friend Billie Tyson called and told me she and her husband had been the victims of a con. She'd like to hire both of us to find the people responsible."

"What happened?"

"We're going to meet tomorrow so she can fill me in. Sound interesting?"

"I'll be glad to help. How about your other case? Anything new to report?"

"The search is on for Pamela's missing letter."

"Any clues?"

"Nothing exciting. It's buried in mounds of papers she's been collecting for most of her adult life. I have to sift through several file boxes and stacks."

"What's so important about it? Are we going to get to solve another riddle?"

"Again, nothing as thrilling as a mysterious riddle. The letter gives her permission to build onto her shop."

"So we both have jobs. Peace reigns once again in the Fairweather household."

"I'm taking advantage of this peace to do a little art," I said.

Uncle Val had used the upstairs parlor as his study. When we first saw it, it was a typical Victorian parlor with overstuffed chairs, a marble-topped table, an old phonograph, and bookshelves filled with leather-bound copies of the classics. I kept the table with its fancy glass lamp and the bookshelves, but the phonograph and chairs went to an antique dealer. I moved in my easels, paper, and art supplies and converted the space into a studio. The light was perfect, and there was plenty of room to spread out my projects and leave them until I'd finished. I was halfway through a landscape of the fields around our house and spent a constructive hour shading in some grass and getting the clouds just the way I wanted them. In this blissful state, I forgot about Wendall and Larissa, Pamela's letter, Denisha's concerns, even poor frozen Baby Doe. But something nagged at the back of my thoughts. I finally put down my brush and gave the picture a critical look. It wasn't the picture. The picture was coming along fine.

It was my growing indecisiveness about children. For years I'd been completely against having a baby, and I'd told everyone there was no way I was going to change my mind. Now I wasn't so sure. A little boy would be all right, but my mother would snatch up a little girl and try to turn her into a pageant princess, just as she'd done to me. No, Jerry and I wouldn't let that happen. Our little girl could be an artist, or a musician, or even a private investigator.

Wait. What was I saying? I was not going to have a baby! My wonderful, orderly life, remember? Investigate, paint, sit on the porch, repeat as necessary. That's what I liked. Having a baby would change all that.

But you could handle it, my little inner voice said in a wheedling tone. You're a strong woman who can handle anything, as your husband pointed out, and you could definitely keep your child out of your mother's clutches.

"Be quiet," I told the little voice. "No baby. Not now."

Just as Jerry announced supper was ready, and I came down the stairs, Austin Terrell and a little blonde girl rode up the pathway through the field and parked their bikes under one of the large oak trees in our front yard. Austin's hair was in its usual colorful spikes, but he didn't come galloping into the house in his usual rodeo style. He waited for the girl and knocked politely on the screen door.

I let them in. "Hello, Austin."

"Hi, Madeline." He turned to the girl beside him. "This is my friend, Kennedy Marshall."

"Hello, Kennedy," I said. "Nice to meet you."

She shook my hand. She was indeed a beautiful little girl with a sweet smile. She was dressed all in pink, her blond hair held back with a pink headband.

"Nice to meet you, too, Mrs. Fairweather."

"You can call her Madeline," Austin said. "She doesn't mind. Is Jerry here?"

"He's in the kitchen."

I followed them to the kitchen where Austin made his introductions, and Jerry asked Kennedy if she'd like to stay for supper.

"No, thank you," she said. "As soon as my mom picks up my sisters from piano practice, we're all going to Deely's."

"Kennedy has three sisters," Austin said. "Madison, Tyler, and Reagan."

"Are your parents interested in politics?" Jerry asked.

"Yeah," she said. "How did you know?"

Austin obviously had a plan. "I wanted Kennedy to meet you, Jerry, 'cause I knew you'd be interested in seeing the Wow System in action, so maybe we could bring it over sometime."

"Sure," he said.

Austin grinned at Kennedy. "See? I told you he'd say yes. Well, we gotta go. See you later."

There didn't seem to be anything romantic about Austin's behavior, but I had to find out. At the door, I said, "Austin, hang on a second. I have some more paper for you."

Austin had shown a talent for sketching and liked the type of drawing paper I had. I went upstairs and grabbed a handful. As I'd hoped, Kennedy went on out to her bike while Austin waited on the porch.

"I see you have a girlfriend, Austin."

He looked scornful. "She's not my girlfriend."

I didn't think so. "She's awfully pretty."

"She's got the only Wow in town. That's the only reason I hang out with her. Thanks for the paper."

"Well," I told Jerry when I returned to the kitchen, "that's the easiest case I ever solved."

"So Denisha has nothing to worry about?"

"Austin said the only reason he hangs out with Kennedy is because she's got the only Wow in town."

Jerry grinned and gave me a kiss. "Oh, I wouldn't say that."

I returned the favor. "Thank you. What's for supper?"

"Chicken and rice."

I helped myself to a large portion and brought my plate to the table. There was a stack of envelopes next to the butter dish. "Is this today's mail? I hope there aren't any bills."

"I didn't see any."

There was one envelope addressed to both of us. The return address was a post office box in Parkland. "Any idea what this might be?"

He brought his plate over and sat down. "Nope. I thought I'd wait till you got home to open it."

"Looks serious." I opened the envelope, took out the letter, and read it. "Oh, my lord." It was serious. "What's this? Jerry, you're being sued!"

"What?" He came around for a better look. As he read, his eyes got wide. "What the hell?"

"This claims you cheated some woman named Denby Forest out of her life's savings. You said you weren't going to do this anymore! You promised."

"Mac, I swear on my life I had nothing to do with this. I never met a Denby Forest. I never cheated anyone out of their life's savings."

I was so angry and upset, I was shaking. Last month, someone Jerry had scammed recognized him and sent her very large boyfriend to collect what Jerry owed her. Fortunately, I had enough money to pay off this man before Jerry became part of the pavement. "How many of these past mistakes are we going to have to deal with?"

He reread the letter. "I'm telling you I didn't do this—here, wait a minute. Look. It isn't something from my past. Check out the date."

The paper stated that Jeremyn Nicholas Fairweather had performed a séance in Millersberg on August 15, whereby he allegedly spoke to her dead uncle and had convinced Denby Forest the uncle wanted her to invest all her money in Double Delite Doughnuts. She did. Double Delite Doughnuts immediately went under, taking her savings with it. She was suing us for a million dollars.

"Think about it," Jerry said. "August 15. Where was I? Here with you trying to fix up my house. When did I ever go to Millersberg? I don't even know where that is."

I was trying to be calm. "Okay, maybe it's a case of mistaken identity. Maybe there's another con man with the same name." Which was highly unlikely.

"Mac, I never use my real name, especially not my full name. This is somebody who knows me."

"That's even worse."

The letter had been typed on high quality paper. At the top was the name "Hadley Boyles, Attorney At Law," the post office box address, and a phone number.

"We'd better clear this up right away." I took out my cell phone and called the number. A recorded voice said, "Thank you for calling the law offices of Hadley Boyles. Our office hours are nine to five, Monday through Friday. If you'd like to leave a message, please do so after the beep. Thank you." The recording beeped, but I didn't leave a message. "They're closed for today, and I'd rather speak to a real person."

Jerry had his own cell phone in hand. "If there is one. I'm calling around."

"You think this is some sort of scam? Why would this woman try to con us out of a million dollars when it's obvious we don't have that kind of money?"`

"I know this is some sort of scam."

I thought of something else. "Wasn't Nell working here on the fifteenth? She could provide you with an alibi."

"I'm not going to need an alibi."

"Jerry, what if this is real?"

He had started to punch in a number. He paused. "Mac, believe me, I'm speaking from experience. Somebody's trying to scare us."

"Do you have any idea who might be using your name?"

"I'm checking with Del right now."

Del was one of Jerry's friends in Parkland. He owned a pawn shop and seemed like a reasonable fellow. "You don't think he did it, do you?"

"No, but he'll know who's in town."

I listened as Jerry held a terse conversation with Del. "Just let me know, okay?" Jerry said. "This had to be sometime this summer. Is Frankie out yet? How about Allan?" He listened for a while. "Could she be holding a grudge?" He laughed. "You're kidding! Okay. Thanks." He closed his phone. "Del says it sounds like something Honor Perkins would do. He's going to ask around."

This was getting even more absurd. "Wait a minute. Honor Perkins? There's a con woman named Honor?"

"Nice, huh?"

"Will you please tell me exactly what is going on?"

"I'm not sure, but Honor may still be mad at me for a little incident that happened a while ago. This may be her way of trying to get back. This letter doesn't look like a real summons. It's nothing for you to worry about. I'll take care of it."

I gave him a long hard stare. He looked so innocent and unconcerned I could see why fooling people came easily to him. After a while, I took a deep breath. "I'm sorry I accused you so quickly, but honestly, your reputation doesn't make things easy."

"My former reputation, Mac. I have a new one now, remember? Camp Counselor Jerry Fairweather?"

"Yes, I'm sorry. I just hate for things like this to keep happening."

"Like I said, I'll take care of it."

Chapter Five

On top of everything else, there was Jerry's séance to get through. We arrived at Deely's to find a small crowd had gathered to watch the spectacle. This didn't bother Jerry in the least. I'm sure he was hoping to drum up business.

Deely didn't stay for the séance, saying he didn't hold with that kind of thing and reminding Annie to make sure everything was locked up when we were through. He had set up a card table and folding chairs in the back room of the restaurant, which was really a storage room filled with boxes of paper plates and napkins and cleaning supplies. Jerry had brought along his own candle. He lit the candle and set it in the center of the table.

"Okay, Annie, you sit here by me. Who's this with you?"

"Two of my best friends and my Aunt Louise, Aunt Gloria's sister. She's really hoping Gloria comes through."

Aunt Louise was a grim-faced woman whose tiny eyes narrowed to mere slits. "Got a few things to discuss with her."

Jerry gave me a wry grin. Let's see you handle this one, I thought.

The women sat down, and everyone held hands. "Mac, if you'd get the lights, please."

I turned off the lights. The faces around the table looked ghostly in the candlelight.

"This may take a few minutes," Jerry said. "Don't be disappointed if nothing happens. The spirit world has its own rules."

Jerry Fairweather rules. I was always amazed that anyone could take this nonsense seriously.

Annie timidly raised her hand. "Will we be able to speak to her directly?"

"Yes, if your aunt comes through, you can ask her your questions." He closed his eyes and took a few deep breaths. "I call to the spirit world. I request your guidance. We wish to speak to Annie's Aunt Gloria. Come to me. Show me the way." There was a pause, and then he spoke in a distant voice. "Annie? Is that you?"

Annie leaned forward. "Aunt Gloria?"

"Yes, child."

Her friends giggled, and Aunt Louise frowned. Annie spoke in a timid voice. "Aunt Gloria, I need your advice. Robbie Wilcox is getting serious, but so is Tim Farris. I don't know what to do."

"Trust your feelings, my dear. Do you love one of them?"

"I think I love Robbie. I'm not sure."

"Tell both young men you need time to sort out your emotions. If the one you love truly loves you, he'll be willing to wait."

Annie looked pleased. Then Aunt Louise broke in. "Gloria, where is my money?"

"What money, dear sister?"

"You know very well what money. The money that was supposed to come to me. I know you were angry with Papa for favoring me, and you took it and hid it, so you'd better tell me right now where it is, or so help me, I'll leap over to the other side and make certain you're twice dead!"

Jerry made some strangled noises in his throat and let go of their hands. He blinked and made a great show of coming back to earth. "Sorry. There was a disruption, and all the spirits disappeared. Did Gloria come through?"

Aunt Louise gave a snort. "Came through and ran off, like she always did when faced with a hard decision!"

"I was real happy with what she told me," Annie said. "Thanks, Jerry."

Aunt Louise smacked the table. "Well, I'm not happy! Turn those lights back on. I want to talk to this young man."

I turned on the lights.

Aunt Louise's face was pinched in tight. "I thought for sure you'd be able to reach her long enough for me to find out where my money is."

Jerry tried to stall. "What money is that?"

"You don't know? You was right there with her, wasn't you? The ten thousand dollars our daddy left us, only half was to come to me, and Gloria ran off with all of it."

Annie gaped at her. "You never told me that."

"That's 'cause you thought so much of your Aunt Gloria, I didn't want to say nothing, but I'm fed up with it now. You see anything in that spirit world that looked like my money, Fairweather? If she told you where it was, you'd better tell me, or I'm going right to the police."

"I promise you she did not say anything to me."

"Huh! Better not be fooling me, young man. In fact, you go into that trance again and get her back here."

"I'm sorry, ma'am, but this was my very last séance."

"I don't believe you. You get her back right now."

"It doesn't work that way. The spirits have to cooperate."

"Are you trying to put one over on me, boy?"

Annie was appalled. "Aunt Louise, it's time to go home." She took her aunt by the arm to steer her out. "Sorry, Jerry. She's been in the root beer again. It makes her crazy."

"I'm not crazy! My sister's crazy if she thinks she's getting away with this!"

Aunt Louise complained and whined as Annie pulled her along. Annie's friends followed, still giggling.

I gave Jerry a long look. "Do I really have to say anything?"

He blew out the candle. "Well, I have to say I'm glad this was my last séance. It's hard to put a spin on little surprises like Aunt Louise."

◇◇◇

I hardly slept at all that night—sorry that I'd lost my temper with Jerry and even sorrier we were still being haunted by his past shady career. What if he was wrong, and this was a real lawsuit, and we couldn't prove it was a case of mistaken identity? His last con had cost us thousands of dollars. At the time, I'd thought this was a huge sum, but it didn't compare with the million dollars Denby Forest wanted. And if Denby Forest was this Honor Perkins, what did she really want besides playing a stupid prank?

Honestly, these friends of his.

In the morning, I stopped by my office before heading over to Flair For Fashion. I sincerely hoped there wasn't more mail. I couldn't take any more surprise letters. There wasn't any mail, but I had a visitor. Wendall Clarke tapped on the door.

"Hope I'm not interrupting anything."

I motioned for him to enter. "Not at all. Please come in."

He came in, followed by Flora, who glanced at me shyly and smiled. "I wanted to talk to you some more about helping with the gallery," Wendall said.

"As I said, I'll be glad to think about it, but my work here keeps me busy." And cleaning up after my husband, I wanted to add.

"Seems to me I recall you winning Miss Parkland a few years ago. Am I right?"

"Yes."

"I thought so. Your mother still lives there, doesn't she? I've run into her at several charitable functions. And you know Chance Baseford, don't you?"

I certainly did. It had taken me a long time to get over Baseford's harsh criticisms of my first art show. "Yes, I do."

"He practically dared me to set up a gallery here, said the peasants wouldn't appreciate it or care. I'm going to prove him wrong, and if you've had similar experiences with the man, my guess is you'd like to prove him wrong, too."

He was right about that.

Wendall leaned forward. "Here's what I have in mind, Ms. Maclin. I'm going to invite the very best artists from this area to show their work in the gallery. I'll get a respected critic and some reputable journalists to come cover the opening, and this will send a loud message to Baseford and others like him that art isn't just for a few snobs in Parkland. What do you think?"

"That's a great idea."

"I'd like to feature your work, of course. Do you know any other artists who should be included?"

"Pamela Finch mentioned that she paints, and there's a local artists' club that meets at the library every month."

"A good place to start. Can I count on your help?"

I really had no excuse not to help, and down deep, a vengeful little part of me wanted to best Chance Baseford. "I'll do what I can."

"Excellent! The workers have already started on the remodeling. I expect to have the gallery ready in a couple of days."

"A couple of days?"

"Oh, yes. I have offered substantial bonuses to the contractors. When I want something done, it gets done." He smiled down at his wife. "Baby, didn't you have something you wanted to say?"

She tugged nervously at a curl of her blond hair. "If you don't mind, Ms. Maclin."

"Please call me Madeline."

"Madeline, I just wanted to thank you for being so kind to me at the party yesterday. You might have noticed that most people there gave me the cold shoulder."

"I did, and I'm very sorry."

"I really hope we can be friends."

I felt a stab of sympathy for this worried little woman. "Certainly. Where are you staying in town?"

"We've rented a house in River Ridge," Wendall said, "just until the gallery is open and running. I'm in discussions with several curators about the position." He handed me his card. "Please call any time. I'm sure Baby would love for you to visit."

River Ridge was Celosia's country club area. I wondered if the neighbors had been as friendly and welcoming as the reception crowd.

"Thank you, I will."

Flora looked at me hopefully. "Come for lunch today if you're not too busy."

I agreed to this, and they both left smiling.

No one was smiling at Flair For Fashion. I arrived to find a group of women, including Bea Ricter, bunched up at the back of the store, arguing fiercely about whose work was suitable for the new gallery. When Pamela saw me, she gestured me over to one side.

"Emergency meeting of the Art Guild. There's been some confusion about who'll be in charge of acquisitions at the new gallery."

"Won't Wendall be in charge?"

"After the reception yesterday, he mentioned he's talking to several people about the curator's job."

He'd mentioned this to me, too. "So what's all the fuss about?"

"We should be the ones to run the gallery. We can't imagine Wendall staying in town to oversee everything. If he's opening an art gallery for Celosia, then Celosians ought to be in charge. If he chooses an outsider, there's a very good chance some of us will never get to show our work."

"Have you talked to him about your concerns?"

"I tried to talk to him yesterday, but he just laughed and said not to worry. He'd take care of everything."

This sounded harmless, but apparently the Art Guild had heard his statement as a threat. "I've just had a conversation with him, and he plans to show local artists' work." At this, all the women turned to look at me. Some of their looks were concerned, but most were unfriendly. This didn't bother me. I'd been the object of hostile stares before—try backstage at Miss Parkland—and these ladies couldn't compete.

"Why was he talking to you?" Bea asked. "You're not even a member of the Art Guild."

"But Madeline's an artist," Pamela said. "Didn't you have something at the Weyland, Madeline?"

At the mention of Parkland's prestigious gallery, I got a few more dagger glares.

"Wendall Clarke and I have both had run-ins with Chance Baseford, an art critic in Parkland. We agreed we'd like to show him that Celosia can have a great art gallery, too."

Pamela addressed the group. "We agree with that, too, don't we? What else did he say, Madeline?"

"What I've just told you. He wants to include local art." I didn't add, *good* local art.

This set the members of the Guild into another tizzy.

"But who's going to decide?"

"And who goes first?"

"How long will someone's exhibit be up? Is it a monthly schedule, or weeks, or what?"

One woman called for quiet. She had red hair and freckles and looked very annoyed. "We're getting nowhere with this. If one member of the Guild has a showing, then every member of the Guild should have a showing. That's the only fair way to do things."

"No," Bea Ricter said, "it should only be the best."

The red-haired woman turned to her. "Good lord, Bea, who are you to say what's best? You make things out of dead wood!"

The group went off again. I'd lived in Celosia just a few months, but I recognized most of the women, including Samantha Terrell, Austin's mother, by face if not by name, having seen them in Deely's or Georgia's Books or at the community theater. They'd always seemed to be pleasant, reasonable people, but the gallery had them all stirred up.

This was exactly like a group of pageant contestants arguing over who got to be in front during the opening number. "Ladies, I know I'm not a member of the Art Guild, but could I make a suggestion? Why don't you sit down with Wendall Clarke and get things straightened out? Pamela made a good point when she said this is a gallery for Celosia, so you should have some say in it."

"I think Pamela should run the gallery," Samantha said, and several others nodded.

I could see Pamela was pleased by this. "Oh, my, no. I wouldn't know where to begin."

"Don't be so modest," Samantha said. She was a small attrac-tive woman with Austin's smile and his tenacity. "You're the only one of us with any experience running a business."

"How hard could it be?" another woman said.

"But what about my store?" Pamela asked.

Samantha had a solution. "Hire an extra salesclerk to watch the store when you're not here. You're never very busy, are you?" Pamela looked at her askance. "That didn't come out the way I meant it, sorry. But you have to admit you have a select clientele."

"Well, that's true," Pamela said. "I still don't think I could run the gallery."

"You could try," another woman said. "We need one of our own in charge."

Pamela appealed to me. "Madeline, did Wendall tell you who was going to run the gallery? Did he ask you to do it?"

"No, and I wouldn't want the job. My main occupation in town is private investigation."

"Maybe you should investigate Wendall Clarke and see what he's really up to," another woman said.

These artists were determined to paint Wendall Clarke as a cad. "I don't think he's up to anything. I think he's giving you a great opportunity," I said. "Tell him you want everyone to be represented. Then if he says no, you'll have a legitimate reason to complain. Pamela, if you don't want to run the gallery, maybe he'd accept you as an assistant."

They looked at each other. Bea Ricter gave a sniff. "I still don't appreciate that dead wood remark, Ginger."

"Well, it is dead wood," the red-haired woman said.

"That does not make me any less of an artist than someone who makes cross-eyed birds out of ping-pong balls."

The group immediately divided into those who thought dead wood was artistic and those who sided with Ginger and her ping-pong birds. I moved away.

Pamela came to me. "Sorry about this. Ever since we heard about the gallery, emotions have been fraying. Some members of the Guild have waited for years to show their work. Many of us have been turned down by every gallery in the state. We see this gallery as our last chance."

"Why haven't you started a little gallery of your own? It wouldn't take much to transform one of the empty stores downtown."

"I'd thought about it, but it would take more time and money than I have, even with the support of the group. Wendall Clarke's plan is a wonderful surprise and a terrible problem."

"It could still work out well for everybody."

She glanced at the group. The women were now arguing about the merits of felt versus velvet. I heard Bea Ricter say, "Well, just because you had one wild night, that doesn't make you any sort of expert," and Ginger answered, "You were just as crazy at that craft show, dancing around like some demented cancan girl. Nobody wanted to see your crocheted petticoats."

"You'd better be quiet, Ginger, unless you want me to mention you-know-what."

Whatever she was talking about was enough of a threat to make Ginger back off, although she attempted a final shot. "Well, there are things about you that people might be surprised to find out."

Bea had the last word. "Not as surprised as they'd be about you."

Ginger turned pink with embarrassment and didn't say anything else.

"I don't see how you could work with all this racket going on, Madeline," Pamela said. "Do you want to come back this afternoon?"

"Sure. I'll check with you later."

As I started out, Samantha Terrell called, "Wait a second, Madeline." She followed me out the door. "I've had enough of their arguing."

"It doesn't take much to stir up a group around here," I said.

"Don't I know it. I thought the Garden Club would explode over all that Mantis Man business a few months back. You remember that, don't you?"

I sure did. Celosia's legendary monster had caused plenty of real and imaginary trouble. "I didn't know you were an artist."

She laughed. "I'm not. I'm making a scrapbook for Austin. That's as close as I get to art. Pamela saves things left over from her pictures for me, scraps of paper, ribbons, buttons, things like that. I'd just stopped in to get them and got caught in the middle of that." She swung her purse over her shoulder. "I wanted to make sure Austin isn't bothering you with all this about a Wow System. He said he'd asked Jerry to buy one."

"Jerry would be happy to buy one. He loves all the latest gadgets."

"I just don't want Austin to become a pest."

"He's not. He's a great kid. We both get a kick out of him."

She gave me an appraising look. "The two of you are really great with children. Any plans to start your own family?"

"We're thinking about it."

"Well, I really appreciate all you've done for Austin. He loves both of you."

"Thank you," I said. "What's your take on Wendall Clarke and the gallery? Could the Art Guild handle running it?"

Samantha glanced back at Flair For Fashion, where the women were still arguing. "This is different from the Garden Club. Anybody can plant flowers or pull weeds, but when it comes to their art, these ladies are very passionate. The problem is some of them aren't very good."

"But art is subjective."

"And I don't want to be subjected to some of their stuff. Austin's kindergarten pictures are better than some of that."

I figured Samantha might know something about all the major players in this drama. "Is Pamela serious about running the gallery? Could she do it?"

"I think she'd be perfect. She's the most levelheaded of that bunch."

"And Wendall Clarke?"

She shrugged. "I never had any problem with him. He was a grade ahead of me in school, and the only thing I remember about him was he was a big guy who talked loud and had lots of friends."

"Larissa Norton?"

"A very proud girl. Stuck-up, as we used to say. Her family was poor, and I think she was ashamed of that."

"How about Flora? Had you met her before?"

"No. I don't know a thing about her." Her cell phone jangled. "Oh, excuse me, Madeline. That'll be my husband wondering where I am. I'm supposed to meet him for lunch."

Time for me to investigate.

Chapter Six

I took a short walk down the street to the site of the new gallery, which had been vacant ever since Jerry and I moved to town. It was an unremarkable building, one story, smooth and gray, with double glass doors and all glass along the front, one window proclaiming Arrow Insurance in black and gold letters. Workmen were already hammering and painting, moving out leftover shelving and boxes, cleaning the wide front windows, and sweeping up dust. One of the workers was our handywoman, Nell Brenner. She stopped what she was doing and came to the door.

"Come in and have a look, Madeline. See what you think."

I admired the space inside, the high ceilings, and smooth wooden floor. "Perfect."

Nell wiped her large hands on her ever-present overalls and tucked a stray strand of short blond hair under her baseball cap. "I know it's causing all kinds of ruckus with the Art Guild, but it's good business for me. Wendall's offered a bonus if we get done by Friday."

This was Tuesday. "That soon?"

"Well, the place is in great shape. Just needs cleaning, some paint. Turn the water and electricity back on and you can put all the art in you like. And let me show you this." I followed her to the back of the store. "Here's an office. The insurance company left all the furniture and filing cabinets. There's even an intercom system if people want to use it, a two-way mirror to keep an eye on the store, a mini-fridge I guess nobody wanted, even one of those old adding machines. Once everything's clean, Wendall can move on in."

I checked out the mirror, which gave a good view of the main room. "He's not likely to stay in Celosia, is he?"

"Nah. He's got business elsewhere. And he sure don't need to hang around here, not with that new wife of his on his arm."

"I've noticed the reaction."

"I guess it's to be expected. Everyone knows Wendall left Larissa Norton to marry another woman. But Larissa didn't do herself any favors. Wendall's always been very ambitious. Larissa didn't understand that. He wanted to give her everything, and for some reason, she didn't want him to."

"That sounds odd."

"Only thing I can figure is since Larissa was so poor growing up, she felt like he was wasting his money." One of the work-men came up to ask her a question about the color of the walls. "Yeah, everything along that wall is cream," she told him. "The ones up here are pale willow and off-white." She turned back to me. "You might have a case pretty soon. I hear the ladies of the Art Guild are ready to kill each other."

Nell manages to hear everything that's happening in town. "The big issue is dead wood versus ping-pong balls. I'm keeping out of it."

"Just put everybody's stuff in here. Plenty of room."

"That was my suggestion, but it doesn't look like that's going to happen." Saying that reminded me of Wendall telling Bea "That's not going to happen."

"Nell, what's the deal with Wendall and Bea Ricter? She tore into him at his reception and told him he needed to do the right thing."

"Can't say as I recall anything in particular. Bea was always one of those intense social climbers, always jealous of anyone's success. Married some rich fella from Raleigh and moved there for a while, but the marriage didn't work out, so she and her son came back here."

"She has a son?" I envisioned a round, angry little boy.

"Yeah, but he's grown, lives somewhere else. Visits her every now and then. From what I hear, Bea didn't get much out of the divorce. That could make her cranky." Nell picked up her can of paint and paintbrush. "Gotta get back to work. Whenever the Guild declares a truce, the walls will be ready."

While Nell returned to supervising the remodeling, I walked back to my car and called Jerry to see if he had any leads on Honor Perkins.

"No," he said. "I called that number several times and got the same recording. I also called my pal who's a real lawyer, and he said we would've received more than just a plain letter. I promise you this is a scam, Mac. When you get home, let's drive to Millersberg and find this Denby Forest."

Something I definitely wanted to do. "All right. You're on your own for lunch. I've been invited to the Clarkes'."

"Tell Baby Flo hello from me."

The house Wendall and Flora were renting in River Ridge was huge and modern with an oddly slanted roof that made the house look as if it might take off and fly away. Inside, the rooms looked cold and formal, but there was nothing cold or formal about Flora Clarke's welcome when she answered the door.

"I'm so glad you could come! Wendall has business in Park-land, so it's just the two of us. I thought we'd eat out on the deck, if you don't mind. It's such a beautiful fall afternoon."

The deck overlooked a wooded area filled with bright yellow trees. A lunch of fruit salad, chicken salad croissants, and iced tea had been set on an elegant wrought-iron table. "This looks delicious."

"Please, sit down. I hope you like everything."

I slipped into one of the floral-patterned chairs. "I'm sure I will."

Flora was wearing a dress in soft fall colors and a light gold sweater. A distinctive bracelet made of gold and bright yellow leaves dangled from her wrist. She sat across from me and spread her napkin in her lap. This was my first chance to have a good look at her. She was a beautiful woman, her face further enhanced by an expertly applied layer of makeup, including subtle pink rouge and matching lip gloss. A soft gray eye shadow complemented her blue eyes, which appeared to be larger, thanks to eyeliner and thick false eyelashes. And if I wasn't mistaken, all that golden hair was not her own.

"Have you seen the gallery?" she asked. "It's going to be a wonderful place."

"I stopped by just a little while ago. Looks like it'll be ready in no time."

"Wendall went to Parkland to interview a potential curator. He wants to find the perfect person."

"Has he considered hiring someone from Celosia?"

"You know, I told him that might be a good idea, but he didn't agree. I thought it might help things." She sighed. "Madeline, I haven't known you very long, but I feel as if I can confide in you."

"I'll be happy to listen."

Once again, she played with a curl of the golden hair. "It's like this. I didn't set out to ruin anyone's marriage. Wendall and I fell in love at first sight. It just happened. We couldn't help it. He was so unhappy because Larissa never understood his big plans. As for my ex-husband, he had no ambition whatsoever, and whenever I got him to try something, it always fell apart. I'm sorry Larissa is still so angry, but Wendall and I were meant to be together."

"Sometimes these things happen, Flora."

"He wants to give this town something grand and important. I think that a beautiful new art gallery would be just the thing."

To make the town forgive him? "I hope people will appreciate it."

"Oh, I think an art gallery is a splendid idea," she said. "People need the arts, you know. Well, of course you know. You're an artist. But were you really Miss Parkland?"

"Yes, I was."

"You didn't want to continue?"

"I entered Miss Parkland because I wanted to and I needed the money, but from the time I was very small, it was all my mother's idea."

"People always said I should be in pageants, but I was much too shy to be on stage."

"Being in a pageant will take care of your shyness, believe me." I liked Flora, but there was something forced in her friendliness, as if she were trying too hard to be agreeable. She'd make a great pageant girl. No, that wasn't fair. She was new in town and had been thrust into an unpleasant situation.

She took a sip of tea. "But you're really a detective, Madeline. Have you solved any mysteries?"

"When I first moved to town, I helped solve the murder of a Miss Celosia Pageant contestant."

"Murder at a pageant? That must have been very strange."

"It was a *Twilight Zone* moment. But having pageant experience came in handy." And one of those handy experiences was the ability to tell a fake smile from a real one, and I wanted to believe Flora's was real. "Then not long after that, a director wanted to use my house for the set of a monster movie, and someone killed him."

"And you solved that mystery?"

"Yes, and next, an unpopular teacher was found dead at the elementary school, and it turned out she had been murdered. I didn't think I'd find much work in Celosia, but every now and then somebody goes wild."

She gave a little laugh. "Well, if you find me murdered, you'll know who done it. Larissa Norton."

I sincerely hoped not.

"Besides Larissa, did Wendall ever tell you anything about Bea Ricter? She seemed very upset at the reception. Do you have any idea what she meant by telling him to do the right thing?"

Again she toyed with the curl of hair. "I'm not sure what's going on there. He is doing the right thing by opening this gallery. Maybe she's afraid he won't let her show her work."

"He also told her, 'That's not going to happen.'"

"He said she was still angry about something that happened a long time ago. He knew not everyone in Celosia would welcome him back. Sometimes when you're that popular, you have a lot of people who are jealous." Flora picked up a croissant and took a dainty bite. "There comes a time when you have to let things go."

That was true, but I sensed there was more to this than some petty high school envy. "Did he mention what that something was?"

"Well, now, that's the odd thing, Madeline. Bea's angry at him, but she won't tell him why. I think they need to sit down and straighten things out."

Well, it was usually sex or money. "Did they have a relation-ship at one time?"

"I don't know. That doesn't seem likely, does it?"

"Does he owe her money?"

"I don't know that, either." Her hand went back to her hair. Maybe she was afraid it was going to fall off. "I'm just glad we're not planning on living here. Why don't we talk about something else?"

I spent a pleasant hour and a half with Flora and promised to visit again. Before I went back to Pamela's shop, I stopped by Celosia High School, located out near the highway. The school looked new—a sprawl of light-pink brick buildings with shiny green roofs connected by covered walkways. The parking lot was as large as the football field. I found a visitor's spot, parked, and went into the office where I was given a visitor's badge and directed to the media center. There a helpful student showed me the yearbooks from the years Wendall, Larissa, Pamela, and Bea had gone to Celosia High.

Wendall looked the same, only darker. A long list of accomplishments was under his name. Larissa and Pamela had been very attractive. Teenage Larissa's hair was down past her shoulders, and her eyes were soulful. Young Pamela's hair still misbehaved, but in a different style. However, the high school version of Bea was a revelation. Her hair was long and curly, and her eyes crinkled as she smiled. Her picture practically glowed. She looked young and radiant and ready to face the world. So maybe there had been some sort of relationship with Wendall. Maybe he broke her heart. That kind of pain could last a lifetime.

All three women had been in the same clubs; all three were on the soccer team. I looked for the picture of the team in the athletics section of the yearbook. There they stood, side by side on the field: Larissa, Pamela, and Bea. At one time, they must have been friends.

What happened?

◇◇◇

I drove back to Pamela's shop, where I spent a not-so-pleasant hour and a half digging through another file cabinet. When my eyes began to cross, I went home. It was not quite time for Denisha to be out of school. Jerry was waiting for me on the porch. He wanted to go to Millersberg right away, but I told him I'd like to wait and give Denisha the good news about Austin and Kennedy.

"Then we'll go to Millersberg. We can stop back by Baxter's for supper."

Jerry agreed. "All right, but I want to take care of this problem as soon as possible."

"Any idea what caused this problem? Sounds like you and Honor have a history."

"Just a history of cons, that's all."

"Look me in the eye and say that."

He did. "Just a history of cons, that's all." He looked exactly the same.

"I can never tell when you're lying."

"Okay, now I'm going to tell a lie." He kept his gaze right on me. "I really don't like Baxter's barbecue."

"You sound the same."

"That's the whole idea. Keep eye contact and speak in a neutral tone. But I promise, Honor and I were only friends and partners in a few schemes."

"And one of those schemes went south and she's blaming you? Any idea which one?"

"I think I know, and it was sort of my fault. You don't want the details, do you?"

I really didn't. "Maybe later. What have you been doing today?"

"Taking charge of my own destiny."

"That could mean a lot of things."

"Job-hunting."

"Great! Any luck?"

"I've set up a couple of interviews for later in the week, one with Tecknilabs, and one with Southern Foods. Both are sales positions. I don't have any experience with sales, but it can't be that much different from running cons. You're trying to get people to buy something you make them believe they can't live without."

"I can see where that might work for you."

"I've also been practicing. You can have a private concert while you wait for Denisha."

I sat on the porch while he played selections from *Oklahoma*, occasionally putting his own spin on the tunes, so I heard "Oh, What A Beautiful Morning" reggae style, and "Kansas City" as a slow blues. Around three-thirty, Denisha rode up on her bike, hopped up the porch steps, and plopped into a rocking chair.

"Whatcha got for me, Madeline?"

"Good news," I said. "I investigated the problem and found out Austin is only interested in Kennedy because of the Wow System. He told me so himself."

"You didn't mention me, I hope."

"Not at all."

She nodded as if mulling over this information. "Well, that's what I thought, but I wanted to be sure. Thanks, Madeline."

"My pleasure. And it didn't take as much time as I planned, so I owe you a refund." I handed her three dollars back.

"Okay." She solemnly shook my hand. "What are the chances of Jerry buying a Wow?"

"I'll have to ask him."

"Because if Jerry has one here, then Austin won't go to Kennedy's."

"If Jerry has one what?" He walked out in time to hear.

"A Wow System," Denisha said.

"Depends on how much it costs."

She handed him the three dollars. "Here's a start."

He laughed. "I'm not going to take your money. Mac and I are going to Millersberg this afternoon. I'll check on the prices."

"It's important," she said. "If you have one, then Austin will stop hanging around Kennedy so much."

"I will definitely look into it."

She thanked him and rode off.

"Denisha's a good name," Jerry said. "Not as forceful as Hortensia, though."

Hortensia was the name he'd given our non-existent daughter. "Where did that come from?"

"I looked up some names on the Internet. I was trying to find Honor. She used to have a website."

"Scam Artists dot com?"

"Fly By Night dot com."

"You're kidding."

"Nope. You put it out front so people can't say they weren't warned. But it's not there anymore. She either changed it, or moved on."

"Well, let's move on and see if we can find her. I'll drive."

On the way to Millersberg, Jerry went down a long list of baby names.

"How about Adelaide?"

"Too old-fashioned."

"Ambrosia?"

"Isn't that some kind of coconut dessert?"

"Cephorah?"

"Too Biblical."

"Dauphine?"

"Sounds like a cough medicine."

"Guess it's Hortensia, then," he said.

"Why are you naming a baby that might not ever be?"

"You said you'd think about it."

"That's a long way from having one."

He looked at my expression, folded the list, and put it in his pocket. "How was lunch with Baby Flo?"

"Interesting. According to Flora, Wendall left Larissa because she didn't understand or appreciate his ambitions. Flora left her husband for the same reasons. Apparently, he was a slacker, and she had more expensive tastes. She's quite dazzling, but my experienced pageant eye noticed a lot of her glamour is store-bought."

"Such as?"

"Besides the fake eyelashes and fingernails, she had very realistic hair extensions and loads of makeup, but she's one of those women who can carry off this look. No wonder the other women hate her. But I like her. I think she's a really sweet person who's caught in the middle of a highly charged emotional situation."

"Was Wendall there?"

"He'd gone to Parkland to find a curator. Flora and I agreed it would be better if he chose someone from Celosia."

He grinned. "Like you, for instance?"

"Oh, no. Don't go there. I was thinking of someone like Pamela Finch. At least she's had experience running a business."

"Does Pamela want to do it?"

"She acts all flustered and modest, but I believe she's been dreaming of an opportunity like this."

"Is her work any good?"

"It's not too bad. Larissa made some very disparaging remarks about it, though."

"So if Pamela ran the gallery she could display her work and thumb her nose at Larissa."

"I'm sure that's occurred to her."

"What about the other members of the Guild?" Jerry asked. "Suppose Wendall chooses Pamela? Won't there be intense infighting over whose work goes where?"

"I'm sure that's going to happen no matter who Wendall chooses. Here's something else I found out. Larissa, Pamela, and Bea were all on the high school soccer team, and from the picture, you'd have to believe at one time they liked each other. And since all three were very attractive girls, I think Wendall played the field."

"The entire soccer field."

"I wouldn't put it past him. I think he broke Bea's teenaged heart, and she has yet to forgive him."

"That's the secret grudge she's holding?"

"According to Nell, Bea married a fellow from Raleigh and the marriage didn't work out. Maybe that guy was Mr. Rebound."

"It's a good theory."

"Never underestimate the power of teen angst. But let's take care of your problem first."

I rarely see Jerry look grim. Even his choice of ties for the trip was serious: little white skulls and bones on black.

"Believe me, I'm ready," he said.

Chapter Seven

Millersberg wasn't much more than a suburb of Parkland, a bedroom community with its own post office and strip malls. Even though it was small, I thought we might have some difficulty locating Mrs. Forest. I had underestimated Jerry's network. We parked at a gas station, and he called someone named Peedee, who knew everyone in town and gave him an address.

"I think you'd better let me handle this," I said as we drove to Denby Forest's house. "If you're wrong, and this woman really is Denby Forest, then you shouldn't confront her. We could get in even deeper legal trouble."

"Mac, I'm telling you, this has to be a con."

"Just let me go in first and talk to her."

He stewed a while then relented. "Okay. Honor Perkins is a large woman. When I last saw her, she weighed close to two hundred pounds, but she could've lost weight. She has dark hair and dark eyes, which she could disguise with a wig and contact lenses. She also has a slight lisp, but you have to listen hard to catch it."

"All right."

"You have to have some excuse for visiting Mrs. Forest. What are you going to say?"

"I'm going to tell her you conned me, too."

He looked impressed. "That's very good. I am so proud."

Unfortunately, Denby Forest was a tiny elderly woman with gray hair piled in a bun, little granny glasses, and no trace of a speech impediment. She looked exactly like a woman who would be easily taken in.

I introduced myself as Madeline Maclin and asked her if she'd ever had a séance with someone named Jerry Fairweather.

"My goodness, yes, I have," she said. "Are you from the police?"

"I've also had a séance with Mr. Fairweather." Which was true. "A séance which did not turn out very well for me. I'm trying to find Mr. Fairweather. Would you mind if I asked you some questions about your experience?"

"Not at all, not at all. Come in."

We sat down in her dark little living room. "Mrs. Forest, could you tell me what happened?"

"Well, I heard from some friends of mine in town about this young man who was an accomplished medium and could speak to those who'd passed on. I was in desperate need of some financial advice, and the only one I trusted was my dear departed uncle. Mr. Fairweather was able to contact him through a séance we held right here in this very room. He put a candle on the table and my uncle spoke right through him! At the time, I found it all astonishing. I know now it was all a dreadful lie. Through Mr. Fairweather, my uncle advised me to put all my savings into Double Delite Doughnuts, so I did. The company failed, and I lost everything."

"When was this?"

"This past August, August 15."

"Could you describe this man?"

"Oh, my, yes. He was very handsome, very charming."

My heart sank. "Do you remember anything else?"

"He had light brown hair."

Oh, dear.

"And the most beautiful gray eyes. You don't see that very often these days."

Oh, brother. "Are you absolutely sure about this, Mrs. Forest?"

"Well, aren't all con men supposed to be good-looking? It's part of their performance. I still can't believe I was so taken in.

So sad, isn't it, that a young man like that has to resort to cheating old ladies?"

"Oh, I agree." Believe me, I agree.

"What did he take you for, dear?"

"Practically everything I had."

"Well, dearie, I've done something about it, and you should, too. I got a lawyer, and I'm suing that young man."

"How did your lawyer know where to find him?"

"I was so lucky to have a dear friend in Celosia who said she'd heard that name before. Imagine my surprise when it turned out to be the same man!"

"I would like to speak to your friend." Boy, would I.

"Oh, I'm sorry to say she's passed on just last week."

I thought of a better idea. "Mrs. Forest, what if I found this man for you? Would you be willing to sit down with him and have some face-to-face negotiations and settle out of court? If you've lost your life's savings, paying a lawyer and court costs might be difficult for you."

"Would you be able to find him?"

"I'm pretty sure I can. I'm a private investigator, and I'd do this free of charge for you. Or if you prefer, you can get a mediator or an arbiter, but I believe that would cost you some fees, as well."

She looked daunted. "Well, that's awfully generous of you. Let me think about it."

I gave her one of my cards. "Please call me when you decide. Thank you for all your help, Mrs. Forest."

"You're welcome," she said. "Can you see yourself out? My leg's acting up today."

When I got back in the car, Jerry took one look at my face and said in disbelief, "It wasn't her?"

"Denby Forest is a wizened little grandma who remembers you quite well and wants every drop of your blood."

He started to get out of the car, but I caught his arm. "Jerry, no. Not yet. I told her I'd find you, and the two of you can settle this out of court. I don't want you bursting in on her."

"Mac, I never use my real name! I have never been in this town!"

"Maybe you forgot. Maybe you've been run out of so many towns, they all look alike."

He slumped back in his seat. "Come on," I coaxed. "We'll have some Baxter's barbecue and talk about this. She didn't look like she could afford a lawyer."

"She can if she gets a million dollars."

"Not if we don't have a million dollars."

Usually a trip to our favorite barbecue restaurant can calm any storm, but neither the juicy sandwich nor the crunchy fries helped Jerry settle down.

"I was so sure this was some scheme of Honor's." He squeezed the ketchup bottle with unnecessary force. "I still think she's got a hand in this somewhere. Maybe she hired a little old lady to play Mrs. Forest."

That seemed way too elaborate for me. "Just relax. She has a dear friend in Celosia who's just passed away."

"How's that going to help?"

"All you have to do is light a candle and call her up."

He gave me a very ornery look and then his scowl faded into a reluctant grin. "Okay. I deserved that."

"We'll take care of this, Jerry." My phone beeped and I checked it. "A message from Pamela," I said. "Uh, oh. Looks like more trouble with the Art Guild. Her text message says, 'Disaster! New curator chosen! Call me!!' Double exclamation marks."

"Then you'd better call her."

I punched in Pamela's number and barely said hello before she started in.

"Madeline, you would not believe what Wendall's done! He's hired some woman from the Silver Gallery in Parkland, a complete stranger, and the two of them have final say on whose work is good enough to be displayed. He's invited the Art Guild to meet her tomorrow, and I know this meeting is going to be a total disaster!"

"Have the members of the Guild told Wendall about their concerns?"

"He said he'd answer all our questions at the meeting, but he's not going to listen to us! He's got his mind already set on what he wants."

"I know this is going to be difficult," I said, "but why don't you wait and see what really happens? You might like this new curator. She might be open to your suggestions."

Pamela would not be comforted. "I don't know how that's possible. She's not from here. She doesn't know us."

When we moved to Celosia, Jerry and I had run into this same small-town mindset. If I hadn't solved several murders, we'd still be outsiders. "Then she'll be able to have unbiased opinions about your work, right?"

There was a moment of silence on the other end of the line, as if Pamela hadn't considered this. "I don't know. I just have bad feelings about all of this. Can you come to the meeting? You're not an official member of the Guild, but you're an artist and we need your support."

There was no way to get out of this. "All right."

"Tomorrow at two at the gallery," Pamela said and hung up.

"Pamela's just like you," I told Jerry. "All in a wad about something you can't control."

"I take it from your conversation that Wendall has brought in some snooty curator from New York City."

"Close. She's from the Silver Gallery in Parkland. That's snooty enough to send the Guild into a tailspin. I'll find out tomorrow at two."

"I've got your next murder case for you," he said. "I predict someone's going to take Wendall out."

"I hope not. He's just trying to do something for the town. Want another order of fries?"

"No, thanks."

Things were serious when Jerry didn't want seconds. "Let's head on to Billie's, then. You might be able to use your powers for good."

Billie's house was at the end of Pumpkin Lane in a neighborhood only a few streets over from my mother's. Knowing Billie's early taste for all things gaudy, I expected the house to be different. It was a brick Colonial with a circular drive and boxwoods. Billie's appearance, however, more than made up for her bland surroundings. She had put on a little more than fifty pounds, but she was still the loud, flashy girl I remembered. Her sequined top had a butterfly design that spread its wings over her ample chest, and she had a ring on every finger. Billie's mother had always insisted her daughter's hair be the poofiest in the pageant. Now Billie's hair was closely cropped to her head with a fringe of bangs. Huge earrings dangled from her ears, and in honor of my visit, she was wearing one of her many crowns.

Her laugh bounced off the walls. "There she is! Madeline Maclin! The moment we've all been waiting for! Grand Supreme Pixie Dust Winner!"

I gave her a hug. "Good grief, how do you remember that?"

"Because that crown should have been mine, of course! My singing was better than your awful violin playing any day." She turned to greet Jerry. "And this must be Jerry, con man extraordinaire, or you'd better be, to help solve this mystery."

He shook her hand. "Pleasure to meet you, Billie. So what happened?"

"Come inside and I'll tell you all about it."

The living room, like Billie, was extravagant and bedazzled, with zebra-patterned furniture and huge china cabinets filled with her crowns, ribbons, and sashes.

I peered in one cabinet at a photograph of Billie as Little Miss Acme Carpets. "Why in the world did you keep all this stuff?"

"Oh, I think it's hilarious. Don't you have yours?"

"My mother has a shrine."

Billie took off her crown and placed it on a side table. "Let me get you a drink. You want iced tea or something stronger?"

"Tea would be fine, thanks."

While she was gone, Jerry looked in the cabinets. "Here's one of you, Mac."

There was eight-year-old me standing in my rigid pageant pose. I had on my best fixed smile, a pink dress that probably cost my mother twelve thousand dollars, and a hairstyle that could withstand hurricane-force winds.

"I don't know why you didn't like doing this," Jerry said. "You look so happy."

"Ha, ha."

"Billie looks happy, too."

Billie, standing beside me, had an equally glazed expression. "She's annoyed because I placed higher than she did in that pageant, but she has to keep smiling. We all did."

Billie returned with a tray and glasses of tea. She set the tray on the zebra-striped coffee table and handed us each a glass. "Now, let me tell you my tale of woe. Last week, my husband and I got a letter in the mail saying we'd won a night out to the Parkland Dinner Theater's gala. Of course, we were skeptical, so I called the number on the letter and was assured there was no catch. We'd been chosen from a mailing list, and we assumed it was the theater's list, because we're theater supporters. Gala night, a limo came to the house, and the driver told us not to worry, everything had been paid for. We went to the gala and had a fabulous time."

"Let me guess," Jerry said. "When you got home, a few things were missing."

"A few! Practically everything! Our wide-screen TV, our computers, my jewelry box, Harold's golf clubs, and all of our best wine. *You* tell *me* what happened."

"A week or so before the letter came, did someone come to your house, maybe asking you to take part in a survey, or someone asking about a house for sale on your street, anything like that?"

Billie's mouth hung open a moment. "A woman came by who said she was from the neighborhood improvement committee."

"Did you invite her in? Even for just a few minutes?"

"We stood in the foyer and talked. She wanted to make sure I knew about the revised garbage pickup schedule and the proposed club house renovations. Oh, my God, Jerry! Was she casing the joint?"

"That's one way of putting it. She got a good look so she could decide if the investment of a gala ticket was worth a burglary."

"This is unbelievable. She bought us a night out?"

"She and her partner or partners paid for your evening, probably as an anonymous donation, and the theater sent you a perfectly legitimate letter. The bad guys knew exactly when you'd be away from your home and when you'd be getting back."

"But we have a security system!"

"Are the controls near the door?"

"Yes, that little panel right there."

"Your neighborhood committee woman got a good look at that, too. These are pros. They know how to disarm all kinds of alarm systems."

"Is there any way to catch these crooks?"

"Probably not. Your stuff's insured, right?"

"Yes, but still, I really hate that they got away with it. Does it sound like a gang you know? The Gala Gang, maybe?"

"It sounds like a gang I'd rather not know," he said. "The stuff my friends and I do—that I used to do—was never this daring. Tricks, sleight of hand, little cheats, you know? I never broke into anyone's house to steal things. You called the police right away, I hope?"

"They don't have any leads."

"What did this woman look like?"

"Well, I have no room to talk, but she was plus-size, like me. Full-figured, as I like to put it. Very nicely dressed. Dark hair."

Jerry's attention was caught. "Bit of a lisp?"

"Now that you mention it, I believe she did. Good grief, do you know her?"

His expression darkened. "I have a really good idea who she is."

"The next time you see her, tell her I want my stuff back. No, here's what I want you to do. Set the cops on her. People like that shouldn't be allowed to run free."

"I agree with you completely, Billie."

Billie and I spent the rest of our visit reminiscing about our horrible pageant years, but Jerry was pretty quiet. Much quieter than usual. I'd seen that preoccupied look before, and it worried me.

When we got in the car to go home, Jerry slammed his door shut. "I can't believe Honor would do something this extreme."

"How well do you actually know this woman?"

"She was one of my first friends in the underworld—she and Jeff and Rick and Del. We had a lot of fun. This is not fun."

I'd never met Jeff, but Rick was the same Rick who'd become entangled in the death of the movie director who was using our house for *Curse of the Mantis Man*. After I solved the case and cleared Rick of murder charges, he'd agreed to leave us alone. So far, Del had acted like a gentleman. Honor sounded like something else, something dangerous. Would Jerry do something equally dangerous to stop her?

"What are you thinking, Jerry?"

"Until I find her, I can't do anything."

"Tryouts for *Oklahoma* are tonight, right?" I wanted to make sure he was occupied.

He must have tuned in to my concern. "Don't worry, Mac. I'm not going to charge off in all directions, but we are definitely going to catch her."

◇◇◇

When I dropped Jerry off at the theater, I noticed Bea Ricter among the crowd of excited people waiting to audition. "Is there a role for Bea in this show?"

"She'd make a good Aunt Eller," he said, "the cranky but loveable matron of the plains."

"Cranky I can see, but loveable?"

"That's why it's called acting." He gave me a kiss. "Sure you don't want to hang around?"

"No, thanks. I'm afraid Evan will shanghai me into the show. Call me when you're ready to come home."

He went into the theater, and I sat for a while in the car. I'd told Jerry I had no desire to make contact with the pageant world, and this was the prime reason why. Talking with Billie had brought up a host of unwanted memories. I'd wasted too many of my childhood evenings in theaters and hotel ballrooms, all dressed up in stiff, jeweled dresses, my head piled with heavy hairpieces and congealed with hair spray. Just the sight of those giggly younger girls waiting to audition made something cringe inside. They looked like they were having fun. It was never fun for me to parade around on stage, fearful that a wrong step or a tentative smile might cost me the crown my mother wanted so desperately.

Whew. Enough soul-searching. I was no longer six, and my mother was no longer on the hunt for Little Miss Perfect. Now I was Miss Ace Detective and could do exactly as I pleased, and it pleased me to go home to see what I could find out about Honor Perkins.

I spent about an hour online with no success until I remembered Mrs. Forest claimed she'd lost her fortune by putting all her money in Double Delite Doughnuts. I looked up Double Delite and found the company was still in business with steady sales. Okay, so was Mrs. Forest also a swindler? When I looked her up, all I found was a picture of her and several other elderly ladies at church functions, including the sale of a cookbook with recipes from the congregation. I looked up the account of the robbery at Billie's house, which appeared to be an isolated incident in the neighborhood. None of this fit.

When I picked up Jerry, he reported that auditions had gone well, and that the tall, scholarly looking young man standing with Bea was her son, Ferris.

I did a double take. "You're kidding, right?"

"Nope. Must take after his dad."

Ferris Ricter had dark curly hair and glasses and was actually smiling, something I'd seen Bea do only in her yearbook pictures.

"He came to give her a ride home. Seems to be a regular guy. Joked that his mom wasn't a fan of the movie or the wheel, but chose 'Ferris' after an old boyfriend. I asked him if he'd like to be in the orchestra, but he said he was in Celosia for only a few days."

"Well, what do you know?" Ferris escorted his mother out. "Has Bea said anything else about her feud with Wendall?"

"A lot of grumbling about people keeping their promises."

"She doesn't seem the type of person who'd want to be in a musical comedy."

"That's where the keeping promises comes in. Apparently, she'd promised Evan she'd try out. I heard her tell him she'd do the role, but then they'd be done. Evan says she does keep her word."

"And gets really angry when other people break theirs. So Wendall must have messed up big-time with her."

"I wonder what he promised her."

"Flora said Bea wouldn't tell him."

"Oh, so there are many things he's done wrong, and Bea wants him to guess."

A group of young women went past, all calling "Good night."

Jerry waved good-bye. "You're going to have a case pretty soon, Mac. Those girls would kill to play Laurie. Fortunately, there is a clear front-runner."

"Good." I had enough to worry about. The growing discontent among the members of the Art Guild, the break-in at Billie's, and most of all, the mysterious Honor Perkins and her connection to Jerry. He'd told me he wasn't going to charge off in all directions, but that's exactly how I felt, pulled this way and that with no answers in sight.

Chapter Eight

"Camp Lakenwood! Camp Lakenwood!
Where sex is wild and free!
Camp Lakenwood! Camp Lakenwood!
Come share a beer with me!"

I buried my head under my pillow. How many more months until June?

"Breakfast is ready!"

Jerry then launched into another unacceptable verse of the Camp Lakenwood song. The only way to stop him was to get up, get dressed, go downstairs, and express my concerns. But once again, my stomach rebelled.

Good lord, I thought as I staggered into the bathroom. Have I miscounted my pills? I checked my birth control pill dispenser. Everything was in order. I simply could not be pregnant.

By the time I came into the kitchen, I had things under control. That is, until I smelled what Jerry was cooking, and he said, "Cinnamon toast and sausage coming up."

I really wish he hadn't used that phrase. "Just the toast, please, and some coffee."

Fortunately, he'd turned away to check on the sausage. "I've been thinking about what we should do about Mrs. Forest, Mac. Don't wait for her to call you. I think you should find me and haul me in to talk to her. That way, I'll be able to see what her game is."

"What if she doesn't have a game?"

He faced me. "I have never been to Millersberg. I swear on whatever you want me to swear on." I must have looked like I felt, because he frowned. "Are you still feeling queasy? Maybe you should go to the doctor."

"I don't think it's anything to worry about."

I could tell Jerry wasn't convinced, so I changed the subject. "I forgot to ask if Bea got a part in the show."

"This is top secret info, but I think I can trust you. Bea is Aunt Eller, mainly because no other woman her age tried out. Evan will post the cast list later today, and I predict many hearts will be broken. Nice try changing the subject, by the way, but I still think you should see a doctor."

His argument had to wait because my cell phone rang. The caller ID said "Nell Brenner." "It's Nell. I hope she's calling to say she can come by today."

She wasn't. "Thought you'd like to know somebody tossed a brick through the gallery window last night."

"Uh, oh." Celosia has its share of troubled teenagers, but I had an idea someone was sending a more personal message.

"Dad's got some people investigating. If you want to have a look, you'd better come now. As soon as they're done, we're fixing it."

"Thanks. I'll be right there." I closed my phone. "Someone threw a brick into the gallery window."

"Not very subtle of them. How many members does the Art Guild have?"

"When they met at Pamela's shop, I counted eight, including Pamela, and I can't rule out Larissa."

Jerry handed me a plate of cinnamon toast and brought his plate loaded with toast and sausage to the table. "Eat what you can. I won't be offended."

I nibbled a corner of toast. "Thanks. I'll stop by the drugstore and get something for my stomach."

He handed me my coffee. "Why don't I come to town with you? I can get in some more *Oklahoma* practice this afternoon."

"Sure."

"After we come back from Millersberg."

I knew he wasn't going to let that go.

Yellow police tape kept a small crowd back from the front of the gallery. Bits of glass littered the sidewalk and dangled dangerously from the jagged edges of the broken window. Nell's father, Celosia's chief of police, and two other officers gathered information from the shopkeepers and a thin man in jogging clothes.

Pamela Finch was there, and as soon as she saw me, she hurried over.

"What did I tell you, Madeline? Didn't I say I had bad feelings about this?"

I was glad Jerry came with me because I really didn't want to deal with her and her bad feelings. I wanted to look around. He picked up on this right away.

"Pamela, did you have a premonition?" he asked. "That's my specialty, you know. Tell me all about it."

I left her pouring the whole story of the slighted Art Guild into Jerry's ear while I walked over to Chief Gus Brenner and asked if I could have a look at the crime scene. Nell gets her large frame, blond hair, and small sharp blue eyes from her father. The chief's a gruff, no-nonsense man, but now that I've helped solve three murders, he's more willing to answer my questions.

He jotted another note on his notepad. "Not much to see. We have a brick and a broken window. Must have happened early this morning." He gave a nod toward the thin man in jogging clothes. "Mr. Carson was out for his morning run and called it in. Do you have any ideas?"

"Wendall Clarke hasn't made too many friends with the Art Guild."

"So I've heard." He closed his notepad. "We've given him a call, and he's on his way. Is he a client of yours?"

"Not yet."

"Keep me posted." He called to his daughter. "It's all yours, Nell."

Nell already had a large piece of plywood to cover the opening. As she and another worker maneuvered the board in place, I walked back to Jerry and Pamela.

"I was just telling Jerry I can't imagine any member of the Guild doing this," Pamela said. "There must be someone else in town who doesn't want a gallery here. You need to find out who that is, Madeline."

"Are you hiring me?"

"You know, I think I will. I don't want people to think we're capable of this. Our main goal is to promote the arts and give local artists the opportunity to shine. How much do you charge for—oh my gosh, there's Wendall. He's going to be furious."

A sleek black sports car drove up and parked behind the police car. Wendall and Flora got out. Flora looked upset, but Wendall seemed to shrug off the incident. He was dressed in his usual black and gave his black scarf an irritated toss.

"We got here as soon as we could," he said to Chief Brenner. "What's the damage? Just the window?"

While Chief Brenner explained what had happened to Wendall, Flora timidly approached us.

"Good morning, Flora," I said. "I believe you've met Pamela Finch. This is my husband, Jerry Fairweather."

Pamela gave her a slight smile and a hello. Jerry shook her hand. "Sorry about the window, but Nell will have it repaired in no time."

Flora tugged at that same curl. "I hope so. It's really upsetting to think someone hates us so much."

I knew Pamela wanted to stay aloof, but Flora's sad words must have melted her resolve.

"Dear me, I certainly don't hate you, Mrs. Clarke," she said. "I want us to work things out. In fact, I'm going to hire Madeline to find out who did this."

Flora turned her big blue eyes to me. "Oh, that's right. You're a detective. Wendall and I should hire you, too."

Wendall came up in time to hear this. "Hire Madeline for what? Are you talking about discovering who broke the window?

I'm sure Madeline's a fine detective, but we're not going to bother her with something as trivial as this. It was probably just some kids. Nothing to worry about. We can have this fixed before our two o'clock meeting. Good morning, Pamela." He offered his hand to Jerry. "Wendall Clarke."

"Jerry Fairweather. I'm Madeline's husband."

"And a lucky man. Madeline, we'll see you at the meeting, I hope? You, too, Jerry. It's open to everyone."

"Yes, we'll be there," I said.

"Good. Come on, Baby, we have a lot to do before two o'clock." He took her arm and ushered her back into the sports car.

Pamela dug into her purse. "I don't care what he thinks. I'm hiring you." She wrote me a check right then and there. "I'd better go open my store. When can you come over?"

"Jerry and I have business in Millersburg this morning. How about after the two o'clock meeting?"

"That sounds fine. Hopefully by then you'll have some idea who did this."

The plywood was up and secure, so Nell motioned us in. "Figured you'd want to look around."

Jerry and I stepped into the gallery. The plywood blocked some of the light, but we could still see the area, now painted and ready for art.

"This is a great space," Jerry said. "The Art Guild should be thrilled."

"Didn't Pamela tell you the whole sad story?" I asked. "Thanks, by the way, for the diversion."

"You're welcome. Yes, I heard the Saga of the Spurned Artistes. Which one's most likely to heave a brick?"

"Searching for clues right now."

There wasn't much to search. A few stray chips of glass sparkled on the wide expanse of bare floor. Paint cans and drop cloths were piled in one corner. A ladder was propped against the office door.

Jerry pointed to a large can in the corner. "There's a trash can to root through."

"Dad's men have been through it," Nell said. "It's all yours."

Jerry and I found dried paint stirring sticks, curls of cardboard, wads of masking tape and paper, and a calling card that read: "Larissa Norton, Piano Lessons," with her phone number and address.

"Did the police see this card?" I asked Nell.

"Yeah, she stopped in yesterday to see if one of the painters wanted his son to have lessons. Guess he didn't."

"Did she say anything about the gallery?"

"Well, I figured she just wanted an excuse to see it. She looked around and sniffed as if she wasn't impressed. I would've been surprised if she was."

I put Larissa's card in my pocket. "I'm sure your dad knows the Larissa and Wendall story."

"Everyone knows it. You have a whole town full of suspects."

"Before you grill the whole town, let's go to Millersberg," Jerry said. "We settle things with Mrs. Forest, and then you're free to investigate the Case of the Unwanted Gallery."

"What's happening in Millersberg?" Nell asked. "That's a little squat of a town."

"Jerry has some unfinished business there."

Nell knew all about Jerry's business. "Who'd you rile now, junior?"

"A Mrs. Denby Forest. And I didn't rile her. Somebody's playing a joke."

She picked up a broom and a dustpan. "You look mighty serious for it to be a joke."

"That's because the joke's on me, and I have to clean up afterwards."

Nell chuckled. "And here I thought you'd gone straight."

"I'm trying. Can I help it if the world won't let me?"

I checked my watch. It was a little past ten. "Okay, Jerry, let's go, and when we get there, let me do the talking."

"Only if you stop by the drugstore first."

We stopped by Health Aid Drugs and the pharmacist recommended an over-the-counter remedy for upset stomach. On our way to Millersburg, Jerry asked me if I'd noticed Flora's nervous hair-tugging.

"Yes, she did that a couple of times during lunch. I'm guessing she wants to make certain her hair stays on."

"That's probably it."

"What else could it be?"

"I've been in the game too long. I'm always on the lookout for tells."

"Tells?"

"Little giveaway habits that people are unaware of. Comes in handy when you're playing poker."

"Or solving crimes. You don't think Flora broke the window, do you?"

"She's the last one you'd suspect, isn't she? Maybe she's not happy Wendall's spending all this money on the gallery."

"Well, that's a thought. I'll invite myself to another lunch and find out."

We arrived in Millersberg and drove to Mrs. Forest's house. She was surprised to see me.

"Back so soon? And you've brought Mr. Fairweather." She shook her finger at him. "You should be ashamed of yourself, young man."

Jerry hung his head. "He's very sorry," I said. "He wants to make things right, but he doesn't have a million dollars. Is that the amount you lost?"

"Not exactly. Please come in."

We sat down in the parlor. "I'm still amazed you were able to find him so quickly," Mrs. Forest said.

"That's my job."

"Well, I would be willing to settle for ten thousand."

I could tell it was taking all of Jerry's self control to remain silent.

"We could set up payments, say, a thousand a month for ten months? I think that's more than reasonable."

"Would you excuse us for a moment?" Jerry and I stepped back outside. He was about to pop.

"Mac, this is classic. You always start on the high end, scare the hell out of the mark, and then act like you're doing them a big favor to settle for the amount you wanted in the first place."

"You're certain this is a con?"

"I want you to try two things. One, mention that we're getting the police involved. If she's scamming us, she won't want anything to do with them. Two, tell her I'll have to pay her in cash, and I promise you she'll light up like a Christmas tree."

We returned to the parlor. Somewhere in the back of the house, a cat yowled.

"I'll feed you in a minute," Mrs. Forest called to it.

"Mrs. Forest," I said, "you're not the only one with a complaint about Mr. Fairweather's activities. Would you accompany us to the police station and add your complaint to the list?"

She rubbed her leg and grimaced. "Oh, I'd love to, but this leg of mine gives me so much trouble if I ride anywhere. I believe we can settle this ourselves without involving the police, now can't we? Mr. Fairweather looks like a man who learns from his mistakes."

I was beginning to see what Jerry was talking about. "I really think you should go to the police." Jerry tried to look contrite.

"Just pay me what you owe me, young man, and I won't press any charges."

"That's very generous of you," I said, "but Mr. Fairweather's current financial situation is somewhat unusual. He would have to pay you in cash."

Mrs. Forest brightened. "Why, that would be most acceptable."

"Merry Christmas," Jerry said, sotto voce.

"I'll see to it." I stood up to shake her hand when the cat yowled again. Jerry ran past me and down the hallway toward the back of the house.

Mrs. Forest gasped in alarm. "What's he doing?"

I heard another voice, a slight scream, running footsteps, a crash, and a "Damn it!" from Jerry. Then the back door slammed twice.

Mrs. Forest wrung her hands. "Oh, no, he's getting away!"

What in the world? I hurried to the back. Jerry came limping across the backyard. "What was all that?"

"Her partner," he said. "The way that cat kept howling I had a feeling someone else was back here, listening in, in case things got ugly."

"What did you do to your leg?"

"Tripped over the cat."

"Was it Honor Perkins?"

"I couldn't tell. It was somebody large, though, and whoever it was screamed like a girl. Can I talk now? There are a few things I want to say to Mrs. Forest."

But when we got back to the parlor, Mrs. Forest was gone.

"Bad leg and all," Jerry said. "It's a miracle."

To my surprise, he went back to the kitchen and looked through all the cabinets.

"Do you need a snack?" I asked.

Satisfied with what he found in the cabinets, he checked the refrigerator and then moved down the hall. I followed and watched, mystified, as he looked in all the rooms and all the closets.

"Jerry, what are you doing?"

"A real con woman would be living very light," he said. "From the look of things, I'd say Mrs. Forest actually lives here. Plenty of food in the kitchen, lots of clothes in the closets and junk that accumulates over the years. Check out the dresser. Family photos, pictures of her cats." He took a deep breath. "That lived-in smell. Well, most of it's cat, but you know what I mean."

"Then what's going on?"

"A real con woman wouldn't have all this stuff. She'd fold her tent and get out of town, but I have a feeling Mrs. Forest is just somebody's stooge. She won't leave her cats, or all these family pictures. I don't think she's going anywhere, and if she does, it'll take her a while to pack. Let's go get some lunch and come right back. She won't be expecting that."

I agreed to this plan. "I want to apologize for doubting you. Mrs. Forest sure had me fooled."

He grinned. "You gotta watch out for the little old ladies."

Chapter Nine

We found a diner on Millersberg's Main Street. I was hungry enough to eat some tomato soup and grilled cheese sandwich. Jerry reminded me to take the medicine. My stomach hadn't given me any trouble since this morning, but he insisted I try the pills.

"Unless you want me to haul you off to the nearest doctor."

"No, thank you."

We gave Mrs. Forest about an hour to return and settle down. Then we went back. Jerry parked the car several houses down and suggested we split up.

"You go in the front. Tell her the police have arrested me and she's safe. I'm going in the back."

I didn't bother to ask if he could get in. One of his dubious skills is his ability to pick locks. "Don't scare her. You'll give her a heart attack."

"She's not the one I hope to scare."

Mrs. Forest was puzzled to find me at her door again.

"Mrs. Forest, good news. The police caught Mr. Fairweather."

She opened the door a little wider. "Oh, my, well, that's a relief. He frightened me, bounding out the door like that." She turned and spoke over her shoulder. "Did you hear that?"

I could see someone else sitting in the parlor, a very large woman with long black hair cut in bangs straight across her forehead and keen dark eyes.

"Yes, now say thank you and good-bye," this woman said.

"This is my niece, visiting me for a few days."

I didn't think so. "I didn't realize you had company. I won't bother you any longer."

I figured I'd given Jerry enough time. Sure enough, he appeared from the kitchen.

"But I will," he said.

Mrs. Forest gave a squeak of terror. The other woman jumped up and appealed to me. "Oh, my God, it's that madman! He's come back to kill us! Call the police!"

"Give it a rest, Honor," Jerry said. "That's my wife."

The woman stared at me for a moment and then gave a burst of laughter. "I don't believe it! You can't fool me, Jerry, but I sure as hell fooled you."

"Not for long."

Jerry looked as angry as I'd ever seen him. I thought I'd better jump in. "I'm really his wife. Madeline Fairweather. And you must be Honor Perkins."

She was still chuckling to herself. "The one and only. You've met Denby Forest. Take a bow, Denby."

Mrs. Forest's eyes darted from Honor to Jerry to me and settled on Honor. "You said there wouldn't be any trouble."

"And there won't be, right, Jerry? Now we're even."

"Even for what?" I asked. "I didn't appreciate your joke."

"Oh, now don't get your knickers in a twist, Mrs. Fairweather. Jerry owed me for a bank examiner swindle. Now we're done."

"Bank examiner swindle?" Just when I thought I'd heard it all.

Jerry gave me a look to say, not now. "All a big misunderstanding. Honor, if you'd waited where I told you to, you would've gotten your cut."

She shook her head. "Oh, there was a lot more to it than that."

Mrs. Forest tugged on Honor's sleeve. "When do I get my money?"

Honor rolled her eyes. "I told you I'd pay you. Chill out."

Mrs. Forest pointed at me. "This woman's a private investigator. If you don't give me my money, I'll hire her to track you down."

Honor looked interested. "So that card you gave her was the real deal?"

"Yes, and since I'm not too happy with you right now, I'd take the job."

She chuckled again. "See what comes of working with amateurs, Jerry? Let me pay Denby off, and then we can talk about old times."

I'd had enough. "No, if you and Jerry are through playing jokes on each other, we'll go. We have a meeting in Celosia at two."

"You actually live in Celosia?" she said to Jerry. "I thought that was another one of your cover addresses."

"I inherited an old house there."

"Still doing the séances?"

"No, I've reformed, which is more than I can say for you."

"Aw, a little harmless prank."

"No, I'm talking about a D and S on Pumpkin Lane."

She paused. "Oh, really?"

"The woman you robbed is a friend of Mac's. She gave me a good description. Who are you working with? And more importantly, are you crazy?"

"I'm sure I don't know what you're talking about."

Mrs. Forest tugged harder. "My money."

"Yes, yes." She kept her self-satisfied smirk. "It was fun, though, wasn't it, Jerry? Admit it. Nothing like the rush of a good con."

"Not when I'm on the receiving end," he said. "And not when you're involved in breaking and entering."

"Can we talk about this later?" She pried Mrs. Forest from her arm. "All right, all right, you'll get your money. Is there somewhere we can meet?"

"We're going to talk about this now."

"In front of the—?" She gave a little nod indicating Mrs. Forest, and one indicating me.

"Mac's not a mark and never has been. We can talk outside if you don't want Mrs. Forest to hear."

"I just want my money," Mrs. Forest said.

"Pay her off and come on."

Honor sighed theatrically. "All right. Give me a minute."

Jerry went out the back door to stand guard while I covered the front in case Honor decided to make another run for it. After a few minutes, she came out the front door and gave me an appraising dark-eyed stare.

"So you're really a private investigator, huh? I thought you were a beauty queen."

"Beauty queen's not exactly a full-time job. The pay is lousy and no one takes you seriously."

"But it makes a great cover, doesn't it? Have you solved any crimes?" Her tone bordered on condescending.

"A few. Including murder."

She backed up in mock fear. "Oh, a tough gal. Not exactly Jerry's style. You know he always went for the baby-doll blondes. What was that woman's name? Olive? Olivia?"

"Olivia."

"Yeah, he was hanging around her for the longest time. What did you do to pry him away? You must know some pretty good tricks, yourself."

"No tricks."

"Well, we ran some great schemes. He's never told you about any of them?"

"He's told about some of his adventures, but he never mentioned you."

She had a pretty good poker face, but I could tell this bugged her. "Wild times, I'm telling you. What's it like being married to him? Never thought he'd settle down."

"Never a dull moment," I said. "Especially when we have to confront his old con buddies."

"Aw, you don't have to worry about me. I was only fooling around. I apologize if I upset you." She turned to call, "I'm out here talking to your wife, Jerry."

He joined us. "Okay, I want details."

"Nothing to tell," Honor said. "I did the scope, that's all."

"Who asked you to? Who are you working with? Nobody in our circle went that big."

"You know I can't tell you that, Jerry." She glanced at me. "Sorry about the D and S. Insurance paid for your friend's stuff, didn't they?"

"What's a D and S?" I asked.

"Dinner and a show. It's also called the Broadway. Really kinda harmless."

"What if my friend and her husband had come home early?"

Honor shrugged. "Everybody hightails it out of there."

"You were involved only with the setup?" Jerry asked.

"Yes, and what's it to you? You're out, right? No more cons? At least, that's what Rick tells me."

Jerry hesitated. I could tell he was torn between wanting to help his former partner in crime and letting her deal with the consequences of her shady actions.

Honor pressed another button. "So now that you're a law-abiding citizen, you're not going to rat on me, are you?"

"No. But you can't keep doing this kind of thing."

"I repeat, what's it to you?"

He took another long pause. I knew he wanted to be loyal to his friends, but wasn't there a limit? I wondered if this was going to be the final cut in that knotty rope that tied him to his con man past. "I guess it's nothing to me. You said we're even, so we're even. Come on, Mac."

Honor gave him a jaunty little salute, but gave me a look that bordered on hostile. "Till next time."

Oh, there'd better not be a next time.

Jerry didn't say much on the drive back to Celosia, except to express concern that if Honor had moved on to the larger more dangerous cons, he wouldn't be able to help her.

I wasn't so sure we'd seen the last of her. "So all this with Mrs. Forest and the million dollars was just an elaborate prank to get even with you. Is this something you and your friends did all the time?"

"Honor's the only one who got a kick out of conning us. I suppose it made her feel superior. She never could do card tricks or pick locks, and she wasn't the physical type to be a bait girl. Maybe she was jealous." He rubbed his forehead. "I don't know. I can't believe she's in this deep."

"I hate to say this, but we should call the police. She could lead them to the people who actually robbed Billie's house."

"I can't rat on her."

"But I can. She has to know that's what I'm going to do."

Jerry heaved a sigh and didn't answer.

◇◇◇

He was still in a thoughtful mood by the time we arrived at the gallery for the two o'clock meeting. A new window gleamed with the words Celosia Art Gallery in swirling gold letters.

"At least it doesn't say Clarke Art Gallery," I said. "I don't think that would win him any more fans."

Rows of chairs had been set up inside. Besides Pamela and the members of the Art Guild, I saw Larissa Norton, her arms folded, her lips in a thin line. I recognized a reporter from the *Celosia News*, the head of the downtown merchants' association, and a young policeman.

Flora was seated in the first row. She was wearing a pink suit with rows of gold buttons and lots of gold jewelry, including the bracelet with the little gold and yellow leaves. She looked gorgeous but maybe a touch too flashy. I would've attempted to be more subtle. The curl of hair was getting quite a workout.

Jerry and I took the two seats next to her. She leaned over to me. "Thanks for sitting with me. I didn't want to come, but Wendall insisted."

"Everyone will settle down."

"I don't think Bea Ricter ever will. And Larissa is here. I want to sink into the floor. Why did she come?"

"Just curious, I suppose."

"I wouldn't want to be anywhere near my ex. She was probably hoping the gallery would be a big flop."

Wendall stood facing the group. Standing next to him was a severe-looking, dark-haired woman all in black. Wendall held up his hands for silence. "All right, everyone, I know you're anxious to find out more about your new art gallery. We're very lucky to have secured the services of a very fine curator from Parkland's Silver Gallery. Let me introduce Sasha Gregory."

The dark-haired woman gave a brief nod.

"Sasha and I will be happy to review any and all submissions. Just see her after the meeting. We plan to hold a reception and grand opening next Saturday, where you can see the best artwork Celosia has to offer. Does anyone have any questions?"

Bea Ricter was already waving her hand. "Why didn't you get a curator from here? No offense to Ms. Gregory, but we have plenty of qualified people in Celosia who could run this gallery."

"Who did you have in mind?" Wendall asked.

"Me, for one! I could run this place!"

A few people laughed and there was a general muttering from the Guild for her to sit down and be quiet.

She glared at the crowd. "I could! What do you have to do? Pick the artwork that goes on the walls, pick the artwork that goes in the display cases. That's all there is to it. I could certainly do a better job than someone who never lived here. She won't know whose work is good and whose is just crap."

Pamela spoke in a tense whisper. "Bea, please. I think it's a little late to present your case. Wendall's already hired Ms. Gregory."

"What about Larissa, then? I know they're divorced, but she knows all about running a business."

"Hush, Bea, for God's sake."

Bea flopped back into her chair. I wasn't sure it was possible, but Larissa sat even stiffer. Her voice was dark with sarcasm. "Thank you, Bea, but I have no desire to have any dealings with this gallery."

"Then why are you here?" Bea asked.

"It's a public meeting. I have a right to be here."

Sasha Gregory raised a slim hand. Her voice, by contrast, was low and calm. "If Sasha may say something." When she had everyone's attention, she continued. "Perhaps there is some concern that, not being a native Celosian, Sasha will not be a fair judge of your art. Sasha assures you, everyone will have a chance to be represented in this gallery. Sasha will be happy to speak to anyone about this. The goal of this gallery is to advance the universality of art in your community, not exclude artists because of visionary differences."

No one said anything for a long moment. I wasn't sure how many in the audience understood what Sasha Gregory had said, and the fact that she referred to herself in third person had even given me pause. Jerry was trying not to laugh. Quite a few people gave her narrow-eyed looks, as if to say, "Are you putting one over on us?"

Wendall rubbed his hands together in a satisfied manner. "Well, then, I think that says it all. Any further questions?"

Despite Pamela's efforts to stop her, Bea waved her hand.

Wendall smiled politely. "Yes, Bea?"

She stood up, rearranging her patchwork skirt. "I just wanted to say that although I appreciate a gallery, I don't like the way you steamrolled in and set everything up without consulting us."

"I did consult the Celosia Chamber of Commerce, the city commissioners, and the downtown merchants association. As much as I value your input, the Art Guild is basically a social group without any real clout. I don't think someone opening a new landscaping business would need the approval of the Garden Club."

This did not sit well with the members of the Guild. Fortunately, the reporter from the *Celosia News* had some questions.

"Mr. Clarke, what will the hours be for the gallery?"

"Ten-to-five weekdays and Saturdays, one-to-four on Sundays. Free admission. And Sasha hopes to bring some exhibits from Parkland on a regular basis."

Bea Ricter wasn't finished. "Didn't you forget a place for children?"

"Not at all. There's a special room in the back for children to have hands-on experiences and after-school classes. I hope you'll check it out." He looked around the group. "Any further questions? No? Then those of you who wish to display your work, if you'd please fill out one of these forms and make an appointment with Ms. Gregory. We have some refreshments over here. Please stay and enjoy yourselves."

As Bea continued to seethe, and members of the Art Guild made a dash for the forms, I made my way over to Wendall.

"All in all, that went very well, I think," he said. "I was expecting more resistance, but I think people understand I can't feature everyone right now. I have to go with the best. Once the gallery's established, maybe I'll have time and room for them."

I didn't like that "maybe." "For the grand opening, it would be a tactful gesture to have a sample of everyone's work."

"I'll think about it. However, I definitely want some of your work to be the first we display."

I didn't want to get in the middle of this. "I don't have anything ready right now."

"Even some pencil sketches would do. I'll see that Sasha leaves an appointment open for you."

I could feel the anger around me as members of the Art Guild heard every word.

"That's not necessary, Wendall. I can wait."

"Nonsense! You're the only one with any real talent."

Before he could say anything else to make me the most popular girl in the room, I asked him for a word in private. We moved to a corner of the room.

"What's this about, Madeline?"

"If you want my advice, in order for the gallery to move forward in a positive way, you need to clear things up with Bea. There's obviously some unresolved issue between the two of you."

"I really thought we'd settled our differences." He lowered his voice. "Madeline, we all do things when we're young that we're not proud of. You're a beautiful woman, and I imagine you could've had any boy you wanted in high school. I had a good time in high school, too, and well…let's just say I may have led some girls on. Apparently, Bea hasn't forgiven me."

"You had a relationship?"

"A one-night stand, I'm afraid. I thought I was quite the stud back then. But she shouldn't feel bad. I slept with a lot of girls because they threw themselves at me. However, I'm not that wild teenage boy anymore, and I'm going to try to make amends if she'll let me."

We were interrupted by Bea's strident voice.

"Where did you get that?"

We turned to see Bea grab Flora's wrist where the little leaf bracelet dangled.

Flora tried to back away. "Wendall gave it to me."

"That bracelet is mine! Give it to me."

For a moment, Flora's eyes narrowed, and I thought she would haul back and give Bea a good thump on the nose. I saw Jerry get ready to referee. Then Flora's look of bemused innocence returned. "My goodness. If you're that sure, you can have it."

She started to take the bracelet off, but Bea gave it a rough tug. The bracelet snapped, and all the little leaves clattered to the floor. Bea kicked the leaves and rounded on Wendall.

"So much for your promises!"

Most of the people were busy filling out the forms and getting appointments from Sasha, or at the tables filling plates with refreshments, and missed this little drama. Bea stormed out. Flora rubbed her wrist and shot Bea a look of pure loathing before turning a sweet, big-eyed gaze to Wendall, who hugged her.

"Are you all right, Baby?"

"I didn't mean to cause so much trouble."

Behind them, Jerry was looking at Flora thoughtfully. I was wondering how Flora got a bracelet that apparently Wendall gave to Bea. "Wendall, do you know what that was all about?"

"Oh, a little misunderstanding, that's all. If you'll excuse me, I believe that policeman is here to have a word with me about the incident yesterday."

Flora gave a little wave. "Good-bye, Madeline. Good-bye, Jerry. Thanks for sitting with me."

Jerry picked up one of the yellow leaves. "That was interesting."

"Yes, if Wendall's left his bad boy past behind, why does he have Bea's bracelet? And why was Flora wearing it?"

He gestured toward the long line at the sign-up table. "Well, one thing's for sure. The gallery's not going to be a flop."

"The whole thing is so schizophrenic," I said. "The members of the Art Guild are still angry at Wendall, and yet they knocked each other over getting in line for an appointment with Sasha, who, by the way, must imagine she's Queen of Artlandia. I don't believe I've ever heard anyone consistently refer to herself in third person. Madeline's not sure what to make of it."

"Jerry says it's hilarious."

◇◇◇

We walked the short distance to Flair For Fashion. Pamela had yet to arrive, so the door was locked.

Jerry reached into his pocket for his keys. "I can get us in, if you like."

I wasn't in any hurry to wade through the paper. "All that mess can wait." I leaned back against the door. "I saw that look you gave Flora. What's up?"

"That little baby doll act she's got going is very convincing."

"You think it's all an act?"

"I'm not sure. I thought for a moment I was going to have to peel her off Bea. But Bea could test anyone's patience. I wanted to smack her myself."

"Well, a lot of women play up to men that way. And Wendall confessed he'd been a studly dude in high school, so he's used to being fawned upon. I was right about his relationship with Bea. She is a woman scorned."

"And still angry after all these years?"

"Don't you remember the first woman who broke your heart?"

"There were so many."

The policeman who'd been in the gallery came up the street. "Ms. Maclin, Chief Brenner would like to know if you have any news for him."

I took out my phone. "I'll be glad to call him."

The chief was interested in what I'd found out in the meeting. "Wendall has hired a curator from the Silver Gallery in Parkland named Sasha Gregory. The members of the Art Guild are happily signing up for gallery times, and Bea had an altercation with Flora Clarke. Something about a bracelet Mrs. Clarke was wearing that Bea felt was hers. Flora handed it over, and Bea left in her usual style."

"Was Larissa Norton at the meeting?"

"Yes, but no words were exchanged, just hateful looks."

He thanked me and hung up.

"Need some help looking for the letter?" Jerry asked.

"Yes, but first, I have to call Billie and tell her about Honor."

"Yeah, I know. If Honor's smart, she's already left town."

I hadn't meant to give her a head start, but if it made Jerry feel a little better about my decision, then I'd let him think that. I called Billie and told her the woman who scammed her was Honor Perkins, a professional con artist.

"And she robbed my house?"

"No, she gathered information for the burglars, but she may be able to lead the police to them, if they can find her."

"Thanks, Madeline. That's a start, at least. When are you coming back for another visit?"

"Soon, I hope." We said good-bye, and I hung up. "Jerry, you said you never used your real name, and I remember Rick doesn't use his, either. Why does Honor use hers?"

"Sheer egotism. She figures she'll never get caught."

"And explain something else. What exactly is a bank examiner swindle, and why did Honor feel compelled to pay you back?"

He looked apologetic. "I'm not proud of this one, okay? Honor set it up, and then I called the mark—I mean, this woman—pretending to be a bank examiner, and told her there was something wrong with her account and could she help catch the dishonest bank teller? The woman went to the bank, made a withdrawal, and then took it outside and handed it to me. I said I'll mark it and redeposit it."

"But you kept it, and half was to go to Honor."

"She wasn't where she was supposed to be. I had to get out of there."

This was worse than I thought. "You stole some poor woman's hard-earned money."

"As I said, not proud. And it wasn't very much. We didn't take her life's savings, just two thousand dollars."

"People fall for that?"

"All the time. But I didn't do it again. Way too risky."

"What else haven't you done again?"

"Whatever I've done, I promise I'm through. I have to set a good example for Hortensia."

"Do I have to have a baby to make you reform?"

"Yes, exactly. You see right through me."

I had to smile back. "I know what you want. You want a little con baby to use as a shill or whatever it is you call it."

He snapped his fingers. "That's it. That's her name. Shilleeta."

"I don't think so."

"Shilleeta Decoy Fairweather. That's sheer poetry."

Pamela came hurrying up the street. "Oh, there you are, Madeline. My apologies." She unlocked the door. "I meant to give you my key. I need to go back and sign up for a time to bring in my work. Can you keep an eye on the store, as well?"

"I can do that while Mac's working," Jerry said.

"Thank you. I'll be back as soon as I can."

We went inside Flair For Fashion. Jerry looked around the shop. "Very elite. Very trendy."

"Very expensive."

"Where's this letter supposed to be?"

I showed him the cluttered room. "Welcome to Needle in a Haystack."

"Good grief. I'm beginning to think everyone in Celosia is a hoarder."

It was true that several of my former clients had disorderly homes. "You can look through that stack near the door. That way you can see if anyone comes in." He took a chunk of the leaning stack and began to thumb through the pages. "The letter should be from Daniel Richards, and it gives Pamela permission to remodel the building."

We worked in silence for a while, and then Jerry said, "Are you going to put any of your work in the gallery?"

"I think I'd better give everyone else a turn first. Some of the Guild ladies looked a bit testy." I closed one file drawer and opened another. "Nothing in that one but receipts."

"Nothing in this stack but order forms."

"I meant to tell you if you find anything that pertains to the Art Guild, stack it on this chair."

"Okay." He gave me the full force of his beautiful gray eyes. "Mac, I really am sorry I didn't tell you about my other crimes."

"Apology accepted."

He grinned and gave the door a little nudge with his foot, closing us in. "I think the store will be safe for a few minutes, don't you?"

"There's not a lot of room in here."

"We'll manage."

We managed. Then we managed some more. And we managed to be through before Pamela came back. She was so excited about getting an appointment with Sasha, she didn't notice our slightly disheveled appearance.

"Have any luck?" she asked.

I didn't dare look at Jerry. "Not yet."

"Well, I'm so relieved Ms. Gregory is going to consider my work. You don't mind leaving early, do you? I want plenty of time to look over all my pictures. I need to decide on just the right ones to show her."

"We don't mind."

Pamela practically pushed us out. "Okay, thanks. See you tomorrow."

We stood in front of the store for a few moments while Jerry retied his tie and I pushed my curls back into order. Down the block we could see cars still parked on both sides of the street at the gallery.

"Shows no sign of slowing down," Jerry said. "Maybe the problem will take care of itself."

"I don't know. That was quite a blowup between Bea and Flora."

"She dropped her wounded little flower act for a moment. I'm not sure if she meant to."

"Bea would provoke anybody." I hunted in my purse for my keys. "Please don't tell me Flora's another of your con artist buddies. Honor is more than enough."

"I don't recognize Flora from any past dealings. As for Honor, she won't bother us again."

I did not believe that for one minute.

Chapter Ten

When we got home, Denisha, Austin, and Kennedy were waiting for us on the porch.

"Rats," Jerry said. "I forgot to see about buying a Wow System."

"Looks like the three of them are getting along. Maybe all is forgiven."

We got out of the car and were immediately surrounded by the kids.

"Jerry!" Austin said. "Did you get a Wow?"

"No, I'm sorry, guys. Mac and I got involved with something and I completely forgot."

Austin was down for only a moment. "That's okay. We can go to Kennedy's."

Denisha didn't look happy with this decision. Kennedy had another question.

"I saw you had a piano," she said to Jerry. "Do you ever give lessons?"

"No. I suppose I could, though."

"I take lessons from Mrs. Norton, but I don't like her. She's really strict."

"I've never tried, but I guess I could," he said. "Show me what you know already."

While all three kids and Jerry experimented with the piano, I checked the answering machine and was surprised to find a message from my mother asking me to call. When I called, she was unusually cheerful. I soon found out why.

"Madeline, I hear Wendall Clarke is opening a gallery in Celosia. What a piece of luck for you! I hope you're going to show your work there. He's such a character. Have you met that new wife of his? She's at least fifteen years younger. Quite the little princess. She used to be married to Stan Bailey, you know. Talk about an upgrade! Bailey never amounted to anything. I'm not surprised she left him. When can I come visit?"

I was almost speechless. Mother never wanted to visit. She's resigned to the fact that Jerry and I are married, and she's become a little more tolerant of my artistic endeavors, mainly because I had a successful showing at one of Parkland's premiere galleries. This gave her a new set of bragging rights. But she'd never shown any interest in seeing our new home.

"You're welcome any time, Mom."

"What's Jerry doing these days?"

"Oh, he's musical director for the Celosia Theater." I made it sound as lofty as possible. Even though Mother says she loves Jerry, she's baffled by his refusal to take any of the Fairweather fortune and is not a fan of his carefree lifestyle. If she knew of his past shady dealings, it would knock her perfectly ordered world off its axis.

"That sounds impressive, Madeline. I hope it pays well."

"We're doing all right."

"I suppose you still have your little agency?"

My little agency. Thanks, Mom. "Yes, I'm working on a couple of cases."

"One of my friends said she thought she saw you at Billamena Tyson's yesterday."

In some ways, Parkland is as small a town as Celosia. "I stopped by to visit."

I braced myself for a lecture on why I didn't take the time to visit my own mother since I was right there in the neighborhood, but instead, she latched on to the pageant connection. I should have known.

"Are the two of you thinking of entering Mrs. Parkland? She

still has a reasonably good voice, and if you practiced every day, you could have your talent in shape in a couple of weeks."

After my last pageant, I'd sold my violin. I was never going to play "Orange Blossom Special" again. "We talked about other things."

"She's let herself go, but you still look wonderful. You could easily win."

Was *she* ever going to let go? "I'm kind of busy right now."

There was a long pause. "Well, I'm very interested in seeing the new gallery. Maybe I'll drive over there later this week."

"I'll be glad to see you." I meant it. Could my mother and I finally attempt a real relationship?

By the time I got back to the parlor, Austin and Denisha had already left, and Kennedy had called her mother to see if she could switch piano teachers.

"She says she'll think about it," she said to Jerry. "I guess I'd better go. Thanks."

"You're welcome."

As she skipped out, I said, "You'll never guess who wants to visit us."

"The stork?"

"No. My mother."

He was impressed. "Really? What brought this on?"

"The new gallery. She wants to see it."

"Did you tell her to come on down?"

"She said she may drive over next week." I still couldn't quite believe it.

"This news deserves a fanfare." Jerry played several impressive chords on the piano, started a cheery tune, and then slid into a minor key. "Uh, oh. What would she think about being a grandmother?"

I sat down on the piano bench beside him. "That's not high on her list. And I'm afraid if we had a girl, she'd try to make her into a pageant princess."

"Then we'd better have a boy."

"I'd rather have dinner." I gave him a hug. "What's on the menu tonight?"

"Spaghetti."

I waited, but my stomach did not object. "Great. I'm going to paint for a while."

"I'll be in Oklahoma."

I worked in my studio for about an hour, but this time I couldn't concentrate on my paintings or lose myself in the creative process. I kept thinking about Honor Perkins. On top of my usual concerns about Jerry's old con buddies, Honor seemed like a woman who was not likely to let Jerry go. I thought there was a lot more to her scheme than payback for a past con job. I wondered if he knew she had feelings for him. Probably not. My husband was very clever about many things, but he didn't always connect the emotional dots. It had taken him forever to realize I was his perfect choice.

On second thought, maybe I was wrong about Honor. Maybe she just missed the good old con days and having Jerry as a partner. But my pageant days had taught me quite a bit about jealousy. That's what I saw in Honor's keen dark eyes.

It was almost seven-thirty when I came into the kitchen. Since it was Wednesday night—church night—Jerry didn't have to be at the theater. He was piling a heap of spaghetti onto his plate. "Someone from the choir called and said they were having some kind of retreat meeting tonight, so I wasn't needed," he said. "I figured you'd come down when you got hungry. I didn't want to disturb you."

I helped myself to some spaghetti and took my place at the table. "You've already disturbed me. I need to know what other schemes of yours are likely to cause trouble."

"I'm not sure I can remember all of them."

"Try."

He gave himself another helping of sauce and sat down at the table. "Well, let's see. Besides the séances, Jeff and I ran a lot of little cons, the knife trick, simple bar tricks with matches and coins. With Rick it was the fake unicorn pictures, pet psychics, and the purse scam. Del and I ran some fob off games and twinkles. I guess that leaves Honor and the bank examiner con, the one I told you about."

"Anything else?"

He shook his head. "I believe that's it."

I wound some spaghetti around my fork. "So no more of these friends hold grudges, or want you back in the game, or have angry victims hunting them and, by association, you?"

"I hope not. I'm really sorry about all this, Mac."

I can't stay mad at him for long. "I know. I'm just worried about our future. The next threat might not be a practical joke."

"You have to understand that for me none of these cons were about cheating folks out of their money. It was about seeing what I could get away with. It was a lot of fun for me."

"It was illegal. You're lucky you weren't caught."

"That's why I stopped. I'm a married man and possibly a father."

"You always turn the conversation around to that, don't you?"

"Now that I've given up my cons, I have to find another way to entertain myself."

I set my fork aside. "Okay, suppose, just suppose we had a baby. Since I set up my agency in town, I've been lucky to have enough work, but I can't count on my fellow Celosians to kill each other on a regular basis."

"Then you'll be happy to know I emailed my resume to several more companies."

"That sounds encouraging. What did you put down under experience?"

"'Sidekick to an extremely successful private investigator.' No, the word I used was 'associate.' We'll see what happens." Jerry gave me another searching gaze and then moved his chair so he could put his arm around me. "What's really bothering you about this, Mac?"

What was really bothering me? I wasn't sure. "Maybe I still feel pressured. You know that's all Bill talked about."

"Because he saw his wife as a baby-making machine. What's he got now, six?"

"Number four is on the way."

"The more children he has, the more manly he feels. You know that's not true with me."

"I'm coming around to the idea. But what about my mother? She'll have our child in pageants from the day it's born."

"Nope. I will con her out of that idea."

"It would be worth having a baby to see you do that."

"So we have a deal?"

My phone rang. "Hold that thought."

It was Nell. "Madeline, are you busy?"

"Just having supper."

"Got a bunch of pictures to hang at the gallery. You mind stopping by and giving me some advice?"

"I can be there in about twenty minutes." She thanked me and I hung up, relieved to have postponed the baby deal for the moment. "Nell needs my help at the gallery. Care to come along?"

Nell unlocked the front gallery door for us. "Thanks for coming. I'm not sure where all this stuff goes."

The stuff was a stack of paintings and a pile of sculptures. I recognized Ginger's ping-pong creations and Bea Ricter's distressed wooden frames. Several of the frames were in pieces.

"What happened there, Nell?"

"Found them like that. Guess they got knocked over."

With Jerry's help, we hung the pictures and placed the sculptures in the display cases. Then we cleared all the packing materials, plastic bags, and strips of tape.

"What about Bea's broken frames?"

"Just leave them there, I guess. She can do what she wants with 'em. We can put the trash out back." Our hands were full, so Nell pushed the back door open with her hip and stepped outside. She did a little side step and almost tripped over something. "Good lord!"

The something was Wendall Clarke, stretched out in the narrow space behind the gallery's back door. As I hurriedly punched in 9-1-1 on my phone, I saw a shadowy shape hurry around the corner, get into a car, and speed away. Jerry sprinted after it, returning after a few minutes to say he couldn't see the license plate, but the car was a newer model beige Accord.

"Sounds like Larissa Norton's car," Nell said. She set her trash bag aside and bent down with me over Wendall. "Is he dead?"

I carefully felt Wendall's wrist. "I'm afraid so."

There wasn't much light, but I saw a large chunk of wood by Wendall's head, the same type of wood Bea Ricter used for her artwork. His forehead was scraped and dark with blood. The same dark bloodstains were on the piece of wood.

Nell's voice was shaky. "What's he doing out here? He didn't say anything about coming back to the gallery tonight."

"Are you certain that was Larissa's car?"

"I'm pretty sure. You think she lured him back here to kill him?"

I thought it more likely Larissa would kill Flora. "I don't know. A lot of people were angry with Wendall."

In the distance we could hear sirens. The EMTs would be here in a few minutes, but they'd be too late to save Wendall. The police would be here, too, so I had a few minutes to look around. I was almost certain the piece of wood was the murder weapon. From the mark on Wendall's forehead, I figured he must have known his assailant for anyone to get close enough to hit him. If I wanted to attack a man that large, I would've tried to come from behind. Wendall's murderer must have been someone he knew and someone who took him completely by surprise.

The light was too dim to examine the scene quickly, and before Jerry and I had the chance to check the rest of the yard, a police car drove up. Chief Brenner was first on the scene, followed by the ambulance.

As Nell explained matters to her father, she managed to get control of her voice. "I called Madeline to help me hang some pictures. We were taking out the trash when we found him. You might want to have a word with Larissa Norton. We saw her car driving away."

I pointed out the piece of wood. "Looks like he was hit by that. It's the kind of wood Bea Ricter uses for her picture frames, so you might want to talk to her, too."

Chief Brenner gave me a sharp glance. "Anything else?"

I could truthfully say no.

"All right. On your way home, stop by the station and give them your full statement. You, too, Jerry, and you, Nell. Are you all right?"

She took off her cap to give her hair a brief swipe, then put her cap back on. This simple act steadied her. "It was a real cowardly act, Dad. Never expected someone so big and full of life as Wendall to die like this."

My thoughts exactly. No matter what opinion people had of him, Wendall Clarke had been a force of nature, and to see him lying crumpled on the ground had been a shock.

"You gotta catch his murderer, Dad."

The chief was not pleased someone had killed a prominent hometown man. "I plan to."

"Can we go with you when you tell Flora?" I asked him. "She doesn't have many friends in town."

"Yes. Wait for me at the station."

Wendall's body was taken away, and the piece of wood bagged as evidence.

After we gave our statements to the police, Jerry and I went with the chief to the Clarkes' house. Flora met us at the door, and as Chief Brenner explained what had happened, she shuddered and began to cry. I put my arm around her shoulders.

"Come sit down, Flora. We'll find out who did this."

Her voice caught on her sobs. "I thought it would be me. These were Wendall's friends. I know they weren't happy with him, but he knew them. He went to school with them. I'm the stranger. Why didn't they kill me instead?"

I led her into the living room, and we sat down together on the sofa. "We're not certain it was someone who knew Wendall." Although I thought the odds were good it was.

The chief got out a notepad. "When did your husband leave the house this evening, Mrs. Clarke?"

"A little after eight."

"Did he say where he was going? Was he meeting someone?"

"He said he was going to the gallery, that's all. He usually likes me to go with him, but he said I didn't need to come this time, and he'd be right back." When she realized Wendall would never be right back, she collapsed into tears.

The chief waited until she was able to speak again, his small blue eyes showing sympathy. "What happened after the meeting this afternoon? Did anyone say anything to him that you might have perceived as a threat?"

"N-no, they were all making appointments with Sasha, and they seemed glad to do it."

"I have to ask where you've been all evening."

She gulped back more tears. "I've been here by myself. You have to believe I would never hurt my husband."

"It's a question I have to ask."

"There's no one who can vouch for me. I haven't got a single friend in this town. Madeline's the only one who's been kind to me. Madeline." She looked at me as if seeing me for the first time. "I want you to find out who killed Wendall."

I could tell the chief wasn't happy. "The police will handle this investigation, Mrs. Clarke."

"I want all the help I can possibly get. I can afford it. Madeline, will you take the job?"

I ignored the chief's glare. "Of course."

He tried to talk Flora out of it, but she stayed firm. Finally he agreed as long as I promised not to get in the way. Flora wanted to see Wendall, and Jerry and I went along to support her. Afterward, I asked if there was a relative or friend she could call who could stay with her, or if she'd care to come to my house for the night.

She caught both my hands in hers. "I'll be fine, Madeline, thank you so much. I'm going to call my sister. She lives near Parkland and can be here in about twenty minutes."

"I'll be glad to stay with you until she gets here."

"No, no. You've done more than enough for me. I'll talk with you tomorrow. I want to be alone for a little while."

"Well," Jerry said as we got into the car, "what was that about not enough work for you in Celosia?"

"I'd better be careful what I wish for." My hands began to tremble, and Jerry took the keys.

"Let me drive."

We switched places, and I sat back into the passenger's seat and fumbled with my belt. "It's like Nell said, Wendall was big and full of life, and for someone to murder him like that..." I didn't know what else to say. I finally got my seat belt fastened, and we started for home.

Jerry gave me a few minutes. "So what do you think, Mac?"

Time to think like an investigator. Don't think about Wendall's lifeless body. Think about how you can solve this. "The wood is from Bea Ricter's frames, but Wendall was a tall man, and Bea's very short. She would've had to jump up to hit him on the forehead. Same thing with Flora. But Larissa's tall enough and angry enough to have done it."

"He just stood there and let her do it?"

"I suppose if she took him by surprise, and he didn't see it coming."

"What about Flora?"

"You heard her. She doesn't have an alibi, and she knew Wendall was going to the gallery. Wendall left for the gallery around eight o'clock and told Flora he'd be right back. Nell met us there at eight-thirty, right before we found him, so whoever killed him worked quickly."

"My money's on Larissa, then. Motive and opportunity and her car at the scene of the crime."

"I'll talk to her tomorrow."

"Good luck," Jerry said. "Even when she's not a suspect, she looks capable of murder."

But since opening my agency, I'd found out anyone was *capable* of murder. It was the people who actually went through with their plans you had to stop, and that's what I was determined to do.

Chapter Eleven

I didn't sleep very well. I dreamed I saw Wendall lying at the gallery door and all the members of the Art Guild stood around his body, laughing and pointing. Then they pointed at each other, exclaiming, "You did it! You did it!" until the chorus of shrill voices woke me. I shivered and snuggled closer to Jerry, who made his half-asleep grumbling sound and put his arm around me. The dream slid into a pageant where Honor Perkins was crowned Queen of the Con Artists, and I snatched the crown off her head and ran so fast she couldn't catch me. Satisfied, I managed a few more hours' rest before morning.

At breakfast, I thanked Jerry for holding off on another verse of "Camp Lakenwood."

He handed me my coffee. "From all that thrashing around last night, I didn't figure you'd be in the mood."

"Thrashing's all done. I'm ready to get started on this case."

Cast members of *Oklahoma* called Jerry and asked if he could meet them at the theater to work on their songs. He also had a job interview today, but said he could catch a ride to Southern Foods, so I dropped him off at the Baker Auditorium. Before going to Larissa's, I stopped by the crime scene. The gallery was closed, encircled with yellow police tape. I knew the police would've gone over the backyard and gathered every scrap of evidence, but I wanted to have a look for myself.

There were large footprints in the dirt and the sparse grass was flattened where Wendall's body had fallen. The trash bags were still where Nell had left them. I could see the prints of her shoes and mine and Jerry's and some other prints that may or may not have been Larissa's. The rest of the yard was grass out to a fence of faded boards. This yard was bare. I figured any stray pieces of trash had been picked up by the crime scene team.

I didn't want to cross the police tape at the gallery's back door, so I walked around to the other side of the fence. A small parking lot backed up to the rear entrances of a shoe store and a gift shop. Beside piles of cardboard boxes there were large plastic trash cans and a few broken and discarded display racks. The trash cans were empty. The murderer could have easily parked his or her car in this lot, gone around the fence, killed Wendall, and driven away. But how did the murderer know Wendall would come to the back of the gallery around eight o'clock—unless he or she called him?

I went into the gift shop and asked the owner if she had seen any strange cars in the back lot yesterday evening.

"There was just one," she said. "I left a little after six yesterday, and there was my car and Jan's and a dark blue Honda. I figured it was someone at the gallery."

"Jan runs the shoe store?"

"Yes, Jan and I usually walk out together. Celosia's pretty safe, but no sense taking any chances. It's kind of isolated back there. And just this morning I heard that somebody attacked Wendall Clarke on the other side of the fence. That doesn't make me feel very good."

"You're right to be cautious. Did you see anyone get in the Honda?"

"No."

"Had you noticed any strange cars this week?"

She thought for a few moments. "I guess that was the only one. Some people asked us if they could park there yesterday afternoon when they had that big meeting at the gallery. Of course we said yes. But when Jan and I are gone, anybody could come around and park there."

I thanked her for her help and started out when something caught my eye. On the counter next to the cash register was a glass dish filled with odds and ends, a pair of sunglasses, a key ring, some small toys, a child's sock, and a gold button.

"Is this your lost and found department?" I asked.

"Yes, I find things everywhere."

"I lost a button just like this off my jacket. Do you mind if I take it and see if it's the same one?"

She handed the button to me. "No problem. I found it out back yesterday when I left."

"Thank you very much." I put the button in my pocket. It wasn't off my jacket, but I bet any amount of money it was off Flora's fancy pink suit jacket. And why would she be wandering around a back parking lot? And who was driving the dark blue Honda?

◇◇◇

Larissa Norton's house was almost as elegant as Wendall Clarke's in River Ridge, but Larissa's was located on a quiet shady street closer to town.

She did not want to speak to me. She stood in her front doorway, arms folded. At first, I thought her arms were gripped tight out of anger. A closer look revealed she was trying to keep from shaking.

"I don't know why you're here, Madeline."

"Nell and I saw you leave the gallery last night. I want to hear your side of the story."

"No, you don't. Like everyone else in this town, you think I killed Wendall."

I didn't miss that her voice caught on his name. "Did you?"

I thought her face couldn't get any stonier, but it did. "You can't talk to me like this! You have no idea what it's like. Why are you sticking your nose where it doesn't belong?"

"Believe it or not, I want to help you." She made a disbelieving sound. "Do you want to go to jail? Do you want to be accused of killing your ex-husband and spend the rest of your life in jail, or possibly get the death penalty?"

"No!"

"Then if you didn't kill Wendall, why not tell me exactly what happened?" She didn't answer, and for a moment, I thought she was going to go back into her house. "Larissa, I didn't grow up in Celosia. I didn't go to Celosia High. I don't have any preconceived notions about you or your relationship with Wendall. I've been hired to find out who murdered him, and if you have information that will help bring that person to justice, then why not tell me?"

She stared at me as if I didn't understand what had happened. "He's dead, Madeline. Wendall's dead! You don't know what that means."

"That's why I'm talking to you. I want to know what it means. You're obviously very upset, and I sympathize. At one time, he was your husband. You must have loved him very much."

She took a deep breath and calmed down. "Yes. Yes, I did. At one time."

"Then would you please help me find his killer?"

She still kept her arms folded tight. "Wendall called me and said he wanted to talk."

"About what?"

"I don't know! I found him lying on the ground."

"Did he specifically want to meet you in the back of the gallery?"

"He said come around to the back. He wanted to talk in private. You'd better believe I wanted to talk to him! I wanted to know the real reason he decided to come back to Celosia. Opening an art gallery was a flimsy excuse. He could have his gallery anywhere. He had to know how much it would hurt me to see him with Flora. I couldn't believe he hated me so." She shuddered. "I could tell he was dead. I couldn't comprehend that. I suppose I was in shock. I didn't want to be there with him. That must have been when you saw me leave."

"Did you see anyone else? Another car? Did you hear anything?"

"No, all I wanted to do was get away. And of course the police found my fingerprints on that piece of wood. I'd taken those stupid pictures apart."

"Bea Ricter's pictures? When was this?"

"Earlier that day. After the meeting, four-thirty, maybe. Do you know she had the nerve to approach me at the afternoon meeting and ask me what I thought about Wendall's new wife? You heard how she was in the meeting. So when everyone was gone, I accidentally on purpose knocked over the stack of junk she'd hauled into the gallery and broke her frames."

"You destroyed another artist's work."

"You can't call Bea Ricter an artist. She's an idiot. She doesn't deserve to have anything in any gallery."

"You're mad at the whole world, aren't you?"

She took another breath. "I suppose it looks that way."

"I know you probably won't believe me," I said, "but my first husband and I went through some rocky times before we decided to call it quits. It wasn't easy, and I still wonder about what I did wrong. But you can't let this eat you up."

She gave me a curious look. "You've been divorced?"

"Yes."

"Someone left you? I find that hard to believe."

"Bill decided to marry someone else."

"Quietly? Discreetly?"

"Yes. We came to an amicable agreement."

"At least your husband didn't have the gall to flaunt his new relationship. I found out the hard way." She held out her hands. "I'd always been ashamed of my large hands. But they were perfect for reaching difficult chords and playing intricate runs, so I told myself to stop being foolish about them." Suddenly, words rushed out. "Then one day, I found a box in Wendall's desk. Inside was the most beautiful pair of white lace gloves. For several wonderful moments, I thought they were a surprise gift for me, until I realized they were too small for these ugly fingers of mine. That started my suspicions. Why would he buy lace gloves? He didn't have any young nieces or cousins to give them to. So that night, I followed him. He drove to another part of town and a young blonde came out of her house and got in his car." She paused and tightened her lips as if holding back a curse or possibly a sob. "I followed them to a motel. I didn't need to see anything else. The next day I confronted him. He confessed to the affair. I divorced him as fast as I could and took him for every penny I was entitled to. But I didn't really want his money. It was never about his money."

"Did you know who Flora was?"

"I'd never seen her before. I found out who she was, and I let her husband know what she was doing. She was married to Stan Bailey then, and he acted as if he didn't care what she did. He wanted to get rid of her. He knew what kind of woman she was." She fixed me with anguished eyes. "I hated Wendall for cheating on me. I hated him for bringing that woman to town and parading her around like some sort of prize. I hated him for setting up that gallery and making everyone love him. But I didn't kill him. Yes, I panicked and I ran, but only because I knew what would happen. I knew I'd be accused of his murder."

"And it happened anyway."

"Somebody knew they could get away with murder because I'd be the perfect suspect, the scorned ex-wife with a grudge."

But somebody else might have a grudge, I thought.

Bea's house was huddled in the woods outside of town, a small dreary structure incongruously shaped like a Swiss chalet. Her car was a sad-looking gray Volkswagen Beetle. Pieces of wood lay scattered on the front yard and stacked in heaps beside the house. Bea also had a herd of fake deer and a wishing well. One interesting feature was that the well and all the bushes were circled with bricks. I took a closer look. Most of the bricks were wedged in the dirt. I could tell they hadn't been moved in a long time. But in a row of bricks surrounding a boxwood it looked as if one brick had been removed and the others rearranged to fill the hole. The bricks were old with smooth edges. I'd have to ask Chief Brenner if I could have a look at the brick that had smashed the gallery window.

Something sparkled from a pile of leaves. I reached down and picked up a plastic bag filled with bits of silver. I shook a few out into my hand. The pieces were little ornate circles, the kind of spacers used in making bracelets and necklaces. Did Bea make jewelry, too? I put the bag in my pocket and went up the few steps to the house. A jumble of wind chimes on the porch made it hazardous to reach the front door. Bea opened the door on my first knock. She glared at me suspiciously.

"What do you want?" She stepped out on the narrow porch and shut the door behind her. "You get off my property right now."

"Okay," I said. "I was just admiring all your bricks."

Bea's little eyes darted for just a second to the bricks lining her bushes. "And what the hell's so special about my bricks?"

"I think one of them smashed the gallery window."

"And you think I threw it?"

"Possibly the same person took their anger a step further and killed Wendall. Whoever it was used a piece of one of your picture frames."

She was so furious, I thought she might pick up a piece of wood and smack me. "You've got two seconds to explain what you're talking about."

"Imagine for a minute, if you can, that I'm on your side. Tell me why it wasn't you."

She hadn't expected that and took a moment to readjust her thinking. "Chief Brenner's already talked to me. I came by the gallery and left some of my work for that Sasha woman to see. I can't help it if a crazy person tore up the frame and killed Wendall Clarke."

"But you were angry with him."

"Damn right! Everybody in town's angry with him."

"Even though he built this wonderful gallery and was giving everyone an opportunity to show their work?"

"By hiring some woman from Parkland who isn't even an American? Sasha? All that about making an appointment and everyone would have a turn? That's just bull. That was just his way of trying to smooth things over."

I guess Bea thought Sasha was Russian. Following that line of reasoning, I'd be French. "You made an appointment, didn't you? If you thought you didn't have a chance, why bother?"

Bea fixed me with her fierce little eyes. "I was willing to play Wendall's game. So why would I kill him? As much as I hated it, he was going to give me that show. I was going to make it happen. But I wasn't going to murder anybody."

"When did you drop off your work?"

"I brought it with me to the afternoon meeting. Sasha said she'd get back to me. Where is she, by the way? Did she go back to Parkland? Maybe she did it. Maybe she wanted the gallery for herself."

I doubted that Sasha Gregory wanted the Celosia Gallery when she could return to the more prestigious gallery in Parkland. "I'll ask her."

"Ask that new wife of Wendall's, too."

"Mrs. Clarke has hired me to find her husband's murderer."

Bea gave a snort. "I knew you weren't here to talk about the broken window."

"What do you know about the window, Ms. Ricter?"

"Oh, shut up about the window! They got another window up. The gallery will close, and some other shop will go in that space."

"Maybe not," I said. "The members of the Art Guild could work together and find some way to run the gallery. Isn't that what all of you wanted in the first place?"

"Some people did. It wasn't what I wanted."

"What did you want?"

"None of your business! Go talk to Larissa Norton. She's suspect number one, as far as I'm concerned."

"Were you here at home last night?"

"I was playing cards with Ginger Alverez at her house."

Since Bea's house was surrounded by wood, I wondered if Ginger's was full of ping-pong balls. "So you settled your differences?"

"Ha! I still think she's a moron, but she plays a mean hand of canasta. We played till about eleven. You can call her. Now go away."

She started to turn, and I took out the plastic bag. "Is this yours?"

She snatched the bag out of my hands. "Where did you find that?"

"In the yard. You must have dropped it."

She didn't say yes, or thank you. "Go away!" She went inside and shut the door. She didn't slam it, but I could tell she wanted to. And before the door closed, I caught a glimpse of more shiny things, lots of them, all colors, as if Bea had her own magical cave of wonders inside her run-down little home. Did she have her own private jewelry store in there? I hadn't seen her wearing any jewelry, and her artwork was as drab as mud, so she wasn't using jewels to make it sparkle.

What was she hiding?

◇◇◇

Ginger Alverez confirmed that she and Bea had had dinner at the Chicken House at six, went back to Ginger's, and played cards until ten forty-five. Flora wasn't home. Chief Brenner told me the brick his officers had found was an old brick with smooth edges. When I mentioned Bea Ricter had these bricks lining her shrubs, he said many people in Celosia had the same.

"When the old high school was torn down, the bricks were available to anyone who wanted them," he said. "Right now, we're concentrating on the murder investigation, so anything you discover pertaining to that would be appreciated."

He spoke politely, but I knew what he was really saying was: Don't withhold any important information, or you'll be in trouble.

"Bea Ricter was with Ginger Alverez last night until ten forty-five," I said. "She left her work at the gallery around two yesterday afternoon. Larissa Norton accidentally broke some of those picture frames after Bea left. She told me Wendall called her around eight o'clock and asked her to come to the gallery."

"Thank you for confirming this information."

But I didn't say anything about the gold button. Not yet.

Back in my car, I called the Silver Gallery in Parkland and asked to speak with Sasha Gregory.

"Such an awful thing to happen!" she said. "Sasha can't imagine who would do this."

I still couldn't imagine why she liked to refer to herself as "Sasha" all the time. "When was the last time you saw Wendall?"

"Sasha left the gallery around four. Sasha had scheduled appointments for all the local artists and showed him my calendar. He approved the list, and Sasha came back to Parkland."

"Was there anyone who wanted to show his or her work and was turned down?"

"No, no one. Not at this stage of the process. Sasha will see everyone's work. Then Wendall and Sasha will—Sasha supposes now she will determine whose work is appropriate. That is, if the gallery stays open. Do you know? Have you heard anything?"

"I don't know the future of the gallery. Did anyone argue with Wendall? Did you notice if anyone left angry?"

"Sasha must confess her head was down practically the whole time, writing down appointments. Sasha didn't hear any arguments. When everyone had gone, Sasha said good-bye to Wendall and left. He said good-bye and thank you. That's all."

I was anxious to share my findings with Jerry. When I called, he was on his way home from his interview.

"Unless you'd rather meet at Burger World."

The thought of a cheeseburger and fries made me slightly nauseous. "I'll see you at home, then."

On my way, I drove by the medical park and hovered for a while outside the doctor's office. I could easily make an appointment and find out for sure if I was pregnant. Well, what if you are? I asked myself. Let's try the emotional test. What if the answer is no? How would you feel? I knew I'd feel relieved, but I was surprised to feel a bit disappointed. And what if the answer is yes? My feelings were still ambiguous, but somewhere in the mix of emotions was the slightest thrill of a challenge. It would be a challenge to raise a child, run my agency, and find time to paint. I was up for this challenge, wasn't I? It wasn't as if I'd have to look after the baby all by myself. Bill wouldn't have been any help, but Jerry was ready and willing to do whatever I needed him to do.

My hand was on the door when my old caution took over.

No.

Not yet.

Chapter Twelve

I argued with myself the rest of the way home. Just go ahead and find out! Maybe after I solve Wendall's murder. I've got too much to think about right now.

I was so wrapped up in my thoughts, I had to stop in the driveway and take another look at the strange car parked in the yard. I didn't recognize the car, but I recognized the large woman sitting on the porch.

Honor Perkins.

Now I was really nauseous. What could she possibly want? I parked my car and got out, wondering if I was ready for yet another confrontation. As I walked up the porch steps, I'm sure my expression said, what the hell are you doing here?

Honor got up and held out both hands as if to forestall my protests. "Before you say anything, I'm not here to cause trouble, honest. I need to lay low about forty-eight hours, and then I'm on my way. You owe me."

I stopped. I owed her? "How do you figure that?"

"You called the cops, right?"

"Right. You'll be happy to know Jerry didn't rat on you."

"I knew you would. I could tell by looking at you."

I took out my phone. "Yes, and I'm getting ready to call them again. Why are you here?"

"Hold on, let me explain. I had originally planned to stay with Mrs. Forest, but she was just a little uncooperative."

From the way Mrs. Forest had insisted on being paid right away, I knew exactly what had happened. "You stiffed her, didn't you?"

Honor grinned and shrugged her wide shoulders. "Let's just say it didn't work out. Can we sit down and talk?"

"I'll give you five minutes."

"All I need."

She arranged herself in one of the rocking chairs. I positioned myself further away. I didn't trust her one bit and was grateful her unexpected visit wasn't later in the day when Austin and Denisha would have been here.

"You can't stay here, Honor. I'm not going to harbor a fugitive."

"Like I said, you owe me. I'll sleep in my car. You won't know I'm here."

"No. You may be one of Jerry's old friends, but I have no loyalty to you whatsoever."

She rocked and smiled as if she hadn't a care in the world. "Oh, there might be a few things about Jerry you wouldn't want to come to light."

"Blackmailing me won't work. Jerry and I have discussed all the cons he's done."

"Everything?"

This made me pause. Before she came upon the scene, I hadn't known anything about Honor Perkins, or the bank examiner swindle, or any of his past dealings with this woman. I believed Jerry was as truthful with me as he could be. Unfortunately, he often omitted things he knew would upset me.

Honor looked pleased with herself. "So, not everything."

"What will it take to make you go away?"

"I need Jerry's help with something. Nothing bad, I promise."

"If it's nothing bad, tell me what it is. Maybe I can help you."

"It's a bit personal."

I'd had enough. "Your five minutes are up."

I was wondering if I could physically wrest her from the rocking chair and heave her into the yard when a small SUV zipped up the drive and Jerry hopped out. As the car turned to go, he called "Thanks" and waved good-bye to the driver. He was almost to the porch when he saw Honor. His reaction was the same as mine.

"What are you doing here?"

"Thought I'd stop by for a visit," she said. "Nice place you got here. Lots of room."

Jerry correctly read my face. "You can't stay."

"Aw, be a pal. Your wife called the cops, so I have to hide somewhere."

"Not here."

"I can pull my car around back and sleep there."

"No." He took her arm. "Look, for the sake of old times, I'll tell you where you can hide, but you need to leave."

She wouldn't budge. "But I need to talk to you about something."

This had all the signs of becoming a fierce tug of war, interrupted by a silver Mercedes coming up the driveway. My mind immediately shifted into overdrive. "Jerry, that's my mother's car."

He let go of Honor's arm. "Great timing."

"What are we going to say?"

He and Honor looked a lot calmer than I felt. "No problem, Mac."

Maybe the two of them were used to facing sudden potentially embarrassing situations, but my heart was doing strange little flutters as I went down the porch steps to greet my mother as she got out of her car. "Hello! What a surprise!"

Mother is tall, thin, and elegant. She decided years ago that color was vulgar and she'd dress only in black and white. She stared up at the house. "Good lord, what it must cost you to keep this up! And it needs painting, Madeline, or are you planning on aluminum siding? Jerry, how are you, dear? What a monstrous house your uncle left you! Are you certain you want to live here?"

Jerry kissed her cheek. "Hello, Cecille. Yes, I like the house very much. It looks better inside. This is a friend of mine, Honor Perkins. Honor, this is Mac's mother, Cecille Maclin."

Honor stood. "Pleased to meet you," she said, sweet as pie. They shook hands.

"Do you also work at the theater, Miss Perkins?"

I could tell Honor was glad for an opening. "Yes, exactly." She glanced at Jerry for a clue. "We're doing a great show."

"*Oklahoma*," he said.

"What part do you play?" Mom asked.

I couldn't help her there, and before Jerry could fill in, she said, "Oh, I'm the mother."

I'm not sure if *Oklahoma* has a mother, but fortunately, Mom's knowledge of musical theater isn't vast. "How nice."

"Can I carry anything for you?" Jerry asked.

"I just brought my overnight bag."

"I'll get it."

"Thank you."

Mother's idea of an overnight bag was a large suitcase and a garment bag, which Jerry hauled upstairs. Once inside, she was a bit mollified by the redecorated living room. She inspected the white sectional sofa, moved one of the blue accent pillows a fraction, and nodded to herself. I expected her to run a finger along the mantel in search of dust.

"I see you have *Blue Moon Garden* displayed, Madeline. Did you design the room around those colors?"

"Jerry and I both like blue, so it was an easy choice."

"I certainly didn't expect anything this elegant. It's too bad the outside of this house looks like a country store."

"I think it has charm."

She gave the painting another long look. "What have you done lately?"

"I'll show you my studio after a while. Come have a look at the kitchen. We've finished in there, too."

The kitchen met with her approval, and she had to agree the view of the fields was pleasant, "If you like that kind of thing." She peered out the back windows. "Is this friend staying here? I don't want to be in the way."

"No, she just stopped by for a short visit." The shorter the better.

"Now what about this gallery, Madeline? When can I see it?"

"I'm afraid there's been a little problem," I said. "The owner's been murdered, so the gallery's closed."

It was typical of my mother that she thought of her own concerns first. "You mean I came all the way over here, and it's not open? You could've called me."

"It's just thirty minutes, and I'm glad you could visit."

Then she realized what I'd said. "The owner's been murdered? You don't mean Wendall Clarke?"

"Yes, and I've been hired to solve the murder."

"Good heavens. So the gallery's closed permanently? What happened?"

"Someone attacked him behind the gallery. That's all we know right now."

"Here in this little town? I wouldn't think anything goes on."

"You'd be surprised."

"I wish you'd give up this idea of being a detective, Madeline. Not only is it ridiculous, it's dangerous."

I didn't want her to get started. "Let me give you the tour, Mom."

Jerry met us at the top of the stairs. He must have done a quick check of our bedroom. I didn't remember if I'd made the bed, but the blue comforter with its pattern of clouds was neat and straight, the pillows in place, and any dirty clothes had been scooped up and put in the hamper. "Cecille, we haven't done all the bedrooms yet, but this is our room, and yours is next to it. I hung your garment bag in the closet."

"Thank you. Now where is the art studio?"

"Right here, Mom."

She stepped into the room. "Well...Well, you've done quite a lot."

As she peered at each painting, I exchanged a glance with Jerry. He grinned and rubbed his fingers together in the sign for money. I nodded. That was coming up, for certain.

"Have you sold any paintings, Madeline?"

"All of these are commissions, except the one I did of Jerry."

"If you'd spend more time on your art, you'd probably sell more. How on earth did you afford all the repairs?"

"Jerry's brother gave him some money."

This brought a gleam to her eye. "And you accepted it, Jerry?"

"For the house, yes."

"Madeline tells me you're the music director at the theater. I'm glad you've found a job you like."

I'm glad you've found a job was what she meant. Jerry grinned. "I've become quite the settled married man. You ladies come downstairs and let me fix you some lunch."

Mom said she'd already eaten, but would love some tea. Honor joined us in the dining room. I could tell she was having a fine time making up stories about her non-existent theater career, and Jerry went right along with her tall tales. However annoyed I was at her, she kept Mom entertained, so Mom wasn't getting in more digs about the house, my agency, or my artwork.

After lunch, Honor said she had to get to the theater for an extra rehearsal. "Jerry, there's one song in particular you need to hear."

"I'm sure there is."

"It's the refrain that's kind of tricky."

"Believe me, I'll take care of it."

Mom didn't see me roll my eyes at him to express my opinion of all the double talk. Honor thanked me for lunch and told Mom again it was a pleasure meeting her. Jerry walked her to the door and must have also walked her to her car because in a few minutes, I heard her drive off. I assumed he told her where she could lay low. Alaska would be a great choice.

Jerry returned to the dining room. "I think I'll make some brownies for the kids."

Mom looked at him askance. "Kids?"

"Jerry's playmates," I said. "Some neighborhood children. They come by after school."

"What for?"

"To see what Jerry's up to."

"Don't they have other children to play with?"

By the time the brownies were done and Denisha, Kennedy, and Austin arrived, Mom was still amazed. I made all the introductions.

"Kids, this is my mother, Cecille Maclin. Mom, this is Denisha Simpson, Kennedy Marshall, and Austin Terrell."

"Nice to meet you, Mrs. Maclin. I see where Madeline gets her good looks," Denisha said in her straightforward way.

Mom was bemused. "Thank you."

"Jerry, has my mother called you yet?" Kennedy asked.

"Not yet."

"I wish she'd hurry up. Mrs. Norton wasn't even there yesterday, and Mom wasn't very happy about it."

This caught my attention. "Kennedy, when was your piano lesson?"

"It wasn't mine. It was Reagan's. Mom took her over there at her usual time, which is four o'clock, and she waited and waited, but nobody was home, and Mrs. Norton didn't answer her phone. Mom left a message, but Mrs. Norton didn't call back until almost seven."

Larissa had been at the two o'clock meeting and left soon after. She told me she came back to the gallery after four. "Did she explain why she missed Reagan's lesson?"

Kennedy shook her head. "No, she didn't, and Mom got mad and said if she couldn't at least call to tell her she wasn't going to be there, then maybe we'd find another teacher. So I don't know why she hasn't called you yet, Jerry."

"That's okay," he said. "If that's what your mother wants to do, she'll get around to it."

All Mom heard from our conversation was "piano lessons." "That would be an excellent way to supplement your income," she told Jerry.

"We'll see." He knew as well as I that Larissa would be even more put out with him if he started taking her students away.

Austin asked Jerry if he'd bought a Wow System yet, which involved a lengthy explanation for Mom. By the time the kids had eaten and exhausted their supply of questions and discussions about the various games you could play on the Wow, Mom was looking even more dazed.

"Tell you what," Jerry said to them. "Why don't you guys come to Parkland with me and help me pick out the best model? Call your folks and ask them."

I handed Austin my phone so he could call his mother. Then Denisha called her aunt, and Kennedy called her mother. All three were granted permission, which sent them into orbit.

"The Wow 300 has Extreme Bowling," Austin said. "You should get that one."

"But they're coming out with Wow 350 next month," Kennedy said. "Maybe he should wait."

"No, I want one now," Jerry said. "Get in the car." The kids ran and piled into the Mazda. "Be right back, Mac."

Mother watched him drive away. "Are those children here often?"

"Every day."

"And their parents don't mind?"

"They've always played here. At least Austin and Denisha have. That's how we met. They were running around in the secret passageways."

"Good heavens. I hope you've closed those off."

"No."

She eyed me. "Those children are here every day. Doesn't that annoy you?"

"No, I like them, and they keep Jerry occupied."

"I don't see how you stand it."

Mom doesn't have to say much to rile me, but the tone of her voice made it difficult for me to control my temper. "Oh, I've gotten used to it. In fact, Jerry and I are talking about having some children of our own."

It's not often that my mother is speechless. She stared at me for a long moment and then said, "I didn't think you wanted children. I thought that was the main reason you left Bill."

"Bill left me, Mom, and there were lots of reasons."

"But this is absurd, Madeline! I don't believe you."

If I could've popped a baby out right then, I would've gladly done it. "I guess you don't want to be a grandmother?"

"That's not the point. I'm just not sure you're ready to be parents. You and Bill could've managed. He has three now, did you know? I believe I heard something about a fourth."

"Yes." Bill always sent me an announcement.

"But to raise a child here, with your limited funds and limited future? I don't think so."

The limited funds I agreed with. The limited future was a slam. "Celosia's a great place to raise children. It's very safe."

"Excuse me, but since you've moved here, at least three people have been murdered. Four, if you count Wendall Clarke. I don't call that very safe." She leaned forward, hands clasped together. "I didn't come out here just to see the gallery. I have a proposal for you, and if you're smart, you'll agree."

What was this?

"I have friends on the Arts Council board in Parkland. In fact, I have quite a lot of clout in that organization. I can get you a position at the Parkland Museum of Fine Art. I also have connections at the English Manor Townhouses in my neighborhood, and there is a vacancy. You and Jerry could move in next week. He can commute to Celosia until this music director job is through. I can't imagine it would last very long, anyway, and then we'll see about finding him something suitable."

I realized my mouth was open. I took a breath. "In case you hadn't noticed, I'm a grown woman, a married woman, with a home and an occupation of my own."

"I'm only trying to help you."

"No, you're trying to control me, which is what you've done since I was born, but those days are over."

"Madeline—"

"Listen to me. Really listen. I hated those pageants, but I did them because it made you happy. What little girl doesn't want to please her mother? Now I'm doing what makes me happy.

I can't be responsible for your happiness because you are never truly happy. Are you?"

"That's nonsense."

I was going to have to play dirty. "You've never said a word about my father. What did he do to make you so miserable?"

She pushed back her chair and got up. "If the gallery's closed, then there's really no reason for me to stay, is there?"

"Don't go. Stay and explain this to me. I want to understand."

"You know your father left us when you were born. I had to take charge. I had to be in control of everything. Otherwise we would have had nothing."

"I'm glad you took care of us then, but you don't have to take care of me anymore."

"I believe you've made that abundantly clear. I'm going home."

I wasn't going to beg her to stay. I helped her carry her things to her car.

True to form, she hadn't given up. "For God's sake will you stop fooling around with these murders? It's not…" she groped for the right words and settled on "proper behavior." I knew she wanted to add "for a young woman who might still become a pageant winner or a prominent artist."

"It's what I want to do."

She looked at me as if to say "How did I raise such an unnatural daughter?" But she replied, "Just be careful." Then for a moment, her guard was down, and I saw real pain in her eyes. "You're all I have, you know."

I had to swallow a sudden lump of emotion. "I know." She gave me a brief hug and got into her car. She drove back down the driveway. I sat down in a rocking chair and took another deep breath. This encounter with my mother had brought up some dark details. I'd known for some time that my mother's marriage had gone off the rails, and she'd refused to have anything to do with men unless she called all the shots.

In her own way, she really cares about you, I told myself. You can't fault your mother for wanting to be in control. Isn't that what you want to do? You've never seen any similarity to her

before, but it's pretty clear you inherited her insane determination to have things your way.

That was going to change.

Chapter Thirteen

After a while, Jerry drove in. He took a large box out of the trunk of the car and carried it up the porch steps as the kids bounded around him.

"Is that the famed Wow?"

"It is. We're going to set it up right away."

"Jerry got the advanced version," Austin said. "It has extreme everything."

Jerry looked around. "Where's your mom?"

"She went back to Parkland."

He handed the box to Austin. "Go ahead and unpack it. I'll be right there." When Austin and Denisha had gone into the house, he turned back to me. "I thought if I got the kids and myself out of the way, you two could have a heart-to-heart."

"There was little heart involved. She had a grand plan, a job for me in Parkland, a townhouse for us, everything nice and neat and controlled. I had to go to the dark side and bring up my father."

"What did she say about that?"

"I know she raised me on her own, and that was tough for her, but she'll never understand that money doesn't mean the same to me. I've got you and this house and I'm managing my own career. You've got your music and all your schemes, legal and otherwise. Mom never got satisfaction out of anything except my titles and tiaras. She never found out who she was and what she wanted."

"I take it she didn't like all this psychoanalyzing."

"Three guesses why I have to be the queen of everything."

Jerry pretended to think. "Well, let's see. You were born a princess, you learned from the best, and you're just naturally bossy."

"I command you to kiss me."

"No problem, your highness."

One kiss led to two and then three, and there would have been many more except for a clamoring from the living room.

"Jerry! Come on!"

I sat on the sofa while Jerry and his assistants hooked up all the wires necessary to run the Wow on our TV. The kids argued fiercely over which game to play until Jerry said, "Let Mac decide."

I looked through the colorful instruction book and chose Extreme Dirt Biking, which was met with extreme approval. After watching the kids navigate the course, crashing and rolling, I went back to the porch to make some phone calls. My first call was to Flora.

"I'm just checking to see how you're doing."

She sounded okay. "Thank you so much, Madeline. I'm all right. I've just been going through Wendall's things."

"Would you and your sister like to come over for dinner? Maybe take a little break from what must be a very sad job?"

"That's so sweet of you. I'll see what she says and call you back."

Then I called Larissa and asked her what she did after she left the gallery.

She was still defensive. "What do you mean, what did I do? I went home."

"You admitted you broke up Bea's picture frames. I know you didn't do that with anyone watching. When did you say you went back to the gallery?"

There was a long pause. "Around four-thirty, maybe five o'clock."

"Was anyone there?"

"No."

Sasha Gregory had told me she left at four. "How did you get in?"

"The back door was unlocked."

"You went in, tore up the frames, and then left?"

"I thought Wendall might be there. I was going to talk to him."

"About?"

"About the gallery, of course."

All of this sounded very unlikely. "Why didn't you just call him, or go to his house?"

"I didn't want to have any possible contact with Flora."

"So when Wendall called you later that evening, you were more than ready to talk with him."

"Yes, I was."

"You didn't meet or talk with anyone in the gallery at four-thirty, five o'clock?"

Another pause. "No."

"Where did you park?"

"What?" she said.

"Where did you park? When you came to the gallery last night, you parked around back."

"What does that have to do with anything?"

"Did you park in the back at four-thirty?"

"No, I parked out front. There were plenty of spaces then."

"Did you notice any other cars?"

"No. I didn't notice. What are you getting at?"

"Maybe nothing," I said. "How long were you in the gallery?"

"Just a few minutes."

Long enough to wreck Bea's frames. "And you went straight home after that?"

"Yes. Is that all, Madeline? I have to go. Reagan Marshall is here for her piano lesson."

"Making up for the one you missed yesterday?"

"Yes. Good-bye."

Just to cover all bases, I called Sasha Gregory and asked her what kind of car she drove and if she'd noticed any other cars in the back parking lot. She told me Sasha owned a black Ford Taurus and had parked in front of the gallery, so Sasha didn't see the cars in the back.

"Did you lock any of the doors when you left?" I asked.

"No, but Wendall was leaving at the same time, and he had a key."

"Do you know if he locked the back door?"

"He followed Sasha out the front and locked that door. Sasha doesn't know if he locked the back." She paused. "You know, Sasha remembers now he told her his key only fit the front door, and he was going to have to get a key for the back."

"So there's a good chance the back door was never locked."

"That's true."

So anyone could get in.

Jerry came out as I was pondering my next move.

"Things are getting too extreme in there for me," he said.

"I doubt that."

"How's it going?" he asked. "Tell me what you found out from Larissa."

"Around eight o'clock last night, Wendall called Larissa and told her to meet him at the gallery. He had something to tell her. She arrived about eight-thirty and found him dead. She says she doesn't know what he wanted to talk about. I also talked with Bea Ricter, who says she brought some work with her to the gallery yesterday afternoon. Larissa admits to breaking up the wooden frames around four-thirty, but she swears Wendall was dead when she arrived for their meeting later that night. Bea was with Ginger last night, so she has an alibi. Oh, and I found this." I took the gold button out of my pocket. "Do you happen to remember if there was a button like this missing from Flora's pink jacket yesterday?"

"Sorry. I don't remember. Where did you find it?"

"On the other side of the fence behind the gallery is a parking lot. The owner of the gift shop found this yesterday and she remembers seeing a dark blue Honda in their parking lot."

"Why would Flora be back there?"

"Good question."

Jerry sat on the porch rail and examined the button. "Well, this looks like it could've come off a man's suit."

"A little gold button like that?"

"Off one of the cuffs, I mean."

"Oh. Yes, I guess it could."

"Which doesn't really help you, because women wear men's clothes all the time."

"And all the members of the Art Guild are women. Oh, speaking of things that sparkle, when I went to Bea's house, I found a plastic bag full of silver spacers in her yard."

"Spacers? For her teeth?"

"Not that kind. Silver or gold pieces that you put between beads when you're making bracelets or necklaces. I also caught a glimpse inside her house, and it looked like a treasure chest had exploded."

"Bea's a jewel thief? Great news."

"This is Celosia, remember? I think we would've heard."

"Okay, so it's her hobby."

"But she never wears any."

"Then what was all that about at the gallery meeting? Did she make the bracelet Flora was wearing? And how did Wendall get it?"

"Maybe it's a keepsake from their high school days. Doesn't Bea strike you as someone who would like to flaunt her jewelry-making skills, especially to all the other women in the Art Guild?"

"Maybe it's crappy-looking jewelry."

"I want to find out, but I used up all my questions, and I've been warned off her property."

Jerry's eyes lit up. "This is a job for Con Man!"

"I just need a peek, that's all."

"I will arrange a peek for you."

"A legal peek."

"You bet."

I took out my phone. "Let me try Flora again. If she's home, I'll visit and see if I can get a look at her pink jacket."

Flora wasn't home. I put my phone away. "I imagine if the coroner's finished examining Wendall's body, she might be making funeral arrangements." How sad, I thought. The gallery opening—Wendall's attempt to make things right with his old friends—was going to be a grand affair. And now Flora had to deal with her husband's murder—unless she had something to do with it.

I didn't like going down that particular road.

Jerry noticed my frown. "Something else?"

"Well, I have to think like an investigator here and toy with the idea that Flora could've killed Wendall."

"She would've had to have jumped pretty high."

"And what's her motive? She'll probably get all his money, anyway."

"You're getting the look you get after going a couple of rounds with your mother."

If I'd thought about it in time, and if I had asked him, Jerry would have borrowed someone's baby for Mom's visit. I had the wild notion of plopping it into her arms just to see how she would react. "My mother doesn't think you and I would make good parents."

"We won't know unless we try. Let's have a baby just to spite her. Spite Fairweather. It has a ring to it."

I had to laugh. "Would that be Spite Shilleeta, or Shilleeta Spite?"

"I can't decide. Let's have twins."

"Let's not," I said. "Where did you put Honor?"

"You know that failed housing development called Tinsley Acres? I told her she could park her car behind one of those houses. No one ever goes out there."

"Did she tell you what she wanted?"

"No, and it doesn't matter. I'm not doing it."

"She said she had some dirt on you, so you'd better come clean right now."

"I'm not only clean, I'm bleached. She has no hold on me whatsoever."

I really wanted to believe that.

◇◇◇

Flora called to say her sister couldn't come to dinner but that she would welcome the distraction. I hoped she would wear her pink suit so I could have a look at the buttons, but she was more properly attired in black. I'd chosen a dark blue dress, and Jerry had on a suit and one of his calmer ties, a dark purple one with little yellow stars. The dining room was one of the few rooms in the house that hadn't needed much renovation. Nell had painted the walls a pale yellow and refinished the dark walnut table. There were six chairs, all decorated with roses carved in the scooped backs and yellow needlepoint cushions, also patterned with roses.

Jerry made a delicious-smelling chicken casserole and a tossed salad. We sat down at the table and passed our plates to him for the casserole.

"How's your investigation coming along, Madeline?" Flora asked.

I handed her a full plate. "I have a few leads."

"Have you spoken with Larissa? And Bea?"

"Yes. Both of them." I took my plate. "Thanks, Jerry. This looks wonderful."

Flora looked down at her dinner. "Such angry women." Her voice caught. "I wish Wendall had never come back to Celosia."

"Did he ever tell you specifically why he wanted a gallery here?"

"He wanted the town to have something grand." She wiped a few tears away. "Could Larissa have killed Wendall? Could Bea Ricter?"

"Whoever killed Wendall had to be fairly tall. That rules out Bea and most of the members of the Art Guild." And you, I thought. "It's also possible Wendall surprised a thief trying to break into the gallery, or someone else from his past who held a grudge."

She gave me her best wide-eyed look. "I can't believe that. I always got the impression that in high school he was a big fun-loving guy who was very popular."

From what I'd learned about Wendall in high school, if he'd been a Wow game, he'd be Popular Extreme. "We'll figure it out."

"What will you do now, Flora?" Jerry asked. "Is there anything we can help you with?"

"I'm moving in with my sister until everything's taken care of. I certainly don't want to stay in Celosia—no offense."

After dinner, she thanked us, and said she was going to her sister's that evening. "I don't want to be in that house anymore. I'll come back later and go through Wendall's things. You'll call me if you find out anything, won't you, Madeline?"

"Yes, right away."

Jerry and I were walking her to her car when, to my exasperation, Honor Perkins drove up. She gave Flora a long hard look, which Flora ignored. She got into her car and drove away. Honor got out of her car, and I was about to tell her to leave when she said, "Well, that's very interesting. What's she doing in town?"

"Who?" I asked.

"Your dinner guest. The grieving widow. Lizzie Bailey."

"Lizzie Bailey? Don't you mean Flora Bailey, who is now Flora Clarke? You know her?"

Honor leaned against her car. "Lord, yes, I know her. We used to call her Bailout Bailey, because that's what Stan had to do every six months or so. She nearly ruined him. What's she doing in Celosia?"

"Honor," Jerry said, "are you telling me Flora Clarke is on the game?"

"Hell, yeah."

"I knew something was up! That hair tug was a dead give-away—which she didn't do during dinner, did you notice that, Mac? But why didn't I recognize her?"

"Oh, she's a pro. Our cons were way too small to interest her."

My suspicions about Flora didn't include this. "You think she's running a con?"

"Duh," Honor said. "Fluttery fluffy little blonde gets rich man to marry her."

"Rich man dies suddenly," Jerry said. "Does she include murder in her cons?"

Honor shook her head. "It's not her style. Fleecing, yes. Murder, no. My money is on the ex-wife. Oh, and on the ex-husband, too. They could be in this together."

"Do you mean Stan Bailey?" I asked. "What do you know about him? Another con man?"

"No, just some poor sap who fell for her charms. I imagine he was glad to be rid of her. I was just kidding about him being an accomplice. He wouldn't have anything against Wendall Clarke."

I wasn't so sure. I recalled Larissa telling me when she'd seen Flora and Wendall together, she'd called Flora's husband to let him know about his wife's infidelity. Larissa had said Stan Bailey acted as if he didn't care, but what if he did care and wanted to do something about it?

"Do you know where he lives?" Jerry asked.

"Let's see, last time I heard of Lizzie, she was living in Bayside. That might be where he's from. She's quite good. Last time I saw her, she was a redhead."

"She didn't seem to recognize you."

"Nah. I never had any real dealings with her. Want me to help you catch Lizzie?"

I was glad to see that Jerry was not intrigued by this offer. "Why are you here?" he said. "Why won't you go away?"

"Hey, be nice."

"Seriously, you need to leave. I'm trying to make a new life here, a con-free life."

"Doing what? Playing for amateur musicals? Playing for church? Good lord, Jerry. Des was always the musician, and you know it."

That was a low blow. I'd spent years trying to convince Jerry that he was just as talented as his older brother. I felt an almost overpowering urge to smack Honor's face, but Jerry remained calm. I could see his thoughts racing.

"Wait a minute. Are you still paying off Big Mike?" he asked.

"Don't be silly. That was years ago."

"He's behind this, isn't he? And you had to go along, or he'd bust you." His eyes lit up. "That's why you conned me. You were hoping to make some money. How many more do you have to play before you're square with him?"

For the first time, Honor looked uncertain. "I never said anything about Big Mike."

"You didn't have to."

I made the time-out sign. "I need an update. Who's Big Mike? King of the Con Men?"

"Something like that," Jerry said. "When we all started out, we learned from the best, and that was Big Mike. As payment for his lessons, we had to give him a cut of our winnings. Well, of course, after a while, that got old, so he got less and less. Apparently, he's still annoyed. I haven't run that much lately, so he hasn't bothered me, but Honor still owes him, right, Honor?"

Another of her large shrugs. "A little."

"Did he set up the D and S at Billie's?"

"No, he didn't."

"And profits from that weren't enough to suit him?"

She gave me a sideways glance. "Could we talk privately about this?"

"Go ahead," I said. "Please settle whatever this is so you can move on. Jerry, I'll be in my studio."

"Thanks, Mac. Honor, let's talk in the living room."

Honor's not the only one with a secret language, I thought, as I went up the stairs.

Thanks to the kids, we had discovered that the heating vent in the studio carried voices quite well from the living room—if the eavesdroppers leaned in. I knew Jerry would make certain that Honor sat in the chair nearest the downstairs vent. Sure enough, in a few minutes, I could hear her distinctly.

"This is between you and me, right? I told you my little prank was more than payback. I needed to get in touch with you."

"I've been living here for months," Jerry said. "Del could've told you that."

"Del might be just the teensiest bit mad at me for double-crossing him on The Widower."

"Good grief, did you scam him, too?"

"That's not important. I need your help."

"Well, you could've asked me instead of going to such elaborate lengths."

"No, you owed me for the bank examiner."

"And we're even. I'm not going to do anything else."

"One more game, that's all. It'll be easy. The mark lives right here in Celosia." Jerry must have started to say no because her voice became more frantic. "Jerry, this is serious. I played one too many pranks on Big Mike, and now he's after me."

"Big Mike never killed anyone."

"No, but he has enough on me to put me away for life. So I cut a deal with him. He says this woman in town owes him, so if I can get what he wants from her, he'll forgive the other things."

"What woman?"

"Her name's Pamela Finch."

I almost fell out of my chair, and from the sound of Jerry's voice, he almost fell out of his, too.

"Pamela Finch owes Big Mike? Now I know you're making things up."

"I promise you I am dead serious, Jerry. They were an item years ago, they had some sort of spat, and she took off with his cash. You know her?"

"Yeah, she's a local businesswoman. But it can't be the same woman. Pamela Finch is thin and wispy, not his type, at all."

"That's her. He said she was skinny and nervous. Who knows why he took up with her?"

"Why doesn't he come talk to Pamela?"

"Oh, he's done with her. He never wants to see her again. And you know as well as I do he has to keep a low profile. He really doesn't need to show up in this kind of town."

"Well, you could scam her. You don't need me."

"Yes, I do. I got it all figured out. Does she know about your séances? You could get her to tell where she hid the jewel."

"First, of all, I promised Mac no more séances. Second, what jewel are you talking about, and third, why should I help you?"

"Jerry." Her voice was hurt. "Have you forgotten I saved your life?"

"Oh, my God. Are you going to hold that over me?"

"That terribly cold winter, that crazed man with a shotgun. Our only chance for survival was to run through the frozen swamp. I dragged you for miles and gave you my coat because yours snagged on the door when we ran, and if I hadn't helped you out of it, he would've caught you. You had pneumonia and a broken arm, and I got you to a doctor before it was too late."

I wanted to say, oh, my God. I hadn't heard this story.

"Yes, it was cold, and yes, I'd broken my arm, but we were not chased by a deranged gunman through a frozen swamp. It was an angry farmer with a slingshot. And you didn't drag me for miles. Maybe one mile. And you did get me to a clinic, but I didn't have pneumonia."

"You could have."

"All right, all right. What jewel?"

"Big Mike gave Pamela Finch a pink sapphire engagement ring. He wants it back. He said if I got it, he'd forgive all my debts."

"Look, I can't promise anything, but I'll try to find out if she has this ring."

"Thanks, Jerry." Her tone changed and became softer, more cajoling. "This will be like old times, right? You and me working together? I know you miss it. You have to."

"Sometimes," he said, "but not enough to go back. Remember the close calls, too, like that night with the angry farmer. We're lucky we weren't ever caught. That luck has to run out eventually, and I don't want to be there when it does."

"But the two of us, we can do anything."

"I'm married now, Honor. It's a whole different game."

Bitterness came back into her voice. "I noticed. And I never would've guessed you'd get married, and I certainly never would've guessed you would marry Madeline, not after all those fancy blondes you went after. What's the deal? What do you get out of it? It has to be boring."

"I want a family."

This set Honor back a moment. "We had a family at Big Mike's."

"Kids. I want kids. As many as Mac's willing to have."

"Is she willing to have any? She doesn't strike me as the mothering type."

Thanks a lot, Honor. I thought Jerry might counter with, "She'll make a great mom," or "She can't wait," to throw Honor off. What he said made me want to run down the stairs and hug him.

"That's for her to decide," he said.

There was a period of silence, in which I imagined Honor was wondering what she could possibly say to change his mind, or what she could offer that could trump his plans for his life as a father. I wasn't sure what upset her more, the fact that he didn't want to join her game, or the fact that he was married. I suspected it was a little of both, with that good chunk of jealousy thrown in. Finally she said, "I guess I'd better go," and then I heard the front door close.

In a few minutes, Jerry appeared at the door of my studio. "You heard all that?"

"Yes, and you'd better believe I've got questions."

"Fire away."

"Did Honor actually save your life?"

"I hate to say it, but it would've been difficult to get out of that particular situation on my own. Considering some of the cons we played, we should both be dead ten times over."

"Pamela Finch and Big Mike. This is not a connection I would ever expect."

"Me, either. Guess I'll find out. We can't let Honor take anything from Pamela, even if Pamela has this pink sapphire ring she's talking about."

"Thanks for what you said about my decision to have children."

"Well, I thought about telling Honor you were already pregnant, but it would be just like her to check up on that six months from now."

"If Honor is still around even one month from now, we will have words." I checked my watch. "Come on, you're going to be late for rehearsal."

◇◇◇

As we drove to the theater, I asked another question, even though I wasn't sure I wanted to know the answer. "What's The Widower?"

"On occasion, I would set myself up as a wealthy widower in search of that one woman who could make me happy again."

"And then take her money."

"Del was always much better at that game than me. It won't work with Pamela because she knows I'm married to you. I'll have to come up with something else."

I'd had enough. "No, Jerry, you do not have to come up with something else. You are going to let me handle this. Your job is to keep Honor away from everyone." I could tolerate Jerry's other friends, but Honor really worried me. Someone who was still carrying a torch for him and going to such elaborate lengths to enlist his help was someone I needed to get rid of fast. "Pamela is part of my murder investigation, so I'll have the chance to ask her about Big Mike. Does he have a last name?"

"Not that I know of."

"Well, if Honor's telling the truth, and Pamela had a relationship with him, then Pamela ought to know."

When we reached the theater, I parked the car. I took Jerry by his purple tie and pulled him in close for a kiss. "I heard you tell Honor no more séances. Thank you."

He returned the favor. "The least I could do, considering I've managed to bring another criminal element into the house. Too bad she doesn't drive a dark blue Honda."

"Or wear a jacket with a missing button. Maybe Stan Bailey drives a dark blue Honda. That would make more sense."

"And he drove over to kill the man who stole his Baby Flo."

"Losing a button off his jacket in the process."

"Damn, you're good," he said and gave me another kiss. "Case closed."

"I have an idea it's not going to be that easy."

Chapter Fourteen

It wasn't.

For one thing, it took Jerry and me two hours the next morning to drive to Bayside. For another, Stan Bailey drove a white Chevy truck. It was parked in the driveway of his large brick house next to a motorcycle and a riding lawnmower.

"There goes that theory," Jerry said as I rang the doorbell. In honor of the mystery, he'd worn his brown tie with the multi-colored question marks.

Stan Bailey was a medium-sized man with a large-sized grudge, but it was also apparent he was through with Flora Clarke aka Lizzie Bailey. When I explained I was investigating the death of Wendall Clarke, he smirked and spoke in a sarcastic tone. "Oh yeah, Lizzie. Let's talk about her. To hear her tell it, I'm the best thing she's ever had in her life. She's so happy. Our future's so rosy. Then a richer man comes along, and boom! Good-bye, Stan. If Clarke's dead, I wouldn't be surprised if she's the culprit. She just about killed me."

"What do you mean by that, Mr. Bailey?"

"Not literally," he said. "She just about killed me financially. Overdrawing our credit cards, 'forgetting' to pay bills, traffic tickets. I'll bet I went to the bank and police station half a dozen times to bail her out of some mess. Thought she'd bat those baby blues at me and all would be forgiven. Well, it was—for a while. Then I saw her game. She just loved me for my money, and when she found out I wasn't as rich as she believed, she left me. I was glad to get rid of her."

"So you weren't upset when she married Wendall Clarke?"

"Hell, no. I even thought about warning him. Then I thought, why should I help any idiot who marries her? Why don't I let him find out for himself what kind of conniving little gold digger she is? Why don't I let her bleed him dry and toss him aside?" He paused in his tirade. "Well, I am sorry he's dead. What happened?"

"He was struck on the head and died as a result of that injury."

Bailey looked thoughtful. "Okay, you can eliminate Lizzie, then. She has the strength of your average mouse. She could barely lift a bag of groceries. Of course, she might have been pretending so I'd have to carry everything." He was still sarcastic but running out of steam. He spoke a little calmer. "I really don't think she'd murder anyone. She just loved money, and I didn't have enough to suit her."

"May I ask where you were Wednesday night?"

"That's my poker night. If you need the names of my pals, I'll get them for you."

"Thanks. And that's your truck?"

"Yep. I used to have a Mustang. Had to sell it to pay all that debt Lizzie had on our cards." The understandable bitterness was back.

"I certainly appreciate your help, Mr. Bailey."

"Yeah, well, if you can do something about that woman, I'd appreciate that, believe me. She's a menace. Let me write those names down for you."

He went into the house. Jerry whistled softly. "And I thought we had money problems."

"Is this typical con woman behavior—run up debts until the husband divorces her?"

"Yep. Then you move on to the next dupe."

"Flora doesn't strike me as that cold-blooded. What if she really loved Wendall?"

He shrugged. "It happens. That's usually when the con artist starts making mistakes."

"Has Flora made some mistakes?"

"So far, I'd say she's been pretty slick. For instance, do you know for a fact she has a sister?"

"Why would she say she has one?"

"To keep people from coming to the house. You thought she was all alone, so you offered to stay with her, didn't you? It gives her a legitimate reason to refuse, and then she can do what she wants."

"You think she was sitting in that house, laughing about how she'd put one over on the town and counting Wendall's money? She's sincerely upset that he's dead."

"If she's a pro, she can make you believe that."

Stan Bailey returned and handed me a piece of paper. "That should get me off the hook. I never even met Wendall Clarke, and like I said, I'm sorry he's dead. Even if Lizzie didn't kill him, you need to make sure she doesn't pull her scheme on anyone else. I hope she's not playing you, too."

After what Jerry had just told me, I wasn't so certain.

"Wrote a couple more names down for you," Stan said. "Come to find out, Lizzie was married three times before me. Wish one of them had warned me."

The husbands' names were Thomas Riley, Ryan Henderson, and Phillipe DuCoeur.

"Thank you, Mr. Bailey."

"Good luck," he said. "Hell, maybe they're all dead."

Jerry and I went to Deely's for lunch, and while we waited on our order, I called Stan's friends. They confirmed he'd been playing poker with them all Wednesday night.

I put my phone away and reached for my tea. "Stan's alibi holds up. I'll track down Flora's other ex-husbands next."

Annie set our baskets of cheeseburgers and fries on the table. "Thought you'd like to know, Aunt Louise won't be bothering you anymore, Jerry."

I thought she was going to say Aunt Louise had joined Aunt Gloria in the Great Beyond, and the two of them were thrashing out their money issues on another plane, but when Jerry asked what had happened, Annie said, "Oh, she's found another medium she's much happier with."

Uh, oh.

Jerry was instantly alert. "Another medium?"

"Oh, yeah. She's just moved to town. Maybe you know her. She calls herself Madam Mystere."

Jerry put down his cheeseburger. "Is Madam Mystere a large woman with black hair and a bit of a lisp?"

"Yes, she is! So you do know her. I'll have to tell Aunt Louise."

"Is Madam Mystere planning to hold a séance any time soon?"

"I think she's having one tonight. I can find out." Another customer called for her, and she hurried away.

"Damn," Jerry said.

I decided it was best not to say anything. I ate my cheeseburger while Jerry toyed with his, his expression preoccupied. After a while, Annie returned and told Jerry that the séance was going to be at midnight.

"Were you thinking of coming?"

Here was a great chance to expose Honor and make her leave town. I thought he'd readily agree, but he surprised me. "No, I'm pretty sure Aunt Louise doesn't want me around."

"How about you, Madeline?"

I gave Jerry a curious glance. He seemed completely uninterested. "Probably not."

"Refills, anybody?"

Jerry said he'd like some more tea, and when Annie left, I leaned forward. "What's going on?"

"I know you asked me to corral Honor, but she and Aunt Louise deserve each other. Maybe she'll tell her something that will make her happy."

"And take her money."

"I'd like to see her get money out of Aunt Louise."

I didn't like the idea of Honor playing tricks on the locals. "Jerry, I really want you to do something about this. Tell Annie and Aunt Louise that Honor is a fraud."

"I don't think Aunt Louise would believe me."

"Well, then, we'll stop by her house after lunch and you can give it your best try."

◇◇◇

Unfortunately, Jerry was right. Aunt Louise lived in a large square house with a huge porch, but she refused to let him even come up the steps. When he tried to explain about Honor, she accused him of being jealous and said she had every right to use as many mediums as she liked to get through to Gloria. Then she told him to get his feet off her yard or she'd call the police.

"Told you," Jerry said as we drove away.

Good grief, somebody had to handle this situation. "All right, then, maybe I can do something about it. Maybe I'll drop in on this séance tonight."

"That's a great idea."

He looked way too calm. "What am I getting into here, Jerry? What sort of séances does Honor perform?"

"She's never done a séance, and she's doing this one only to annoy me, so I'm going to ignore it."

Oh, I think she has a different motive, I thought. She's doing this one because she wants you back. "Maybe it really is better if I go. She won't be expecting me."

"That's why it's a great idea, Mac. Thanks."

Still too calm.

◇◇◇

This was Friday, the day planned for the gallery's grand opening. Instead, it was the day of Wendall's funeral. The service was to be held in Parkland that afternoon. Jerry and I had just enough time to get home and change clothes.

I pushed my clothes aside until I found my best black dress. "I wonder if Flora's sister will be there."

"Don't be surprised if she's too ill to attend."

I was taking the dress off the hangar and paused. "Jerry, I have a better idea."

"Anything's better than going to a funeral."

"While everyone's there, why don't we have a look in the house? I know which one it is, and there's a deck out back. I'm sure you could get in the sliding doors."

"Is there an alarm system?"

"I didn't see one." I looked at my dress, debating my course of action. "Although, I may be able to find out something at the service. It would be interesting to see who's there."

"You go to the funeral, and I'll break into the house."

That had disaster written all over it. "No. Maybe we could leave the service early. Funeral first, then the house."

Jerry sighed and reached for his plain blue tie.

◇◇◇

I expected a large crowd at Wendall Clarke's funeral service, but the church was only half full. Flora sat by herself in the front pew on the right-hand side. In the front pew on the left sat several large men and women who looked as if they might be Wendall's relatives. Pamela and several other members of the Art Guild, including Bea and her son Ferris, were in the middle. Jerry and I sat behind them. I then noticed Larissa sitting across the aisle from us, staring straight ahead, her hands clasped in her lap.

I'm sure Wendall would've found the service too short and too plain; just a hymn, some brief words from the minister, a prayer, and it was over. There were no dark blue Hondas in the funeral procession. We followed the procession to Parkland's Memorial Cemetery and stood off to one side while the minister offered another prayer. Then we expressed our sympathies to Flora, who thanked us for coming.

She introduced the large men and women. "These are some of Wendall's cousins. He didn't have much family, but they were able to come. I told them you were going to find out who did this to Wendall."

"I'll do my best," I said.

"We hope you can," one cousin said. "We weren't real close to our cousin, but we were definitely shocked by this sad turn of events."

Throughout all this, Larissa had held herself apart, ramrod stiff and unsmiling. Pamela kept wiping her eyes with a tissue, but occasionally she'd shoot a glare in Larissa's direction. Perhaps she thought Larissa should be more upset, or maybe she felt Larissa was responsible for Wendall's death. At any rate, the two women didn't speak to each other. Bea's expression was the same: irate. Ferris looked bored, but caught my attention when he casually tossed the knitted scarf he was wearing over one shoulder. This action rang a little bell in my brain and started a train of thought down the tracks. Scarf tossing isn't a genetically inherited trait, but Wendall and Bea had had a one-night stand in high school. Ferris, although he looked nothing like Wendall, was the right age to be his son. What if he was Wendall's son, and Bea had wanted Wendall to acknowledge that? Maybe that's what Wendall meant when he said, "That's not going to happen."

I needed to talk to Ferris. "I need a diversion."

"No problem." Jerry went up to Pamela and Bea. "I think you ladies are the very ones to help plan a memorial service for Wendall at the gallery."

Their attention caught, I was able to speak to Ferris. "I'm sure your mother is sad to lose an old friend like Wendall."

"Yeah. I never knew him, though, or any of these people. We lived in Raleigh with Dad until the divorce."

"Your mother didn't want to stay in Raleigh?"

"She had to come back to Celosia. Turns out Dad wasn't as rich as he said he was. Then Mom got this crazy idea Mr. Clarke would help her out. She said he owed her." He shrugged. "Too late now."

"Why would she think he owed her?"

He turned to check where Bea was. She and the other Art Guild members were deep in conversation with Jerry. He lowered his voice. "She seemed to think Clarke was my father, but he wasn't."

"You're sure?"

"My real father had all the tests that proved he was my dad, but for some reason, after the divorce, Mom got this notion that he wasn't. Doesn't matter now, does it?"

Apparently, it hadn't mattered to Wendall what Bea thought, but Bea could still believe she deserved something from his estate, however misguided this was.

"Learn anything?" Jerry asked as we got into our car.

"Bea thinks Wendall was Ferris' father. She divorced her husband, Ferris' real father, when the money ran out, so I'm guessing she wanted in on Wendall's fortune."

"Blackmail?"

"Possibly. And it looks like business as usual between Larissa and Pamela."

"Flora didn't have a sister. I hope you noticed that."

"Yes, I did."

"So she could be running the long con. Do we have time to scope out her house before she gets back?"

Flora was still talking with Wendall's cousins. "Looks like she'll be busy for a little while. Let's go."

◇◇◇

The deck's sliding glass doors proved no problem for Jerry's special keys, and no alarms sounded as we stepped into the Clarke's rented house in River Ridge.

Jerry closed the doors behind us. "What are we looking for?"

"First, I want to see if there's a button missing off Flora's pink suit."

We found the master bedroom. Flora had packed a lot of her clothes in suitcases, but her pink suit was still hanging in the closet. No buttons were missing.

"Check Wendall's," I said.

Wendall's suits had all their buttons, and none were gold. While Jerry looked through the rest of the closet, I went into the study and looked on the desk. A stack of bills had been pushed aside to make room for a cardboard box filled with a few books, a paperweight, a stapler, and other office supplies. The bills were for clothes, shoes, and jewelry. Flora was an expensive little gal. I wondered if she would benefit from Wendall's will, if he had one.

I continued to look through the box, thinking I wasn't going to find anything useful when down at the very bottom was a cell phone. Was it possible this was Wendall's? I turned it on. The phone still had a little battery power left, enough for me to check through the received calls. Most were from Flora, but there was one from Pamela made on Wednesday around seven-thirty p.m.

Jerry came in from the bedroom. "Find anything?"

"I think so. Judging from all the calls from Flora, I think this is Wendall's cell phone. He got a call from Pamela about half an hour before we got to the gallery." I turned off the phone and put it back in the box. "I need to know what that was all about."

"The only thing I found was more clothes in suitcases. Most everything in the house has been packed up. She's ready to move on."

"I'm wondering why Wendall didn't have his phone with him Wednesday night," I said. "I know the police would've asked Flora about it."

"Maybe they did. Maybe she lied and said she didn't know where it was."

"But why pack it in a box if it holds a clue to who killed her husband?"

"You'll have to ask her."

"I want to talk to Pamela, too. She hasn't said anything about Wendall calling her that night."

We left everything as we'd found it. Jerry locked the sliding door behind us. "I'm all warmed up now. Why don't we have a look in Bea's house?"

"She might be home."

"We can drive by and see if her car's there."

"That could be tricky. Her house is down in a wooded area."

"Even better. But we need to change clothes."

"I don't think I have any camouflage wear."

"Jeans and sneakers will do."

◇◇◇

I wasn't exactly sure what Jerry was up to, but we went home and changed clothes. On the way to Bea's, he asked about the house.

"It's a chalet style, right?"

"If Switzerland were bankrupt. It's small and very shabby."

"A shabby chalet."

"Yes."

"With a balcony."

"A little one."

"Let me know when we're a couple of blocks from her house."

I did, and he had me stop the car at the convenience store on the corner. "We'll walk the rest of the way, and if anyone asks, we're out for a stroll in the pleasant October weather."

It was a pleasant stroll down to Bea's driveway. The gray VW wasn't there.

Jerry looked around. "Okay, we'll wander through the woods and approach the house from the back. She doesn't have a dog, does she? Bea strikes me as a bulldog kinda gal."

"I think it would've attacked me if she did."

The house was quiet and dark. Jerry eyed the balcony, and then, using a trashcan, climbed up. I waited below, expecting at any minute to hear the chugging sounds of the VW. Bea could come home at any time. How would we explain? Oh, we were in the neighborhood and thought we'd break into your house. It's a little hobby of ours. We've already broken into Wendall's. Or maybe she and Ferris had gotten home from the funeral, and he had the VW, and Bea was inside taking a nap. Or she knew we were here and was crouched behind a door with a brick. I was almost ready to call up to Jerry and tell him to forget it when he said, "You're not going to believe this."

"You can't get in?" Maybe that was best. My imagination had us in jail for life.

"No, I can get in. I mean, you're not going to believe what's up here."

Now I had to see. He leaned over the balcony railing and helped me up. He had removed the screen and unlatched the small window. He stood back so I could look inside. The sight was so unexpected it took me a moment to process what I was seeing. Even though the upstairs room was dark, piles of multi-colored jewels glowed like phosphorus in a cave.

"Wow."

Jerry bent over and stepped inside. I forgot all my apprehensions and followed, entranced. We stood surrounded by a wealth of bracelets, necklaces, and rings, heaps of beads separated by color and size in bowls and dishes, more of the silver spacers, larger glass pieces shaped like leaves and fish and stars, and finished projects arrayed on black velvet. I'd had friends into jewelry making, and I recognized the trays for organizing beads, the coils of wire, and the little scissors and pliers. Propped in a fancy silver holder was a stack of business cards with "Bea's Baubles and Beads" written in glittery silver letters.

"Jerry, Bea makes these."

"They're fantastic. Hey, what about this necklace. Look familiar?"

The necklace was a collection of jagged yellow and gold glass crystals, a companion piece to the little leaf bracelet Bea had snatched from Flora.

"Maybe Flora bought the bracelet somewhere, and Bea couldn't stand to see one of her creations on Wendall's newest conquest."

Next to that necklace was another of chunky pastel beads in frosted glass. Jerry pointed out a red and black pendant slashed with silver and a spiky green and coral bracelet fit for a mermaid queen.

"These are works of art," I said. "I can't imagine why she keeps this a secret."

"Maybe she really is a jewel thief."

"No, as gorgeous as all this is, it's costume jewelry. There may be some sterling silver and some gold, but the beads are glass. Still, she could ask some high prices." I looked around at the little room filled with a Fourth of July holiday's worth of sparkle. There was another stack of business cards on Bea's desk from various jewelry stores and dealers. "Jerry, here's a card from the TSN, the Television Shopping Network. That's the network that bought Wendall's perfume bottle design."

"Bea's stuff would look great on TV."

"Here's another TSN card. There are six of them." Bea had scribbled dates on the backs of the cards. "My guess is she wrote down each time she contacted them."

"No luck, maybe?"

"I don't watch the shopping networks, so I don't know, but I would imagine if her jewelry was on TV, the world would hear about it." I didn't want to push our own luck and stay any longer. "We'd better go."

We climbed back out onto the balcony. Jerry closed the window and replaced the screen. We'd both gotten down when we heard a car.

Jerry grabbed my hand. "This is why we came through the woods." We quickly hurried into the safety of the trees. We watched as the VW ambled down the driveway and parked. Bea got out, carrying a plastic bag.

"More loot," Jerry said.

Ferris drove the VW back out the drive. Bea went into her house, and after a while, a light came on downstairs. We waited a few more minutes then circled around to the main road and walked to the convenience store.

"It's official," I said. "I have now gone into mystery overload."

We'd managed to grab a quick snack on the way to Parkland, but that had been hours ago, and my stomach was growling. Growling, but not upset.

We decided to eat in the living room. There was one serving of casserole left over, which Jerry heated for me. He preferred a peanut butter and jelly sandwich and chips. I sat down on the living room sofa, kicked off my shoes, and tucked my feet underneath me. Jerry put his feet up on the coffee table. *Blue Moon Garden* gleamed from its place of honor over the fireplace, its tones of blue and white complementing our walls and furniture.

I pointed my fork at the painting. "My artwork is out for everyone to see. Why would Bea choose to hide her wonderful creations? She enjoys lording over the other women in the Guild. You'd think she would love to flaunt her jewelry."

"Maybe she's saving up for a big reveal."

"Or maybe she's planning some big con. What do you think?"

"I think I will never figure out why women do anything."

As I munched on the casserole, I thought of something else that puzzled me. "If Honor hadn't known Flora was a con artist, I certainly never would've guessed, but wouldn't you say that was genuine grief we saw at the funeral today?"

"Sure looked like it. You want something to drink?"

"Oh, I forgot my tea. It's on the table."

Jerry returned with my tea and a bottle of cola for himself. "What's Pamela's part in all this?"

"Sasha Gregory said Sasha left the gallery at four o'clock. Larissa went back around four-thirty, found the door unlocked, went in, decided to smash Bea's pictures, and then apparently went home. Wendall called her around eight, but according to his phone, he got a call from Pamela at seven-thirty."

"So maybe whatever Pamela told Wendall made him call Larissa."

"Then Larissa hurries over to the gallery and finds Wendall dead around eight-thirty."

Jerry dug in the bag of chips for a handful. "That's her story. She could've bonked him on the head first."

"Wouldn't we have heard that? That's the same time we were there with Nell. We would've heard some sounds of a struggle, voices, something."

We pondered the mystery for a while. "I wonder what kind of car Pamela drives? The owner of the gift shop saw the dark blue Honda at six o'clock. Larissa said she parked out front, and her car is beige. Wendall drives a black sports car. Bea has that old VW. Someone else must have been in the gallery."

"Or maybe someone just randomly parked there. Ask Nell."

"I'll go over to her house and see for myself."

"Do you need backup? I can skip rehearsal."

"No, I'll be fine."

"Speaking of fine, how do you feel?"

"Great. One hundred percent." One hundred percent confused, I wanted to add. I set my empty dish on the coffee table. "We discovered Bea's secret, but I'm not sure what I can do with the information. People keep a lot of things private. Those things don't necessarily make them murderers."

"They may lead to something else."

"And how in the world do you stay so calm? I didn't mind looking around in Wendall's house, but I did a little hyperventilating at Bea's."

"That's because you are an honest person, Mac. You have what I believe are known as ethics."

"You have ethics, too."

"I do now." He set his sandwich down. "When I ran cons, I never used my name, so I was playing a character. It was easy to get away with things when you were someone else."

"But you weren't playing a character when you broke into Bea's. You were Jerry Fairweather on her balcony."

"Ah, yes, but I had a story ready. Always have some reasonable explanation for why you are doing whatever you're doing."

"Checking for termites?"

"That's good. That might work. I was going to say that our cat had run away, and I thought I saw it on her balcony."

"She wouldn't have believed that."

"But she couldn't prove it wasn't true. Have a story ready. Like the Boy Scouts. Be prepared."

"You are the least likely Boy Scout I've ever known."

"Are you kidding? I've got five Breaking and Entering badges." He gathered the empty dishes. "Want anything else?"

"No, thanks."

"We're all out of snacks, so I thought I'd make a cake."

"Chocolate, please."

He leaned over to give me a kiss. "I've also got two Dessert badges."

I sat for a while, gazing at *Blue Moon Garden* and thinking about the beautiful one-of-a-kind jewelry I'd seen at Bea's. Was there some connection between those creations and Wendall's murder? Or maybe Bea didn't feel her work was ready. Oddly enough, I could sympathize. For a long time, I didn't want anyone to see my paintings. I knew something about rejection, and if Bea had been constantly turned down by the TSN, she might have decided not to show her jewelry to anyone.

Not long after Jerry's cake was done, someone gave him a ride to the theater, and I started my search for Flora's other ex-husbands. My computer search program found long lists of Thomas Rileys and Ryan Hendersons. It was going to take a while to sort through all of them. There were only sixteen Phillipe DuCoeurs in the states, so I started with them. Eliminating the very young, I wound up with ten. Luckily, most of them were home when I called. The fifth Phillipe was the one I wanted. Speaking with only a trace of accent, he informed me that yes, he had been married to a beautiful young blond woman named Lizzie Fountaine. She had been too expensive for him to keep, however, and he divorced her after a year. I had an idea that would be Thomas' and Ryan's story, too.

After a while, my eyes began to cross. I needed to get up and move around. I needed to go to Pamela's house. Besides wanting to see what kind of car she owned, I was curious about her relationship with Big Mike. Was the story of the pink sapphire ring another of Honor's scams, or was it possible Pamela had ties to the underworld—connections that may have led to Wendall's murder?

Chapter Fifteen

The car parked at Pamela's was a white Camry. Parked next to it was a car I was surprised to see: Larissa's beige Accord. As I walked up the porch steps, I could hear their voices raised in argument.

Pamela sounded as angry as I'd ever heard her. "You can't possibly think you are entitled to any of that. You hadn't seen Wendall in years! You objected to everything he wanted to do. There is no way you're going to be involved in the gallery."

Larissa's voice was even more harsh than usual. "Don't be stupid. Flora will get everything. She's the sole beneficiary of Wendall's will."

"I don't care about Flora. I only care about the gallery."

"Aren't you listening to me? The gallery isn't yours! It belonged to Wendall, and now it belongs to Flora. She can turn the building into a skating rink if she wants to."

"Why are you here, Larissa? What do you want?"

"I want to know what happened to Wendall."

"You know very well what happened. You were angry with him and you killed him."

I thought the next sound I would hear would be choking noises as Larissa attacked Pamela, but she became unexpectedly calm. "I didn't kill him. Maybe you were so angry because he hired that Gregory woman that *you* killed him."

"Wendall was killed with a piece of wood Bea used for a picture frame. I saw you break up Bea's pictures."

Now Larissa's voice was scornful. "No, you didn't. How could you have seen me?"

"That mirror in the office. It's a two-way mirror."

There was a long pause. I imagined Larissa staring at Pamela in surprise. "And just what were you doing there?"

"I came back to the gallery to talk to Wendall. I thought he might be in the office. I heard you come in, and then I saw you attack Bea's pictures. You were so angry I thought you might attack me, too, so I stayed in the office until you left."

Larissa's voice got very intense. "You listen to me, you little sneak. Yes, I broke up Bea's pictures, not that anyone could tell the difference, but I did not kill Wendall."

"Then why were you seen running away from his dead body?"

"I knew people like you would jump to conclusions, that's why. Maybe you stayed hiding in the office, waiting for him so *you* could kill him."

Pamela snapped. "Get out of my house! Get out!"

I quickly stepped off the porch and got into my car before Pamela flung the front door open, and Larissa came out. Pamela was so furious, she didn't notice me or my car. She slammed the door shut. I got out of my car as Larissa walked up to hers.

She stopped short. "What are you doing here?"

"Pamela invited me to have a look at some of her paintings."

"This might not be the best time. We just had an argument."

"I didn't think you were speaking to each other at all."

"Not usually."

I couldn't see Larissa's face very well in the fading light. She shook her head. "All I know is she's crazy to have the gallery. Maybe she'd do anything to have it."

"You told me when Wendall called that night he wanted to talk to you in private."

"Yes."

"You still don't have any idea why?"

She sighed. "I've been thinking and thinking about it, Madeline, and I don't know. If he wanted to say he was sorry for everything he'd done to me, he missed his chance a long time ago. I don't think he'd choose the back door of his gallery to do that, anyway."

"Would he have offered you a job at the gallery?"

"I would've refused it."

"Then why did you go, Larissa?"

I didn't think she was going to answer. Then she said, "I never thought he'd come back. I never thought I'd see him again, and I just…I don't know. Even after all this time and all the hurtful things he did…" She broke off. "I hate myself for being so soft, for even entertaining the idea that he'd come back to Celosia to see me. Is there anyway you can understand that?"

The words of the "Willow Aria" went through my mind. *Willow, if he once should be returning, pray tell him I am weeping, too.* Larissa was still very much in love with Wendell and interpreted his phone call as an invitation. "Yes," I said.

"And on top of everything else, Bea was trying to make something out of that one night she got lucky in high school, parading that boy around, trying to make everyone believe Wendall's the father."

"She told you this?"

"Why do you think I got so angry? Otherwise, I never would've touched her stupid pieces of wood. How dare she make up such a story?"

I found it oddly sad that Larissa still wanted to protect Wendall's reputation. "According to Ferris, Wendall wasn't his father."

"In any event, Bea feels entitled to Wendall's money. So do I, but feeling entitled gets me nowhere. It all goes to the little fortune hunter."

"You were friends with Bea in high school, though, weren't you?"

"She was such a goody two-shoes back then, talking about waiting until she got married to have sex and planning the perfect home and babies. If she spouted that nonsense off to Wendall, no wonder he dumped her."

Pamela's front door opened, and she stepped out on the porch. She stared at us in an accusing manner. "Are you still here? Who's that with you?"

"It's Madeline," I said. "I'd like to see your paintings, but if this isn't a good time, I can come back."

"No, no, come on in. Larissa was just leaving."

Without another word, Larissa got into her car and drove off.

Pamela greeted me at the door. She was shaking, her hair standing on end. "I suppose you're wondering why Larissa stopped by."

"She said you two were talking about the future of the gallery."

"That's one way to put it." She clasped her hands together to keep them steady. I wondered if the trembling was a reaction to the argument, or if Pamela had other reasons for being so unsettled. "You can talk to Flora, can't you? Tell her she doesn't have to close the gallery."

"I'm sure she wouldn't mind discussing it with you."

"After the way this town treated her, I don't think she'd want to have anything to do with us."

"She's not going to stay in Celosia, but she might want to have the gallery as a tribute to Wendall."

"Well, she might, at that. Come have a look at my paintings. Watch your step."

I needed to watch my step as Pamela's house was small and crowded with furniture and knickknacks. Nothing matched anything else: not the chairs, the lamps, the rugs, or the curtains. It looked as if Pamela had bought one of everything that ever existed in the furniture world. The walls were covered with her flower paintings and collages. She quickly forgot her quarrel with Larissa and her concerns about the gallery as she happily explained each one.

"Now these are some of my very first attempts. You can see I didn't have a good grasp of leaves then. This is a Daisy Series, and over here next to the fireplace is my Aster Series. Of course, I had to have a Celosia Series."

The paintings of celosias showed the feathery flowers in their bright pink, yellow, red, and orange varieties. "Very realistic."

"You haven't seen any of my collages. This is the holiday group over here."

The collages were globs of cloth and small objects from Christmas ornaments and tinsel to valentines and lace. The Fourth of July collage sported toy flags while toy spiders dangled from the Halloween collage. The one that caught my eye, however, was the Veterans Day collage. Among the red, white, and blue ribbons sparkled several gold buttons.

I pointed to that collage. "This one's interesting. I like the buttons."

Pamela straightened the picture. "Those represent the uniforms of our servicemen. It's my newest collage. I just finished it."

I took a closer look. The buttons were exactly the same as the one the owner of the gift shop found in the back parking lot, the same button I had in my pocket. I recalled Samantha Terrell saying Pamela gave her leftovers for her scrapbook. "You must have a large storage area to keep all your materials."

"No, I give lots of things away," she said. "I don't like to use the same ribbons or buttons for more than one picture, and my house is too small to keep everything. I usually keep a bag of scraps in my car in case I run into Samantha or someone who can use them."

"Well, these are unique. The buttons are a clever touch."

"Thank you. I got them off one of my uncle's old suits. I didn't need all of them, though, so I gave the rest to Samantha."

And dropped one behind the gallery.

"Would you care for something to drink, Madeline?"

I followed her to her kitchen, which was just a crowded as the rest of her house. She cleaned off a spot on the small table, moved a stack of magazines off a chair, and invited me to have a seat. "You'll have to excuse the mess. I don't often have visitors. Did you find out who broke the gallery window? Not that it matters that much anymore."

I was almost certain Bea Ricter was the brick-thrower, but I had no proof. "I'm still working on it. Flora Clarke has hired me to solve Wendall's murder. That may take a little more of my time."

"Oh, of course."

"When was the last time you saw Wendall?"

"Wednesday afternoon at the meeting."

"Did you get to make an appointment with Sasha Gregory?"

She took a pitcher of tea from the refrigerator and poured some in a glass. I noticed her hands were steady now. "Yes, of course. She was really very agreeable. I didn't think she would be. Lemon?"

"No, thanks." She handed me the glass. "You didn't come back later?"

"There was no reason to come back."

"What about the phone call?"

She looked startled. "Phone call?"

"To Wendall." I bent the truth slightly. "The police found his cell phone. You called him at about seven-thirty Wednesday night."

"Oh, that." She gave a little laugh. "I'd forgotten that. Just voicing some concerns about the gallery." She busied herself getting another glass of tea. "Making one last plea. Turns out it was the last, wasn't it?"

"What did he say?"

"He said he was certain I'd be happy with the way Ms. Gregory ran things." She didn't sit down. She leaned against the kitchen counter. "Madeline, I have the awfullest suspicion Larissa killed Wendall."

"Because he divorced her and married a younger woman?"

"You have no idea how angry that made her."

"I'm sure she was upset, but it's a big leap to murder. I'm more interested in knowing what you were doing hiding in the office."

She sputtered a denial for a few moments and then realized I wasn't buying it. "How did you know?"

I took the matching button out of my pocket. "The woman who owns the gift shop behind the gallery found this in the parking lot when she left at six o'clock, and I happened to overhear some of your argument with Larissa. You were at the gallery around four-thirty, weren't you? That's when Larissa said she was there. You were able to get in the back door because it wasn't locked."

She pulled out another chair and sat down heavily. "Yes."

"Like Larissa, you hoped to talk to Wendall, but he wasn't there. You heard someone come in, so you hid in the office. You saw Larissa smashing Bea's pictures, but were too afraid to confront her. When you called Wendall to voice your concerns about the gallery, did you tell him this had happened?"

"Yes. He needed to know. He said he'd come over and take care of everything."

Wendall had then called Larissa and asked her to meet him at the gallery. "Did you see anyone else that evening?"

"No. As soon as Larissa was gone, I got out of there." She looked at me pleadingly. "Madeline, you don't think I had anything to do with Wendall's death, do you?"

Pamela was a tall woman, too, almost as tall as Larissa. But what was her motive? If she killed Wendall, she killed her dream of having an exhibit. Pamela watched me anxiously, as if she expected me to leap up and declare: "You're under arrest!"

"Pamela," I said. "If there's anything else you need to tell me, tell me now."

"I swear I did not kill Wendall Clarke."

I took a deep breath and tried to organize my thoughts. The Mystery of the Gold Button had been solved, but there was still the Mystery of the Dark Blue Honda. I'd have to start back at the beginning. "All right. I'm trying to cover all the bases here."

She gave a nervous little laugh. "I believe that's why Flora hired you, isn't it? Isn't she under suspicion?"

"She doesn't appear to be tall enough or strong enough to have struck such a fatal blow."

But at this point, I wasn't ruling anybody out. I got up to inspect some of the other collages. One in particular had struck my eye. Everything in it was pink, including a distinctive pink jewel serving as the body for a pink butterfly made of pink lace. As I moved slightly from side to side, the light caught the jewel and a white star appeared in its depths. "This is a gorgeous jewel. Is it from a ring, by any chance?"

"Yes, someone gave me a star sapphire ring, and when things didn't work out, I didn't want to wear it anymore, but I hated to put it in a drawer, so I had a jeweler take the stone out. That particular collage is called 'New Beginnings.' You can tell by the butterflies and all the flowers blooming and the little eggs hatching in the trees."

"I'm sorry the relationship didn't last, Pamela. Is he still here in town?"

"No, this was when we both lived in Parkland. As it turned out, he wasn't the best choice for me." She fiddled with her tea glass. "He was a terrible choice, actually, but I didn't see it. Maybe I didn't want to see it." Then she said something that took me aback. "Madeline, you're so lucky to have a good man like Jerry. You don't know what it's like to love a swindler. I knew Mike was bad news, but I couldn't help myself. I knew his reputation, but I thought I could reform him."

This was exactly what I thought about Jerry. "So Mike was a swindler? A con man? How did you two meet?"

"I may not look like it now, but I used to model. Not professionally, but for some of the larger stores in Parkland. In my day I was quite alluring. Mike came to one of the fashion shows with some of his friends. We hit it off. Then I found out what kind of man he was. He wouldn't change, so we ended the relationship."

"He never asked for the ring back?"

"No. I haven't had any contact with him whatsoever. And I want to keep it that way, Madeline. I don't know why you're so interested in my personal life all of a sudden."

"My apologies. It's my job to ask questions, and sometimes I forget I'm being too nosy. Let me ask you about Bea. Did you know about her claim that her son was Wendall's child?"

"I don't think she had any proof of that."

"Let's say she did. Would Wendall have acknowledged the boy?"

"I don't know. Could Bea have killed him because he wouldn't do that?"

But why get rid of the father you wanted your son to have? Wendall didn't have to say, yes, this is my boy. There were millions of dads who never had anything to do with their children. I could only surmise that Bea wanted child support, and Wendall had said, "That's not going to happen." Besides, Ferris was a grown man. He had accepted the other man as a father, and didn't appear to be dependent on his mother. He didn't need Wendall's money.

I thanked Pamela for her time and left. So Honor had told the truth when she said Pamela and Big Mike had a fling. But if the ring was that important, wouldn't he have found Pamela and demanded it back? Why send Honor after the ring? Or maybe Honor wanted the ring and was hoping Jerry would find it for her.

Now you're thinking like a real con artist, I told myself. Here you are, hoping to reform your husband, and his lifestyle is rubbing off on you. One thing was certain. Honor was trying her best to involve Jerry in something illegal, and I was not going to let that happen. Not for him and not for me.

Chapter Sixteen

I called to let Jerry know I was stopping by my office to check the mail before picking him up. I had a rude surprise when I unlocked my door. The side window was smashed and a chunk of brick lay on the carpet surrounded by shards of glass. A quick look around assured me this was the only damage, and nothing had been stolen. I went outside and around to the window, but there were no footprints or any clues. Some random act of vandalism, or a warning to back off the case?

I gave Jerry another call to let him know what had happened. Then I called the police. I thought they'd send an officer, but Chief Brenner came over.

He surveyed the scene. "Well, someone doesn't want you involved in Clarke's murder investigation. Anything missing?"

"No."

"Leave everything right there. I'll have a word with the neighbors."

I sat down at my desk and glared at the brick, wishing it could tell me who was running around town smashing windows. Then I got up for a better look. I'd seen the bricks in Bea's yard. This one was different. Bea's bricks were old red bricks with worn edges. The one on my carpet was new and pink, and its edges were sharp.

Chief Brenner came in as I bent over the brick, frowning. "So it won't talk, eh?"

I straightened. "I thought this might have come from Bea's yard, but it's not the same color."

He used his pen to push the brick over and examined it from all sides. "We'll dust it and see. Were you here when this happened?"

"No, I stopped by to check my mail."

"The folks next door didn't see or hear anything unusual. Everyone else in the building must have gone home at five, but I'll talk to them."

"Thanks for coming over."

He took out his camera and snapped pictures of the damage. "You caught me just in time. I was heading over to Parkland's crime lab to see if they had anything for me. Do you have anything?"

I didn't want to tell him Jerry and I had spent the afternoon breaking and entering. "I've talked with Larissa and Pamela. Were you aware Bea thought Wendall was the father of her child?"

"How likely is that?"

"Extremely unlikely. Even her son doesn't believe it."

"All right, I'll follow that up, but we're working on this case from a different angle. Seems one of Wendall's business competitors made some threats last month. We're looking into that."

I thought with a town full of angry artists, this line of inquiry was extremely unlikely, too. "Between the two of us, we ought to come up with something."

He motioned to the broken glass. "I'm not so sure you should be on this case, Madeline. The next brick might be aimed at your head. Are you on your way home? Where's Jerry?"

"I'm picking him up at the theater."

"If I were you, I wouldn't go anywhere alone until this is settled."

It was going to take more than a brick through my window to keep me from solving this case.

When I arrived at the theater, the cast was romping through "Kansas City." They looked like they were having fun, except for Bea, who stood scowling, arms folded, as if the cowboys and ranchers had purposely torn up her tater patch with their wild dancing. It was difficult to imagine this angry little woman creating such amazing jewelry. It was not difficult to imagine her running around town heaving bricks at windows.

When the song ended, I leaned over the edge of the orchestra pit. "Is Aunt Eller supposed to be annoyed by all the frivolity?"

"This Aunt Eller is annoyed by everything. Are you okay? Is the office a mess?"

"I'm fine, and it was only one broken window. But the brick was an alien brick. Tell you about it later."

Evan asked for one more round of the dance number. I sat down to watch. Jerry played so well, it was a shame theater paid about the same as art, which was practically nothing. If the arts were as revered as sports, we'd have no trouble making a living. I'd thought about asking Chief Brenner if he needed a reformed con man on the force to help catch other con men, the way some police departments hired former art forgers to expose fake paintings. But Celosia was too small, and there weren't any other con artists, except Jerry's dubious friends. Maybe he'd have some luck with his job interviews.

Rehearsal ended, and Jerry came up out of the pit. "Be right there, Mac. I need to pick up a few things."

Bea saw me, but didn't come over to talk. I chatted briefly with the young woman who was playing Laurie. She'd been a contestant in the Miss Celosia Pageant, the pageant that had led to my first murder case in town.

"Guess you didn't ever think you'd have this much to do in Celosia, did you, Madeline? Are you helping out with the murder at the art gallery?"

I told her yes, I was, but since she was too young to have gone to school with Wendall and wasn't too concerned, she soon changed the subject to *Oklahoma* and talked about the play until Jerry returned and she waved good-bye. Jerry had a paper shopping bag.

"Stuff I need to look through for the orchestra," he said. "We've decided to dress like cowboys, too."

"Jerry Fairweather and His Rootin' Tootin' Cowboy Band?"

"Right now we're the Tumbleweed Quintet. I'm looking for a few more people to join us. There's a violin part." He grinned and arched his eyebrows.

"Keep looking."

We started up the aisle and he asked, "Now what did you mean about an alien brick?"

"You know what the bricks in Bea's yard look like? This one was different."

"Maybe she's expanding her brickyard."

"Maybe she didn't do it. Hasn't she been here all night?"

"Yes. Are you saying someone's trying to frame her? Why break your window?"

"I don't know. But it was definitely a warning."

On the drive home, I told Jerry about finding the ring. "Pamela has the pink sapphire stuck in one of her collages."

"Will it come off?"

"Do you honestly think if I get it, Honor will give it to Big Mike? I think she wants it for herself. The only way to ruin her game is to get Big Mike and Pamela together. Can you get him here, or do the two of you have issues?"

"Big Mike and I settled our differences a long time ago. He told me I was like the little brother he never had."

"Not the son he never had?"

"Big Mike is big, but he's not that old."

"Well, call him up, or light the bat signal, or whatever it is you do in Con World."

Jerry looked doubtful. "That could be a little tricky. He likes to keep a low profile."

"But not beyond your skills."

"I'll see what I can do. I've also been wondering if she really does owe him anything. He was usually an easy-going guy."

At home, Jerry said he was hungry again, so he made a grilled cheese sandwich. For once, the smells of bread and cheese smelled good, and I asked him to make me one.

"I need a snack before I go to the séance."

He took two more slices of bread from the package. "Well, have fun. I'm going to practice. Want me to wait up for you?"

"Don't you want to hear all the details?"

"I can tell you how it's going to go. Honor will do a pitiful impersonation of a medium, nowhere near as good as me. Aunt Louise will kick her out of the house, and Honor's reputation as a medium will be ruined forever. The end."

"Ruined enough to make her leave town?"

"She'll probably come up with something else, but we'll see."

Aunt Louise wasn't thrilled to see me, but since I'd left Jerry at home, she grudgingly agreed to let me in on the séance. Inside her house, many cats scattered out of my way, except for a large gray one that followed me into the living room. When I joined Aunt Louise and Annie at the séance table, Honor smiled and welcomed me to the circle. She didn't seem the least bit disconcerted, but as Jerry had just mentioned about his own con career, she was playing a part.

"Another seeker of truth."

"How true," I said. Under the table, the cat bit my knee. "Ow."

"Sydney, no," Annie said. "Sorry, Madeline. He's just saying hello."

Hello to my foot, Sydney. I pushed him away.

"Please take hands."

Honor lit a candle in the center of the table and grasped hands with Aunt Louise and Annie. I reached around to grasp their outstretched hands, still fending off Sydney's attempts to chew my knee. "Spirits of the other world, we entreat you to find the soul of Gloria. We ask that you bring her across to answer questions only she can answer."

Jerry was right. Her act was not as convincing as his, but Aunt Louise was buying it.

"We do not wish to disturb the cosmic ether, but there are matters of great importance we must discuss with the dearly departed Gloria. Come to us. Come."

Honor had been chanting with her eyes closed, but a strange scratchy noise made her open her eyes. I thought Sydney was using the table leg for a scratching post. Then Honor's eyes widened and her mouth dropped open as she gave a strangled squeak.

I turned to see what had caused this reaction. Honor stared beyond me. A woman's figure all in black stood at the front window, features hidden by a black veil. A mournful cracked voice spoke.

"Loooouise. Loooouise. How dare you doubt me?"

Sydney streaked from the room. Aunt Louise gave a scream and fell over backwards. As Annie and I scrambled to help her up, the figure raised a trembling hand and pointed at Honor. "And death to this woman who dares summon me!"

Honor stood as if paralyzed.

Annie's face was white and she was shaking. "It's okay," I said. "Stay with your aunt."

I ran out and around the house, but there was no sign of the ghostly figure. I had to admit it had given me a start. My heart was still pounding when I went back inside. The lights were on, the candle was out, and Honor was gathering her things as fast as she could.

Annie was patting Aunt Louise on the back. "It's all right, she's gone." Aunt Louise was still gasping for breath. "I'm calling 9-1-1."

Aunt Louise waved her away. "No, no. Don't call anyone. I'm fine. Get me my root beer."

"That was really impressive," I told Honor. "Too bad she cursed you."

Her voice was shaking. "I don't know how he did it."

"Did what? You think Jerry was behind this? Go outside and look for yourself. There's no way he could've gotten to the house. We have only one car, and I drove it here."

"Then he got someone else to bring him."

"Wouldn't we have heard another car?"

She charged out and went around the house. I followed, also looking for any signs of my wayward husband, but there was nothing. Knowing his talent as a second-story man, I even looked up on the roof.

"I'm starting to think Aunt Gloria did come back from the grave," I said. "Wait till word gets around. You'll be able to hold as many séances as you like."

And then I realized Honor's voice was shaking from laughter. "Oh, he's good. He's really good. You should be so proud, Madeline."

"You honestly think Jerry's behind this? How?"

"Oh, we have our secrets. Too bad you're not in the club. I'd better scoot before Aunt Louise gets wise. See ya." She got in her car, and drove away.

Too bad I'm not in the club? I knew this was Honor's not so subtle way of saying she and Jerry had a special connection. She was trying so hard to hang onto him. There was something more to their relationship, something Honor imagined, anyway.

I went inside to check on Aunt Louise. She was swilling down her second bottle of root beer.

"Where is that awful woman?" she demanded. "What was she thinking?"

"But you wanted to talk to Aunt Gloria," Annie said.

"Not like that! I nearly had a spasm! Madeline, you tell Jerry I want him back. At least he didn't frighten me half to death."

Oh, I think he may have already, I wanted to say.

But when I got home, Jerry was on the couch eating cookies and watching TV. He took the remote and muted the sound. "Oh, hi. How'd it go?"

I sat down beside him. "Honor is a fabulous medium. Do you know she was able to call up Aunt Gloria? We all saw her."

"Must have been scary."

"Honor thought so."

"Well, it's not wise to rile the dead. How did Aunt Louise take it?"

"She almost had a heart attack."

"Gee, that's too bad."

I looked right into his eyes. "How did you do it, Jerry?"

"Do what?"

I'm always amazed by how innocent he can appear. "I don't believe in ghosts, and I certainly don't believe Honor set this up. For a moment, she was truly frightened."

"I happen to know she's a bit superstitious. Maybe the spirit world was trying to tell her something."

"Jerry—"

"Do I look anything like Aunt Gloria?"

"Not now."

"And I just magically got myself to Aunt Louise's house and back before you got home?"

That part had me stumped.

Jerry offered me a cookie. "Whatever happened, let's hope Honor got the message."

"Look, if the two of you are going to play horrible jokes on each other, leave me out of it. I have a case to solve." My ghost-busting had made me hungry, so I ate one cookie and asked for another. "These are good. Did you make them?"

"I've been practicing the piano and making cookies all evening. You have to admit that is an iron-clad alibi."

"For most people, yes."

"And assisting with your investigation. I got a hold of Big Mike. He said he'll stop by one day this week."

"Did he have anything to say about Honor or Pamela?"

"We didn't discuss details on the phone. He'd rather talk to you directly."

"Well, good. Thank you."

He put his arm around me and pulled me in close. "I forgive you for suspecting me."

I gave him a long kiss. "It ain't over yet, bud."

Chapter Seventeen

Austin came over on Saturday morning, and after breakfast, Jerry convinced him there was more to life than Wow, so the two of them went out in the back yard to toss a football and tackle each other. I called Nell to ask about repairing my office window and then spent an unsuccessful hour searching through all the Thomas Rileys and Ryan Hendersons, and then decided to call Flora. I wanted to give her an update on the case, and if confronted, maybe she'd tell me which Thomas and which Ryan I needed to talk to.

I was a little surprised when she offered to come over to my house.

"The police need to ask me some more questions, Madeline, and then I'll stop by."

We sat on the front porch. I told her my investigation was coming along slowly, and I then asked her what she planned to do once Wendall's murder was solved.

She was wearing a powder blue suit, a white blouse, and several gold necklaces. She smoothed her silky blue skirt. "Some people aren't happy about it, but it's no secret Wendall left everything to me. I'm going to take some of that money and buy myself a place in Palm Beach. I've always wanted to live there. I'm not moving right away, of course. I'm not going anywhere until I find out who killed Wendall. It wouldn't look very good for me to leave town so soon, anyway. I know some people here think I did it."

"That's true," I said. "Why did you lie about having a sister?"

I thought this might catch her off guard, but as I'd recently learned from Jerry, she had a story ready. "I wanted to be alone, and that was the easiest way to make you feel more comfortable."

"I'd also like to know about your ex-husband, Stan Bailey."

"There's not much to tell. He and I had different ideas about our marriage."

"What about Thomas Riley and Ryan Henderson and Phillipe DuCoeur?"

She kept her expression neutral. "How did you find out about them?"

"I have connections. And during the course of my investigations, I found out you have a reputation. You also have another name. Should I call you Flora or Lizzie?"

She sat silent for a few moments. "It was a game at first, like all the others, but then I truly fell in love with Wendall. I can't explain why I loved him. I'll admit I was attracted to his wealth and power, but he was also a wonderful man."

"I imagine your other husbands were wonderful men, too."

She shrugged. "Not really. They were rich. They were convenient. I suppose you'll want to talk to them."

"I found Phillipe. I'd like to talk to the other two, if you know where they are."

"Thomas is Thomas Allan Riley. He's in Philadelphia. Ryan's in Texas. Dallas, I think. Ryan Peter Henderson."

Her lack of emotion regarding these men puzzled me. "I'm trying to understand. You don't feel any remorse about tricking them?" I'd run into this same problem with Jerry. He was feeling remorse now, but only because he'd been caught.

"Wendall was going to be the last. It was only a matter of time before my luck ran out."

I'd heard Jerry tell Honor this same thing. The smart con artists were the ones who knew when to get out. "You don't have an alibi for Wednesday night."

"No, I don't. But I don't have a motive, either."

"Wendall might have been onto you. He might have threatened to expose you."

"I'll tell you something, Madeline." She leaned toward me. "For a long time, I was worried that he would find out about me and divorce me, but I honestly think he knew and didn't care."

"How do you think he knew?"

She gave a laugh that was more a sob. "He found one of my wigs in the closet and asked me what it was for. He always liked my blond hair, and this wig was bright red. I said Stan had preferred me as a redhead. He said, 'Stan couldn't afford you, could he?' What else could I say but no, he couldn't? Then Wendall said, 'No one can afford you but me, Baby. You don't need any disguises or tricks. I'll take care of you.' He knew, all right, or at least had some suspicions."

"Coming back to Celosia didn't spark old flames with Larissa?"

"She might have thought so, but he told me he felt nothing for her but pity. When they were married, he tried to give her all his wealth and attention, and she rejected it. He had nothing else to give her."

"Did he mention having problems with anyone else in town?"

"Oh, I found out quite a few things about his good old school chums. Pamela Finch used to date a very shady character, and then Bea comes along with all these false claims about her son. I know a con when I see one, and I wasn't about to let her get her hands on any part of Wendall's fortune."

She didn't say, "That was all for me." She didn't have to.

"That dustup you had with her over the bracelet. What was that all about?"

"I found the bracelet in Wendall's things. He told me it was a sample of Bea's work. She made jewelry and was always pestering him to put in a good word for her with the Television Shopping Network, as if he had some magical pull with them, which he didn't. I decided to wear it and see if she noticed."

This was a far cry from the sweet Bambi-eyed Flora I'd first met. "She noticed in a big way."

"Oh, I wanted her to. I wanted her to see she couldn't manipulate Wendall."

"That's my job," went unsaid. These little flashes of menace made me wonder if Flora had a hand in Wendall's murder. She had easily seen through Larissa's neediness and Bea's rampant greed. Could she have played one against the other, all the while retreating to her guise of sweet little trophy wife when things got too hot?

"What about Wendall's cell phone?" I asked.

"His cell phone?"

I couldn't very well tell her Jerry and I had broken into her house while she was still at Wendall's funeral. "It might have some useful messages the police need to see."

"They asked me about it. I packed it away somewhere. I'll have to find it."

"Why didn't Wendall take it with him when he went to the gallery Wednesday night?"

"He left it with me. Mine was broken, and he didn't want to leave me alone without a phone. He was coming right back, so he said he didn't need it." Her voice caught. "He was always thinking of me. Excuse me." She took a handkerchief from her pocket and wiped her eyes. "I can't seem to stop crying."

I wished Jerry was here to tell me if her tears were genuine.

After Flora left, I went back to my computer. My search was a lot easier knowing full names and last known locations. I was able to find both Riley and Henderson, and their stories, as I'd guessed, were very similar to Phillipe DuCoeur's and Stan Bailey's. It would be easy to expose Flora as the con woman she was, but her willingness to help me made me hesitate before calling Chief Brenner. Wouldn't she have skipped town as quickly as she could? Wouldn't she already be in disguise and flirting with potential husband number six? Maybe I was an idiot, but I wanted to believe she was truly in love with Wendall and had nothing to do with his death.

However, I'd seen a cruel and calculating side to Flora Bailey Clarke. If her con had gone too far, it was time for me to call Chief Brenner.

"We have already looked into Ms. Clarke's background," he said. "I'd like to hear your take on her."

"I have mixed feelings. On one hand, she's very sweet and seems to have honestly been in love with Wendall, but on the other, she's got quite a scheme going. I've spoken with her ex-husbands. Their only complaint is she was too expensive to keep, so they divorced her, not realizing this was her plan all along."

"Well, I want to make certain her plan did not include murder. The ex-husbands are all still alive, which is a point in her favor—a very tiny point. The next time you see her, remind her to stay in town. Anything else you can tell me?"

I told him about finding the gold button behind the gallery and how that clue fizzled out, and I told him about my search for the dark blue Honda.

"I can tell you that one," he said. "Bea Ricter drives a dark blue Honda."

"I thought she had a gray VW."

"That's her son's. He's been driving her around while the Honda's in the shop. Any particular reason you need to know about that car?"

But when did it go into the shop? I'd save that question for now. "I'm trying to establish who was at the gallery. That clears that up, thanks."

"I don't have any leads on who threw that brick in your window, Madeline. I hope you're taking my advice."

"I'm at home and Jerry's with me."

"Good. Stay in touch." He hung up.

Next, I called Nell. "Nell, what can you tell me about Daniel Richards?"

"Owns half of downtown," she said.

"Did he sell the store to Wendall?"

"Yep. Well, actually, his son did. Old Mr. Richards hasn't been himself for a couple of years now."

"Daniel Junior has power of attorney?"

"Yeah, he handles everything."

"Did anyone else want the building? I know Pamela did, but she couldn't afford it."

"You'd have to ask Daniel Junior. His number should be in the book."

It was. When I reached Daniels Richards Junior, I first asked if he knew about a letter his father had written to Pamela Finch regarding renovations to her dress shop.

"Yes," he said. "I told Ms. Finch if she had proof my dad gave her permission, then I'd abide by that proof. Dad owned a lot of property in town, and he was notorious for making promises and deals he forgot about even before the Alzheimer's set in."

"Did you or your father sell a building to Wendall Clarke to use for an art gallery?"

"Yes, the old Arrow Insurance building."

"Was anyone else interested in purchasing that building?"

"I'd have to check my records. Can I get back to you?"

"Yes, of course."

"I should have that information for you by this afternoon."

I hung up and went to see how the football game was progressing. It was a good thing there were plenty of leaves on the ground because at one point, Austin made a daring move, tripped Jerry, and Jerry ended up flat on his back. He laughed and raised his arms over his head in mock terror.

"Truce! Don't hit a man when he's down!"

"Yah! Die!" Austin said and made a wrestling leap. Jerry rolled out of the way, jumped up, and kicked Austin in the rear.

"You die!"

"Faker!"

"Sucker!"

As long as no one broke anything, I usually ignored all the rough housing, but something tickled my brain. I'd been supposing that someone tall hit Wendall on the forehead, causing him to fall. What if Wendall was already on the ground when the murderer delivered the final blow? What if he'd been tripped or pushed and then killed?

I gave Chief Brenner another call and asked if the medical examiner's report was complete. He was able to tell me Wendall Clarke had died as a result of the blow to the forehead, and there were other bruises and marks on the back of his head from the fall. But the examiner had admitted it would be difficult to tell which came first. I thanked the chief and hung up. I'd suspected Larissa and Pamela because both women were tall enough to hit Wendall's forehead. I'd dismissed both Flora and Bea as too short. Could Flora be the killer? Bea had the strength to throw a brick hard enough to smash a window, so could she topple Wendall?

I turned my attention back to Jerry and Austin. Jerry was taller, but Austin had more bulk. On the alert for Austin's moves, Jerry could easily evade him. If Bea took Wendall by surprise and cannonballed out of the dark, Wendall might not have had a chance to defend himself.

Now I needed proof that Bea was at the gallery that night and had somehow avoided being seen by Larissa, Pamela, Jerry, Nell, and myself. Ginger Alverez had said she and Bea were together from six until almost eleven that night. A visit to Ginger was in order.

I stepped out the kitchen door. "Jerry, I'm going into town. Do we need anything?"

Austin roared and charged. "Death move two thousand!"

"Uno minuto, Señora," Jerry said and side stepped, toreador style. As Austin whizzed past, he gave him another kick. "Ole!"

"Ow! How do you do that?"

"Middle child, two brothers." He turned to me. "Don't forget the tires."

With everything that was going on, I had completely forgotten I'd told Jerry I would get the tires for the Mazda. "Okay, I'll stop by Fred's on my way. Anything else?"

"Austin's going to need a new rear end."

"Ha, ha." Austin charged again.

Fred's Garage was down a twisty little country road. One bent metal sign pointed toward the garage while another pointed toward a junkyard filled with scraps of cars, trucks, buses, and even an old fire truck. Fred came out to meet me, a dark little man with grease in every wrinkle. He wiped his hands on his overalls.

"What can I do for you, Madeline?"

"Jerry said you had some tires on sale. We need two."

"I can fix you up right away. Come on in. Dennis! Take care of Mrs. Fairweather's car. Won't be but a minute, Madeline."

I gave the keys to the eager young man who trotted up and followed Fred into his shop. The waiting room consisted of cracked leather chairs, an ancient gumball machine, two chipped end tables covered with old hunting and fishing magazines, and a neon sign advertising Laney's Bar and Grill. I noticed the other cars Fred's employees were working on. One was a white station wagon, one was a maroon-colored Buick, and the other was a dark blue Honda.

"Whose car is that?" I asked.

"The Honda? Belongs to Bea Ricter. Got an oil leak."

"When did she bring it in?"

Fred screwed up his face in thought. "Lemme see. Thursday it was. Told her I couldn't get to it till today. Had to find a part." His phone rang, and he went to the counter to answer it.

If Bea didn't bring the Honda to the garage until Thursday, then it could've been in the parking lot Wednesday. I sat looking out the dusty window and wondering until Dennis brought me my keys and said I was good to go. I asked him how he knew oil was leaking from the Honda.

"Oh, that's easy," he said. "It was leaving big old puddles of oil everywhere."

I looked for big old puddles of oil in the parking lot behind the gallery and found them. I asked the owner of the gift shop if she remembered where the Honda was parked. She pointed out the same spot where I found the stains.

Next I went to the Chicken House, a fast food restaurant across from the Wal-Mart store. I'd met Randi Peterson, the young woman behind the counter, when she had been a contestant in the Miss Celosia Pageant, part of my very first successful investigation. Randi's brown curls were secured beneath a Chicken House cap. Her carefully plucked eyebrows always gave her an expression of surprise.

"Hi, Madeline. Welcome to the Chicken House. Would you like to try our Wings 'N' Rings Special today? Five chicken wings and five onion rings plus a drink for three fifty."

"No, thanks," I said. "I hope you can help me with something."

Her brows went up even further. "Are you on a case?"

"Yes. Were you working Wednesday night around six?"

She rolled her eyes and sighed. "I work every night. I'm beginning to believe my mom was right when she said I should've finished high school."

"Do you know Bea Ricter and Ginger Alverez?"

"I don't know Ginger Alverez, but isn't Bea Ricter a little squatty woman who always looks angry?"

"That describes her pretty well. Was she here that night?"

Randi pursed her lips in thought. "Well, I'm sure I'd remember her because she's kind of rude. And she dresses like she's been digging in the garden all day."

"Ginger's a little shorter than me with reddish hair, pale skin, and freckles."

Randi shook her head. "Like I said, I don't know her." She turned to address a co-worker who passed behind her with a load of fries. "Bea Ricter hasn't been in all week, has she?"

"No, thank goodness," the other girl said. "Grumpy old cow."

"Could she have gone through the drive-thru?" I asked.

"I'll see." Randi went to the drive-thru register and talked for a few minutes with the young man stationed there. When she came back, she said, "Josh was on the window Wednesday night and says she didn't come through there. He knows her, too, because she's never happy with her order and always wants extra ketchup or sauce, or something's not right. She usually comes in to eat, though."

"Thanks, Randi. That's very helpful."

"Did she commit a crime?"

"I don't know yet."

"Does it have something to do with that man that got killed at the art gallery? Everybody's saying his ex-wife did it."

"I'm trying to find out the truth."

Now I needed to know why Ginger Alverez had lied.

Chapter Eighteen

Ginger lived in a particularly ugly green brick split-level near the elementary school. She was hanging clothes on a line in her backyard: large jeans I assumed belonged to Mr. Alverez, some child-sized jeans and t-shirts, towels, and dishcloths. She gave me a wary look.

"Oh, hello, Madeline."

"Got a minute?"

"No, actually, I'm kind of busy." She took another towel from her laundry basket.

"This won't take long."

"I don't have time for this. Not everyone likes to answer your questions, you know."

Hmm, she was mighty defensive. Wonder why? "I don't ask hard questions."

"Does anyone ever tell you they don't like you snooping around town all the time?"

"Yes, they do, but I've gotten results."

She kept her eyes on the clothespins as she hung up the towel. "What do you want?"

"The other day, you told me you and Bea had dinner at the Chicken House and then spent the rest of Wednesday evening here at your house playing cards."

"That's right."

"Why did you cover for Bea?"

"Cover?" Her hand shook as she reached for another towel. "I don't know what you mean."

"Bea has quite a reputation at the Chicken House. The folks there say she hasn't been in all week."

"I guess I meant to say Deely's."

"I guess she wasn't at your house, at all. She told me the two of you went to the Chicken House around six, but at six o'clock the owner of the gift shop behind the gallery saw Bea's car parked in their parking lot. For some reason, Bea was still at the gallery. Where were you?"

"I—she might have come over later."

"What's the problem? What does she have on you?"

She started to hang up the towel and then dropped it back into the basket. "Just leave it alone, Madeline."

"Well, I can't," I said. "I'm trying to find out who killed Wendall. I don't think you want to stand in the way of a murder investigation, do you? Or are you supposed to take the fall for Bea?"

She stared at me. "Take the fall? I had nothing to do with it! I didn't even know Wendall that well! He was three years ahead of me."

"And now he's dead. I want to know what happened. Can you help me or not?"

"I don't know how in the world I could help. I had nothing to do with that."

Something told me this was a lot more serious than dead wood versus ping-pong balls. Then a gust of wind made Mr. Alverez's jeans snap, and I had an idea. I remembered the argument between Ginger and Bea and how Bea had threatened her to be quiet unless she wanted Bea to mention "you know what." Ginger had shut up pretty quickly. "That wild night Bea mentioned in Pamela's store. Did something happen at the crafts show you don't want your husband to know?"

She answered way too fast. "No, of course not."

What else could it be? "Bea said everyone would be surprised about you if she spilled the beans. You said you had something on her, but she implied she had the real dirt. What's going on? Why did you let her win that argument?"

She tried to get her voice under control. "It was a dreadful mistake. I'd had too much to drink."

"You got a little too friendly with someone?"

"I only meant to admire his macramé! Things just got out of control."

"Bea needed an alibi, or she'd tell your husband."

Another nod. Another sob. "She said if anyone called, tell them she was at my house all evening. I didn't see any harm in it." She wiped her eyes on the edge of her t-shirt. "Are you saying she killed Wendall? She couldn't have. Why would she kill him? She was going to have her pictures in the gallery. Even I was going to have my ping-pong birds in the gallery."

"I don't know why. Unless she was desperate to run the place."

"Pamela wanted it, too. And what about Larissa? She was there that night and ran away. Or Flora? Where was she? What was she doing that night? And what am I going to do?"

"The first thing you need to do is tell your husband what happened. Then Bea won't have any power over you. Did you see her at all Wednesday night?"

"No." She brushed the last tears away. "I am not taking any sort of fall for anyone, Madeline."

"You won't have to," I said.

I didn't recognize the car in my driveway, but I should have known that someone named Big Mike would drive a shiny black Hummer. He and Jerry were sitting on the porch, and he was indeed big, so big he didn't fit in any of the rocking chairs, but sat on the top porch step as if it were a royal throne. When he and Jerry stood to greet me, Jerry barely came up to Big Mike's shoulder. In honor of Big Mike's visit, Jerry had on his gold tie with a pattern of little black and white dice. Big Mike wore an expensive-looking suit, a silk tie, and fancy shoes that must have taken an Everglade of alligators to create.

His voice was a deep rumble. "So this is the woman who finally caught you, eh, Jerry? Such a pleasure to meet you, Madeline."

When Jerry first mentioned Big Mike, I imagined someone much rougher, more like a gangster, with squinty eyes and a scar. Big Mike's wide face was surprisingly bland, an asset in a con man, I thought, and his brown hair was cut short. He looked like any other successful business man.

"Nice to meet you, too," I said. "Thanks for coming."

Jerry pulled up another rocking chair for me, and we all sat down. "Well, I was curious," Big Mike said. "I hadn't heard the name Pamela Finch in a long time, and if Honor Perkins is mixed up in this, we have a problem."

If Honor was a problem for someone like Big Mike, our troubles just multiplied.

"What can we do?"

"Jerry and I have been talking about that. What exactly did she tell you about this sapphire ring?"

"She said you and Pamela Finch had once been an item, and you gave Pamela a pink star sapphire ring."

"That part is true."

"She said you wanted that ring back, but you didn't want to contact Pamela yourself. She asked Jerry to get the ring so she could return it to you, and you'd forgive all her debts."

"Here's where her little story falls apart. Honor owes me nothing."

"And the ring is worth a lot of money," Jerry said.

Okay, what was Honor's game? "So why didn't Honor pull some sort of scam and get the ring herself?"

"That is the part neither Jerry nor I understand," Big Mike said. "She must want something else."

Oh, I had a good idea what she wanted. "Pamela does have the ring, or at least the stone. It's part of a collage she made. I have no plans to steal it, though."

Big Mike looked thoughtful. "You won't have to."

Before I could worry about what he meant by that, a timer went off in the kitchen. Jerry hopped up. "That's lunch."

Big Mike watched him go and then turned his calm gaze to me. "I understand you're a private investigator. Do you find enough work here in Celosia?"

"Strangely enough, I do. Right now, I'm investigating the murder of a wealthy art gallery owner. Pamela Finch is a possible suspect."

"Pam was a sweet girl. I doubt she'd murder anyone."

"I've pretty much omitted her as the killer."

"Good." His gaze took in the surrounding fields. "Jerry says he's very happy here."

"I'm hoping he'll settle down."

"One of the best I ever taught, but there comes a time when one must stop. I imagine you want to start a family."

"We're in negotiations."

He chuckled. "He said something like that. You know his family life wasn't the best."

"That's why he took up with you, right?"

"I'd say so."

"Did you all live together in some secret underground lair, you and Rick and Honor and the others?"

"More like my town house. And people didn't live there, although occasionally it was a convenient hideout. It was more like a meeting place. I taught everyone a few tricks, we'd eat and visit." He leaned forward, smiling. "I'm no criminal mastermind, Madeline. I just happen to have certain useful skills."

I liked his smile, but then I was supposed to, wasn't I? All part of his tricks. "Here's my problem, Big Mike. I feel certain Jerry can give up his con man ways, but I don't know what else he can do. He's an excellent musician, but that doesn't pay. He loves kids and is going to be a camp counselor, but that's only for the summer."

"Let me think on it."

Jerry called that lunch was ready. We went in to the dining room. Jerry had an array of dishes on the table, including a ham and potato casserole, salad, and a vegetable dish with corn, lima beans, and red peppers. Big Mike sat carefully, but the chair held his weight. He opened his napkin and spread it on his huge lap.

"This looks splendid, Jerry. I have to say I miss your cooking."

"Thanks. There's peach pie for dessert."

"One would think you knew I was coming."

"I thought you might, so I stocked up."

"Good planning." Then Big Mike looked at me and winked. I wasn't sure what he meant, but he gave me a satisfied smile. "Please pass the salad."

During lunch, Big Mike and Jerry entertained each other with stories of past escapades, many beginning with, "Do you remember when...?" and "Oh, that reminds me of the time when..." Jerry told Big Mike about Rick's attempt to cash in on the *Mantis Man* craze here in town, and Big Mike told Jerry about an incredibly detailed con that took a month to set up.

"It was worth it, though. We were able to stop the destruction of a fine old house and put a certain scumbag of a lawyer out of business."

"That sounds more like police undercover work," I said.

Big Mike wiped his mouth with his napkin. "I occasionally feel the need to do a good deed. Now, where's that pie?"

Jerry brought out the peach pie and we all had a large slice.

"Make the crust yourself?" Big Mike asked.

"As usual."

"Very tasty."

When Big Mike finished his pie, he put his fork down across the plate with a decisive click. "About Honor..."

"She may have left town," Jerry said. "I hear she had a traumatic experience at her séance last night."

"Let's assume she's still around. I can get another pink star sapphire and have it sent to you. See what she does with it. I'd be curious to know."

"Me, too."

"If that doesn't solve the problem, call me."

"Do you have any idea who she might have worked with on the D and S at Mac's friend's house?"

"I'll find that out and bring it to Honor's attention. Sounds like the Over the Border Boys. Fairly harmless, but they've been known to turn on each other."

"Over the Border?" I asked. "Mexican or Canadian?"

"Virginian. They'll do a few jobs in North Carolina and then scoot back home where they think they're safe." His smile suggested the Border Boys were anything but safe. "They won't give me any problem, I assure you. Now I'd like some more tea, if you have it."

"Would you like coffee? Wouldn't take a minute."

"Even better, thank you."

As soon as Jerry left, Big Mike lowered his voice. "Madeline, I believe I have a solution to your dilemma, and I don't mean Honor Perkins. This excellent lunch brought home to me the fact that Jerry is a fine cook. Has he ever considered opening a restaurant?"

Yes, Jerry did all the cooking. Delicious breakfasts, lunches, treats for the kids, cookies, brownies. Wasn't he always happy to be in the kitchen fixing something?

"Big Mike, you may have something here."

"I would be happy to look into possible locations, or would you like to use the house?"

When he'd first moved to Celosia, Jerry's then-girlfriend insisted he turn the house into a bed and breakfast, but all the legal issues and restrictions had made Jerry's head spin and he abandoned that project.

"I think a separate place would be better."

"Sound him out on the idea and see what he says."

Jerry returned with the coffee. "Something else you can help us with, Big Mike. Ever hear of a con artist named Lizzie Bailey?"

Big Mike put three spoonfuls of sugar in his coffee. "What's her game?"

"Marries rich men, squeezes them dry, and moves on."

"Black widow?"

"No, at least not until Wendall Clarke's murder. He's the wealthy art gallery owner Mac mentioned. Lizzie's also a suspect."

"Little redhead? Very attractive? Likes to pretend she's shy?"

"She's a blonde right now and calls herself Flora, but that sounds like her."

I took a sip of coffee. "So the shyness is all an act? I've had my suspicions." Especially since I'd seen the colder, calculating side of Flora.

"I would imagine so. No one likes to think a sweet little unassuming lady is a murderer."

"I don't think she's the murderer, but if she's got this shady past, maybe she knows more than she's telling. Although she really seems heartbroken."

Big Mike gave a massive shrug. "Maybe she honestly loved him. Sometimes even the most hardened grifter can fall for a mark. Did Clarke know about her past? If he found out and still loved her, that might have turned her around. Worked for Jerry. Not that I would ever call you a mark, my dear Madeline. You are much too clever."

Like Jerry, Big Mike could lay on the charm. "Thank you." I recalled what Flora had told me about Wendall assuring her she didn't have to use disguises and tricks. He would take care of her because he could afford to. "Wendall knew. That's why I have a hard time imagining her as the killer."

"Remember, the best con artists are heartless."

Flora was heartless—until Wendall. "You don't strike me as heartless, Big Mike."

He laughed his deep laugh. "Keep believing that, my dear."

Jerry and Big Mike reminisced a while longer until Big Mike checked his large gold watch. "It's not a good idea for me to stay too long in one place these days, and we don't want Honor popping up unexpectedly. Thank you very much for lunch, Jerry. Madeline, a pleasure to meet you. We'll be in touch."

As the black Hummer drove away, I said. "Big Mike isn't what I expected at all."

"He was on his best behavior."

"Are you saying he isn't always a perfect gentleman?"

"I'm saying you never want to cross him."

We went to the kitchen where I helped Jerry clean up. "He said something interesting while you were making coffee. What would you think about opening your own restaurant?"

He spooned the leftover vegetables into a plastic container. "That's a lot of work."

"But does it sound like something you'd like to do?"

"Well, I like to cook."

"And you're a very good cook."

He put the container into the fridge. "I don't know, Mac. Guess I never thought of it. Open a restaurant in town, you mean? Most people are happy to go to Deely's."

"When they want burgers and fries. What if you offered a different menu? You're always making me the most wonderful breakfasts. What if you had a breakfast café?"

He scraped the last of the casserole into another container. "Open just for breakfast? That's not a bad idea. But where would we get the money to start a business like that?"

"I have a feeling Big Mike might bankroll you if you were serious about the project."

He licked the spoon clean. "Oh, I see. You two have a plan."

"Think about it. You are an expert at making pancakes and omelets for everyone from seven to eleven. You have the rest of the day free, your evenings are free for shows and choir cantatas, and you make a little extra cash. Unless you've heard anything from your interview."

He opened the fridge and put the second container on top of the first one. "Oh, about that. There's a snag."

"What sort of snag?"

"The fellow who interviewed me at Southern Foods was Dean Snyder." He paused to let this sink in.

Uh, oh. "Snyder. As in Flossie Mae?"

"And Geoff and Sean. Dean's their cousin."

Flossie Mae Snyder was one of Jerry's former séance customers and a big believer in the spirit world. Her nephews, Geoff and Sean, made a living debunking anything paranormal and thought Jerry took advantage of their aunt. "Does Cousin Dean side with the spirits or the Snyder boys?"

"Let's just say I didn't get the job." He put dishes into some hot soapy water. "Tecknilabs said they'd get back to me. I hope another Snyder cousin isn't lurking in the bushes."

"The downside of the small town."

"So this plan of yours is something to consider. I don't have any experience running a restaurant, though."

"Think of it as conning people out of their money for bacon and eggs."

He laughed. "I'll call it the Breakfast Con Café."

"Since you're giving up cons, how about calling it The Good Egg?"

"How about Flapjack City? No, wait. Pancake Palace." He put his arms around me. He gave me a kiss. "What other plans do you have for me?"

"Well, as much as I'd like to stay here and fool around, we have a letter to find."

I'd been concerned about having Big Mike visit. Seeing his old friend and mentor might have made Jerry homesick for his carefree con man days. But he was excited about this new possibility, and if his reputation kept him from getting other jobs, a restaurant of his own might be the solution.

Now I needed to solve this case and get rid of Honor Perkins, not necessarily in that order.

Chapter Nineteen

On the way to Flair For Fashion, I told Jerry about Flora's visit, my discovery at Fred's Garage, and what I'd learned from Ginger Alverez.

"So the Mystery of the Dark Blue Honda has been solved," he said, "and Bea has moved up to Suspect Number One."

"If I can find a motive."

"Well, like Larissa, Bea seems to have a grudge against the world."

"There has to be something a little more concrete than that."

Pamela greeted us in a reserved manner. I could tell she was still irked at me for considering her a murderer. Jerry and I went into the little office. He started looking through the next filing cabinet while I tackled another stack.

He tugged open the next drawer. "What are you going to do about Bea?"

"I'm going to talk to her again and see what she comes up with."

"If she starts throwing bricks at you, you'll know for sure."

I set a pile of paper aside and started leafing through another. "She had to be hiding somewhere in the gallery."

"Maybe she came in after Pamela left. Anyone could get in the back, right?"

"Right."

"There wasn't anything worth stealing, was there? Just Bea's broken pictures and Ginger's ping-pong birds."

We didn't have any luck finding the letter. I needed to stop by my office, and to my surprise, there was a box at my door with a pink sapphire inside.

"Good grief, Big Mike works fast."

"Helps to know the right people."

I turned the sapphire so the light caught in the frosty star. "It looks exactly like Pamela's. How do I get in touch with Honor?"

"Let's go out to her lair," Jerry said.

Tinsley Acres was a failed housing development outside of town. Several giant houses had been built before the developers and the contractors disagreed on terms and money. The houses now sat empty and forlorn on their once green lawns, driveways cracked and windows blank. Honor's car was parked behind the second house, a massive pink brick mansion.

I thought Honor was taking a big chance staying in the area. "I don't get it. With the police on to her, why didn't she leave town?"

"She wanted this sapphire, so now that problem's solved."

I started toward Honor's car, but Jerry went to the front door of the house and knocked.

"I'd be very surprised if she didn't find a way in."

Honor opened the door. She grinned. "Welcome to my home. So nice of you to drop by."

Jerry handed her the sapphire. "We can't stay. Here's what you came for, it's been fun, so long."

He'd taken her by surprise. She held the sapphire up to the light to inspect it. "Wow, that was fast."

"You really ought to think about packing up. I can't promise there won't be a police car checking out the neighborhood later today."

"Jerry—" She gave me a glare. "Would you mind if we had a private conversation?"

"No problem."

I went back to the Mazda and leaned against it while they talked. I couldn't help but notice the builders had left a small pile of bricks by the driveway. Nice new pink bricks with sharp corners.

Jerry stood with his arms folded. Honor fiddled with the sapphire. This time there wasn't a handy air vent, but I could see her expression, and my old suspicions crept back in.

Honor was definitely in love with Jerry.

It all made sense. They'd been partners in crime, ran some schemes, had narrow escapes together, and palled around at Big Mike's. She didn't believe he'd gone straight, so what better way to get his attention than to run some cons to get him involved? Maybe not the break-in at Billie's. I didn't think Honor knew the connection to me there, but she was a crafty woman. She knew about me, and it wouldn't have been difficult to look up my pageant career and see some of the other girls I'd competed against. Certainly by sending him a fake letter about being sued she sucked him in. And horning in on his séances was a joke that backfired when Aunt Gloria showed up. I still didn't know how Jerry managed that.

But a brick through my window? Not a very subtle way of showing her displeasure at me personally, the woman who ruined a perfectly good con man's career—and disrupted what Honor saw as a chance to rekindle her delusional romance.

All this about owing Big Mike was another way to catch Jerry's interest and keep Honor in Celosia. She probably didn't believe he'd be able to come up with a pink star sapphire. Thank goodness he did. I wanted her as far away as possible.

Jerry turned to leave, and she caught his arm. There was no mistaking the look in her eyes. I didn't have to hear her to know what she was saying. *I don't believe it's over. You can't be serious about leaving the game, about leaving me.*

Did Jerry realize this? He must have realized something. Instead of jerking away, he patted her hand and pulled free. For a moment, Honor looked desolate. Then she went back inside, slamming the door behind her.

Jerry came back to the car. "She's a little upset."

"Well, you two have a history."

"Fun for a while."

"It's more than that." He looked puzzled, so I explained. "She's in love with you, Jerry. I think she always has been."

He gave a short laugh. "No way. We're friends, that's all. We hung out at Big Mike's and did stuff together, but we never did anything you'd call romantic."

"Oh, I think hanging out and doing stuff together was very romantic to Honor."

He still didn't believe me. "Well, why didn't she tell me?"

"Jerry, during our college days and after, you went through a whole string of little blondes. Honor knew she couldn't compete. She was happy to be with you when the two of you were running a con. She probably told herself, well, those blondes may be pretty, but they can't cheat people the way I can. Trust me. I know all about appearances."

Jerry glanced back at the house. "I guess I wasn't very sympathetic."

"I wouldn't say it's your fault, but now we know why Honor is staying here."

"If she felt this way about me, why did she decide to do all this now? She knows I'm married."

"When was the last time you saw her? Maybe she's been out of the country, or in jail. Maybe the fact that you're married represents more of a challenge."

"She has to know she can't break up my marriage."

"Jerry, she's a con artist. Anything's possible, right? Oh, and that brick I was telling you about? It used to be on that pile right there."

He stared at the bricks. "You're kidding."

"Your old pal is more dangerous than you think." He started toward the house, and this time I was the one to catch his sleeve. "She may not have you, but she has the jewel she wanted. If she isn't gone by tomorrow, I'll call the police."

He stood in the driveway. For a moment, I thought he might ignore me and confront her. Then he turned back to me.

"Let's go."

◇◇◇

On our way out of Tinsley Acres, Jerry had a phone call from another cast member of *Oklahoma* asking if he'd come by the theater. I dropped him off and decided to stop at Burger World to talk with Deely. He was wiping the counters and straightening the menus in their metal holders.

I sat down at the counter. "Heard you're thinking of retiring."

"Shoot, no. Could use some more business, though. Times are tough."

"What would you say to opening the place for breakfast?"

"Can't get enough help for the mornings."

"What if you had another cook? Someone who's very good at making breakfast foods?"

He stopped wiping. "You talking about you, Madeline? Didn't know you was a cook."

"Not me. Jerry. Breakfasts are his specialty."

Deely rubbed his chin. "Well, now, I'd be willing to give it a try. People are always after me to open for breakfast, but my regular cook, he only likes frying burgers. Jerry ever worked short orders before?"

"I'm sure he could get the hang of it."

"Wouldn't need anything fancy like eggs Benedict or stuff like that. Just the basics. And I can't pay a lot to start. Business picks up, we'll go from there. Have him stop by and we'll talk about it."

"Thanks," I said. And thank you, Big Mike.

When I stopped by my office, the first thing I saw was a piece of plywood in the space where my window had been. It was ugly. It made the room dark. And I decided, why wait? Enough ugly darkness. Honor was an annoying, vindictive woman who needed to be gone right now. I called Chief Brenner and told him I had a very good idea who broke my window, and if he sent a squad car to the second house in Tinsley Acres, the one made of the same pink brick, he could pick up Ms. Honor Perkins, and I'd be happy to press charges.

After speaking with the Chief, I had a phone call from Billie with an update on her break-in. "The insurance paid for everything, and believe me, I'm going to be very careful who I let in the house from now on."

"I'm pretty sure that woman is out of the picture."

"Good. Sure you don't want to enter Mrs. Parkland? Could be fun. I'll help you with your hair and makeup."

"That sounds sooo appealing, but no."

"You won't believe this, but your mother called me and urged me to try to convince you. Isn't she thoughtful?"

"What's *your* mother's number? I'm going to set her upon you."

Billie's hoot of laughter made me hold the phone away from my ear until she'd finished. "Don't you dare! Thanks for your help. And please visit me again soon. Don't make me have to have another burglary to get you over here."

I'd just said good-bye when I heard loud voices outside. I got up to investigate, and to my surprise, Honor and Aunt Louise were on the sidewalk right in front of my office building. Aunt Louise was screeching like a demented crow.

"There she is! There's the woman who called up Gloria and scared me out of my wits! You give me back my money, you thief!"

Honor held both hands up, trying to placate her. "But you wanted to see your sister."

"Not like that! How do I know she isn't going to haunt me the rest of my days? I can't live my life expecting her to pop up like that at any minute. And never once did she say a thing about where my half of the inheritance is hidden! You've got a lot of explaining to do, missy!"

If she'd had a cane or an umbrella, she would've been smacking Honor over the head. I hurried out to break up the brawl.

"Hold on, Aunt Louise. Settle down. Madame Mystere doesn't want a scene on the street."

Aunt Louise had a claw-like hand on Honor's arm. "She'll get a scene and like it! She needs to learn how to control the spirits and not have them jumping out at decent living folks!"

I could tell Honor was trying to get away without breaking Aunt Louise. "Sometimes the spirits are like that."

"Well, I don't like it! Do something about it!"

Annie came running down the sidewalk. "Sorry, Madeline. She got away from me. Sorry, Madame Mystere." She gently pried her aunt's fingers off Honor. "We talked about this, Aunt Louise. No more séances. Gloria's not going to come back."

"It's going to take a six-pack of root beer to convince me, my girl!"

"We can do that. Sorry, Madeline."

Honor and I stood and watched Annie lead her protesting aunt down the sidewalk.

When she was sure Aunt Louise couldn't hear her, Honor said, "Good lord, what a crazy old witch! I thought the experience the other night cured her of talking to dead people. That kind of scene isn't good for business."

"Since you won't be staying in Celosia, your business doesn't matter. Did you just happen to be in the neighborhood?" She probably saw the police car and made a run for it. "Maybe you stopped by to pay for my window?"

She didn't react to this. "I wanted to talk to you."

If she wanted me to beg and plead for her to go away, she was in for a long wait. "We don't have anything to talk about."

"I don't know how you did it, but you changed him. He was one of the best."

"He's still the best," I said. "It's just that his priorities are different."

"What, being a musician? Playing for dinky little community theater productions? Please."

"No. He wants to be a father."

This seemed to deflate her. "So that's true."

"Yes." I decided it was time for a scam of my own. I remembered Jerry had said he'd almost told her I was pregnant. I remembered what he'd told me about making eye contact and speaking in a neutral tone, and considering all my stomach troubles and strange cravings, something might really be true, or true enough to convince Honor. "I have a doctor's appointment next week. I'm pretty sure I'm pregnant."

As I'd hoped, Honor didn't believe that an ex-beauty queen could tell an expert lie. For a moment, she looked at a loss for words. "Oh. That's…that makes things different."

"You can stay in town and run all the little games you like, but Jerry is going to be too happy about a baby and too excited about setting up our nursery to come out and play with you."

She thought it over. "I came here to cause trouble."

"I figured that out."

"I wanted Jerry to see that this wasn't the life for him. I wanted him to be with—to be on my team again. I guess I was wrong. But I don't want to come between him and his son or daughter. That's not my style."

"Thank you."

"I like to think I'm smart enough to know when it's time to move on."

"You could always change, too, Honor."

"Oh, I'm staying in the game." She showed off the pink star sapphire ring sparkling on her hand. "I put one over on Big Mike, and nobody does that."

"So you didn't owe him anything?"

"No, I wanted the ring. Pretty slick, huh?"

Oh, real slick. "Then if I were you, I'd walk away a winner."

"Yeah, I think I will." She started to walk away and turned. "You know, you're quite the con artist, too."

Had she seen through my lie? "Oh?"

"You've got Jerry convinced you're the one for him. Have to give you props for that."

"Jerry figured that out all on his own."

She looked as if she wanted to say something else. Then she gave me her cocky salute and walked away.

I sincerely hoped that was the last I'd see of her.

Chapter Twenty

I went back to the theater to get Jerry. He and the young man playing Curly were going over one of Curly's big numbers, "People Will Say We're in Love."

That's appropriate, I thought as I sat down in the front row. That's certainly what Honor was hoping. Now I was going to have to have a baby to keep her away.

Well, that's an exaggeration. Maybe I would. Could this be the last little push I needed? "Little push" made me think of delivering this phantom baby. What was I so afraid of? Women had babies all the time. If I could solve crimes and fend off crazed murderers with their deadly needles and guns and umbrellas, I could manage a baby, couldn't I? Strap that kid on my back and go fight evil!

That image gave me pause. Wait. Who am I really doing this for? Of course it will make Jerry happy and might be the very thing to settle him down. But what about me? What will I get out of this? Can I fit a baby into my life? Can I be a mom and an artist and a detective?

Damn right I can.

But wait again, Superwoman, I told myself. Isn't this just another case of wanting to control my entire universe? I don't want to end up like my mother, clinging to one single thing, because that one thing might decide to take charge of her own affairs, get up, and leave town. How about letting go? That's something my mother was never able to do. Let go and see what happens. If my agency succeeds, it succeeds. If my artwork sells, it sells. And if I have a baby, it will come along at the right time, and I'll be ready for it. That little push I feel? It's pushing me away from the control panel.

Let go and see what happens.

As if to underscore my new found determination, Curly launched into "Oh, What a Beautiful Morning." If I needed a sign, here it was.

After the rehearsal, Curly thanked Jerry and left. Jerry gathered up his music and came down the steps at the side of the stage.

"I saw you out here laughing, Mac. What's the joke?"

"My life is a musical," I said, "and I am the star."

"Okay. Translation?"

I kissed him. "Let's go to Deely's. We have a lot to talk about."

◇◇◇

I didn't want to say anything to Jerry about my thoughts until he'd had a chance to talk with Deely. If a baby was in the future, we needed to take a good practical look at our finances.

The diner wasn't very busy, so we sat at the counter. Deely came out to greet us, all smiles.

"Say you can cook, Jerry?"

"Yes, sir. I enjoy it."

"I've been wanting to try something different, see if I can get some more business in here. Georgia at the bookstore says you're a good worker. Willing to give you a try."

I wasn't surprised that Deely had asked around.

"Okay." Jerry sat back, his eyes on Deely. "What do you have in mind?"

"I say we start small, maybe eggs, bacon, toast, and grits, work our way up to pancakes and waffles. I got the equipment, even a waffle iron I got from somewhere and never used. I'll order in the supplies and you can start next weekend, and we'll see how it goes. Ever done short order before?"

"No, but I can work fast."

"I'll ask Annie if she wants a few more hours. She can help you. I'm figuring six to ten in the mornings. Hope you don't have any trouble getting up early."

"He's always up early," I said. "And usually singing."

"Well, if he wants to sing in here, I got no problem with that, as long as he gets the orders out. I've written down what we'll need to start a breakfast menu." He slid the list over. "Anything you want to add?"

Jerry read the list. "Gotta have cheese."

"You might have noticed we got plenty of cheese around here."

Jerry handed him the paper. "That oughta do it." The two men shook hands.

Deely gave me a nod. "Madeline here thought it would be a good idea to start serving breakfast, and I agree. More money comes in, I don't have to worry about dragging one of my boys into the business. They really got no talent for it. We'll see how you do. Worth a try, anyway."

Jerry thanked him. "I'm looking forward to it."

We got our cheeseburgers and fries and took our food to a booth. I raised my glass of tea in a salute. "Congratulations. You are now gainfully employed."

"I hope so." Jerry sat down and flipped his tie over his shoulder before applying ketchup to his fries. "Mac, I just thought of something important we need to talk about."

Now that he had a job, he was getting to the subject of children right away, but that was all right. I was ready to talk about it. "We certainly do."

"We're going to need another car."

What? Oh. "Not exactly what I was thinking, but go ahead."

He handed me the ketchup bottle. "You don't want to get up early and drive me to Deely's, do you? And if I take the car, you won't have it until after ten. Why don't I see if Fred has anything reasonable we could buy? Or I could get a motorcycle."

I had to readjust my thinking. Jerry on a motorcycle. Disaster doesn't even begin to cover the possibilities. "Don't rush into anything. We'll work it out."

"And we should probably go back to Tinlsey Acres and make sure Honor's left town."

"She has. In fact, she came to talk to me at my office."

He stopped eating. "She didn't give you any trouble, did she? Was she angry?"

"Maybe, but then I rescued her from the wrath of Aunt Louise."

"Aunt Louise came after her?"

"Honor's crimes caught up with her at last."

Jerry laughed and took the salt shaker. "I'm glad Aunt Louise unleashed her wrath on Honor instead of me."

"She was fearsome."

"What did Honor want to talk about?"

"She was annoyed at me for ruining your perfectly good reputation as a premiere con artist."

He put the salt shaker down. "What did you say?"

Suddenly, I didn't want to tell him about my lie and how it might not be a lie. Somehow, sitting in Deely's surrounded by the incoming crowd wasn't the time or the place for such a major announcement. I wanted us to be somewhere private, somewhere significant. And I had to be absolutely sure I was pregnant.

"I convinced her that you were happy with your new life."

"And she bought that?"

"Yes, and she was tickled with herself for fooling Big Mike."

"Fooling Big Mike? Oh, about the sapphire." He chuckled. "Well, let her think that for a while." He pulled another napkin from the holder. "Now that Honor's out of the way, you can concentrate on your case."

"This case has so many pieces I'm not sure where to look next. I still haven't heard from Daniel Junior about the building, and I'm very curious."

"Because?"

"Originally Pamela wanted the building for her dress shop, but she couldn't afford it. Suppose someone else wanted it, but Wendall got there first. Wouldn't that someone be angry and want the gallery to fail? Or maybe so angry they'd kill Wendall?"

"Okay, but who? You'd need some serious cash to buy the building. Does Larissa have that kind of money? Does Bea?"

"Flora might."

"Why would Flora want an old store in a small town?"

"I know, I know, I'm grasping at straws. I think—" Bea's gray VW came down the street, pulled over, and parked in front of Deely's. Ferris unfolded himself from the car and came into the diner. We heard him order a burger and fries to go.

"Ask him why his mother has a house full of secret jewelry," Jerry said.

"I think I'll be a bit more subtle."

I sat down at the counter next to Ferris. "Oh, hi, Madeline," he said. "Glad I got to see you before I left town."

"You're heading back to Raleigh?"

"Yeah, Mom needed some wheels while her Honda was in the shop, but now it's fixed. I didn't mind hanging around for a few days, but that's my limit. There's not a lot of room in her house, anyway."

But there was room for me to take advantage of this perfect opening. "I agree, it's pretty full."

His eyebrows went up. "Oh, you've seen inside? How did you manage that? She never wants company."

"No, I found something that belonged to her and was returning it when I caught a glimpse. It looked amazing, though. I'm surprised she doesn't want anyone to see her jewelry."

"Oh, she does shows all over Parkland. Bea's Baubles and Beads. That's a mouthful, isn't it? Guess Celosia's too small and she figures she won't sell enough here." Annie handed him his order. He thanked her and put his money on the counter. "Nice talking to you, Madeline. Don't say anything about the jewelry to anyone. Mom's real touchy about it. Of course, if you know her, you know she's real touchy about everything."

"This business with Wendall Clarke, if you don't mind me asking. Has she always insisted he was your father?"

"It's a recent development." He grinned a wry grin. "She's been having these senior moments for some time now. The fact that Dad—my real dad—lost his money really threw her, you know? I'm perfectly happy with my life, but she's never been content. I'm sorry Clarke's dead, and I hope you figure out who killed him."

Even if it's your mother? I didn't ask.

"Well, so long."

I went back to Jerry and we watched the VW chug away.

"I couldn't hear what you said, but he was definitely checking you out," Jerry said.

"I hate to admit it, but sometimes my looks can work to my advantage." I flashed my best beauty queen expression.

His eyebrows went up in mock surprise. "Sometimes?"

"Back to the case, please. Ferris thinks his mom is sliding toward senility in regards to the father issue. And according to him, Bea has jewelry shows all over Parkland."

"Okay, so she enjoys leading a double life. I can relate."

"I can understand why she wouldn't want to sell her jewelry here, but I still can't understand why she wouldn't want to brag about her success." Another thought occurred to me. "If she's very successful, then she'd have lots of money, which is very important to her." I took out my phone.

"Are you going to call her and ask how much money she makes?"

"No, I'm going to call an expert on all things shiny."

Billamena was home and delighted to hear from me. "When can I expect a visit?"

"Soon, I promise," I said. "But I need your help on a case."

"How exciting!"

"Have you ever heard of Bea's Baubles and Beads?"

Billie gasped. "Oh, my word! Madeline, that's only one of the classiest collections of jewelry in town. You should come to one of her shows. It's fabulous. She makes everything herself, so every piece is one of a kind. I have six or seven of her bracelets on right now."

"So you go to someone's house for a jewelry show, like a Tupperware party?"

"Yes, exactly."

"Would you describe Bea? I want to make sure it's the same person."

"She's a little round woman, and she always dresses in beautiful black dresses to highlight her jewelry. Very classy."

"Is she short-tempered and cranky?"

"She's not the gushy overly friendly type, but I wouldn't say she's cranky. Reserved, perhaps."

Jerry was right. Bea was living a double life. "What about the prices on her jewelry?"

"Toward the high end, but well worth it. The bracelets were around eighty dollars each, as I recall. I've seen your mother at one of the shows, so you know they're expensive little baubles."

My mother never bought anything cheap. Instead of trying to find a bargain, she would search for days to find the highest price on an item she wanted. "Billie, let me know when the next show is going to be."

"Are you on the lookout for some bling? Thinking of winning Mrs. Parkland's crown? It's mine, I tell you, mine!" She gave one of her braying laughs and said she'd call me when she found out about the next show.

I closed my phone. "It's the same Bea, only new and improved. Billie said the bracelets sold for at least eighty dollars."

"So Bea is a lot richer than she looks."

"Why, then, would she be so obsessed about having her dinky little pictures in the gallery?"

"You know how people are. They can have everything in the world except one elusive thing, and that's all they focus on."

Deely called Jerry over to discuss a few more things about the breakfast menu. I sat thinking of all the little pieces in this case and how they were not fitting together. I had Flora, an avowed con woman but convincingly grieving widow. I had Larissa, the wronged ex-wife who was seen leaving the scene of the crime. Then there was Bea with her mysterious jewelry career and a yard full of dangerous bricks. And I couldn't completely rule out

Pamela and her gold button. After all, she had ties to Big Mike and his shady world.

But I couldn't figure out a motive for Pamela. She was happy to have her artwork in the gallery. She had no reason to want Wendall dead. Unless, like Bea, Pamela was living a second life as a criminal mastermind.

I just didn't know.

Chapter Twenty-one

I also didn't know if I was pregnant, so Monday morning, while Jerry was downstairs making breakfast, I called the doctor's office and made an appointment.

"We can see you this morning," the secretary said. "How about eleven-thirty?"

I was surprised until I remembered this was Celosia, not Parkland, and getting a doctor's appointment was not as difficult. "That sounds fine, thank you." I hung up. Good, I thought. That's it. No more putting this off. Find out today and deal with it. Then my phone rang. It was Billie.

"Madeline, you lucky thing. There's a Baubles and Beads party today on Burberry Lane in Ash Grove. Let's go."

"Perfect," I said. "What time?"

"It's at noon. It's a luncheon party type thing. Does that work for you?"

Noon. Well, of course it would be at noon today. "Yes, that works. See you there." Hmm, so much for putting things off. I called and cancelled the doctor's appointment, feeling a little sense of relief at postponing the baby news once again.

Jerry had eggs over easy and bacon arranged artistically on one of our best plates, which he handed to me.

I sat down and took a napkin from the holder. "Getting an early start on the weekend?"

"You know, I'm really excited about it. Thanks for mentioning it to Deely."

"You need to share your talent with the world."

He fixed his plate and sat down. "Are we continuing the letter hunt today?"

"Maybe for a little while this morning. Billie called to let me know about a jewelry show at noon."

"Are you going in disguise?"

"I may wait until things are going and then slip in unannounced. I want to see Bea in action."

After breakfast, we drove into town and resumed our letter search, but once again the mind-numbing amount of paper defeated us. Around ten-thirty, I took Jerry home and arrived at Billie's a little early so we could visit.

She met me at the door. Her whole outfit glittered from her rhinestone headband to her bedazzled shoes. "I'm so excited to be part of your sting operation. How are we going to play this?"

"We aren't going to con anyone, Billie. I just need a look at Bea."

"You can see her any time you want in Celosia, can't you?"

"Yes, but I have reason to believe this is a different Bea." We sat down in her living room, and I explained what I'd learned so far. "Jerry and I saw her jewelry collection, but no one else in town has any idea she makes such fabulous creations. I want to know why."

"So do you want me to pretend to be a buyer from New York, or maybe a Hollywood producer who wants to do a story on her and her humble beginnings?"

"No, I'm going to ask her."

"That's no fun."

"You can pretend to be someone else if you like. That's what Bea is doing."

It was indeed a different Bea, a very different Bea, the classy refined version, all in black, with severe makeup and her hair slicked back. The jewelry had been amazing in her dark upstairs room. Here in the host's living room on a long table covered with black velvet it was a dazzling fireworks display of shapes and colors. I recognized the yellow spikes and the frosty chunks of glass, the red pendant Jerry had admired, and the green and coral bracelet. Among the other pieces were silver necklaces as elaborate as spider webs, bronze pieces studded with turquoise, and pearls caught in little silver baskets and strung on long silver chains.

Bea saw me and stiffened. "What are you doing here?"

"A friend invited me. These are wonderful, Bea. I didn't know you made jewelry."

"Thank you. And I'll thank you not to say anything to anyone in Celosia."

"Why not? There are some necklaces here that could be framed and hung in the gallery."

"Certainly not! This is a business, nothing more. I have my own separate artwork, as you well know."

So she was truly blind to her jewelry's artistic worth. "I won't say anything, but I'm curious why you don't want people to know. It's gorgeous stuff. Don't you think they'll like it?"

"Of course they'll like it. But I'm not ready to show it to them."

This seemed odd, but maybe she was planning a big jewelry show to impress everyone. Another woman called her away, so I wandered the room, admiring the jewelry and catching bits and pieces of conversation. Most of the women were trying on the necklaces and bracelets and checking themselves out in the little mirrors Bea had provided. I heard a lot of "That looks fabulous on you," and "You have to buy that." Then one woman asked, "Bea, when are you going to open a store in Parkland? You'd have no end of customers."

"I'm looking for the right place," she said.

"Didn't you check with Olympia Mall?"

"The rent there is too high. I'm happy with my house parties right now."

It was indeed a party. The hostess had a wonderful array of little sandwiches, fruit pizzas, and tiny cupcakes of all flavors. Billie filled her plate. "Isn't this great? Dinner and a show. I'm getting that coral bracelet, I don't care how much it is."

"The green one? That is spectacular."

We took our food to one side of the room where chairs had been set up along the wall. Billie balanced her plate in her lap. "What are you going to buy? I saw you eying that red and silver pendant."

"It's gorgeous, but I'm here on a mission."

"Learn anything mysterious?"

"I'm really surprised by Bea's appearance. You should see her in Celosia. She looks like a little old farm woman who's been working in the fields all day."

Billie indicated her sequined top with its display of bedazzled butterflies and flowers. "Some people prefer to be casual at home. Not me, as you can tell."

"Yes, but this is a drastic difference, almost as if she's two different people: cranky garden gnome and sophisticated socialite."

"Maybe she thinks people wouldn't take her seriously as a jewelry designer if she showed up in her overalls and boots."

"I'm not so sure. When I was more involved with my art, I met a lot of artists who dressed oddly, but their work was so creative and amazing, no one cared what they looked like."

I watched as Bea talked with the other women, showing them how some of the pieces should be worn, and helping with clasps. Occasionally, she shot me a suspicious look, which I returned calmly. I didn't mind keeping her secret, but I was determined to find out why it was so important.

"I meant to ask you if the police ever caught that Perkins woman," Billie said.

"I think she got away. But she won't bother you again."

"She'd better not. Can you imagine having that much nerve? How did Jerry know her?"

"An old friend from Con School."

"Does he have a lot of those?"

"More than I like. This one in particular wanted him back for more reasons than just to play tricks together."

"Uh, oh."

"Jerry didn't see that, of course."

Billie's laugh made everyone in the room pause for a moment. "Of course! It took him years to figure out he was in love with you." She lowered her voice. "This Perkins woman isn't going to be a pest about it, is she?"

"You'll never believe how I finally got her to back off."

"You told her you'd beat her to death with your tiara?"

"I told her I was pregnant."

Billie almost dropped her plate. "Are you?"

"If I could ever get this case solved, I'm going to find out."

"Are you excited?"

I'd forgotten that I hadn't seen Billie in a while, and she didn't know all the particulars. "When I was married to Bill, that's all he talked about. I began to realize that was the only reason he'd married me. He wanted a lot of children so he could brag about his masculinity. You can imagine how that turned me off. And there were other reasons the marriage didn't work."

"But Jerry wants children?"

"Yes, but he doesn't push me. Well, he does, sort of, but in a light-hearted way, and I've come around to the idea. He wouldn't be like Bill, leaving me to take care of everything. He'd really be involved every step of the way. You should see him with the neighborhood kids."

"Well, good luck, Madeline. You must call me the second you know."

The jewelry party was still going strong, and the hostess indicated that everyone could stay as long as they liked, but Billie and I left around two. She'd spent all her money, and I wanted to get home.

I thought about stopping by the doctor's to see if they could work me in, but changed my mind. It was as I'd told Billie. I needed to solve this case first.

Chapter Twenty-Two

Jerry met me on the porch, offering a bowl full of pretzels. I waved it away. "Thanks, but I'm full of party food."

"Was Bea happy to see you?"

"Not at all." I sat down in one of rocking chairs, and Jerry perched on the porch railing. "I should have taken a picture of her. You would be amazed. She looked extremely wealthy and put together. I'll bet she sold over a thousand dollars' worth of her jewelry, and the party wasn't over yet."

Jerry ate a pretzel and tossed another over the rail to a waiting squirrel. "Any clue as to why she keeps her stuff hidden away?"

"I'm sworn to secrecy. She told me she wasn't ready to show her jewelry to people here. I kind of sympathize. I don't like showing my artwork until I'm satisfied with it. How was your day?"

"I've been on the phone with Deely. I think he's as excited as I am. I called Fred, too, to see if he had a car we could afford. He said to check with Reliant Motors in town. You want to go car shopping?"

"We really ought to find that letter."

"I know. I'm trying to put off digging through all that paper."

"It's a pain, but if it will reveal any sort of clue, then I'm willing to shovel through the rest of it."

The squirrel bravely poked its head over the edge of the porch. Jerry gave it another pretzel. "Have you noticed we're always rooting through heaps of stuff? We hunted all through Tori's attic for that key Nathan needed for his inheritance."

"The glamorous life of a private eye." I pushed myself out of the chair. "Let's do it."

◇◇◇

As we pulled open yet another file drawer and tackled yet another stack, Jerry amused himself by singing selections from *Oklahoma* interspersed with bits of *The Ballad of Baby Doe*. Baby Doe made me think of Flora. Once the mystery was solved, she'd be on her way to Palm Beach. Maybe Wendall had left enough money so she wouldn't have to play any more marriage games. Maybe she set this whole thing up so she could live in Palm Beach. Or maybe Pamela was fooling us. Maybe she'd been Big Mike's girlfriend long enough to learn a few tricks. But neither one of these scenarios really worked.

I pulled a piece of paper from the next stack, looked at it, blinked, and looked again. The letterhead read: Daniel Richards and Co. Finally! "Jerry, I think this is it."

He came over to read the letter with me. The letter was addressed to Pamela Finch and stated that she was permitted to make whatever changes necessary to Building 2619, also known as the Flair For Fashion Dress Shop. It was signed by Daniel Richards, witnessed, and notarized.

"Okay," Jerry said. "Pamela can fix her shop. Drinks all around."

"Wait a minute." The next piece of paper was torn, many of the words faded and difficult to read, but I could see Daniel Richards and Co. at the top, along with a name that jumped out. "Jerry, this is addressed to 'Dear Mrs. Ricter.'"

"Can you tell what it says?"

I brought the letter over to better light provided by the desk lamp. "Something about purchasing a building. 'Regret to inform you that another buyer,' then something about other property available. That's Bea's name, though, and the number 2604. What would you like to bet Building 2604 is the gallery?"

"Bea wanted to buy it?"

"And Wendall beat her to it."

"Hello, motive."

I took out my cell phone and found Richards' number. "Daniel Junior was going to look through his records for me. Maybe he can double check this."

"Sorry to have taken so long," Richards said when I reached him, "but I had to search through several of our lists. Our records show a Mrs. Bea Ricter put in an offer on the building, but Wendall Clarke got his offer in first."

"Building 2604, the former Arrow Insurance building?"

"Yes."

"Would your father have sent her a letter informing her of this?"

"I'm sure he did. I have a copy right here."

And I had Bea's copy. I had one more loose end to tie up. "Mr. Richards, do your records show that Pamela Finch put in a bid for Building 2604?"

"No, she did not."

"Thanks." I hung up. "Pamela's in the clear, but Bea wanted the building, all right, and I'll bet you anything she wanted it for a jewelry store."

"But didn't you find out she didn't want to sell her stuff in Celosia?"

"I heard her tell someone at the party that the rent at the Olympia Mall was too high. I'm guessing that rent anywhere in Parkland wasn't going to suit her, but here in Celosia, she could have a large building of her own, a big flashy jewelry store, the kind of gesture that thumbs her nose at the entire town. Only Wendall bought it first."

"What's her letter doing in with all of Pamela's papers?"

"Pamela told me there might be some Art Guild paperwork in all this. Bea used to be secretary for the Art Guild and sent all the papers to Pamela. I'll bet that letter got mixed in with the Art Guild files."

"What now?"

I folded Bea's letter into my pocket. "We'll give Pamela the letter she's been looking for and just keep quiet about Bea's. I want to see what Bea says about it."

Pamela was so thrilled we had found her letter, I was forgiven for suspecting her of murder. Jerry and I drove to Bea's house. The dark blue Honda wasn't in the drive, but just to make sure, we got out and went to her door. She wasn't home.

Jerry got a good look at Bea's front yard. "Are these the famous bricks? She's got enough to bean everyone in town."

"Yes, I'm pretty sure there's one missing from around that bush." I took a closer look. "In fact, there are a couple missing. I wonder what she's planning to smash now?"

"You can ask her. She'll be at rehearsal tonight. We're blocking 'The Farmer and the Cowman,' and Aunt Eller has a part in that song."

I frowned. "What I can't figure is where she was hiding Wednesday night. Pamela was in the gallery office, Larissa was in the main gallery. Where was Bea?"

"In the ceiling, listening through the air conditioner vent?"

"That's where you would be, but I seriously doubt she could climb up into the vent. Let's have a look in the gallery."

◇◇◇

The police had put a lock on the gallery's back door, but Jerry was able to undo it. The minute we walked in, I knew what I'd overlooked. "Jerry, I forgot about the children's room."

"There's a children's room?"

"Yes, Bea asked Wendall about it, and he assured her there was a special room in the back for the kids."

We walked down a short hallway to a small room complete with work tables and child-sized chairs and easels. There was also a large empty closet for supplies. "This is it. This is where she could've been hiding. She would've known Larissa destroyed her artwork. She would've been furious with her, maybe even angry enough to frame Larissa for murder."

"How did Bea know Wendall was coming to the gallery that night?" Jerry asked.

"Pamela was here, too. She saw Larissa smash Bea's pictures and called Wendall to tell him. Bea could've overheard her."

"Pamela, Larissa, Bea—the whole town was here." Jerry shut the closet door. "Did you ever hear Bea confront Wendall about buying the building? I mean, she had to know he was the other buyer. Everyone knew."

I thought of all the times I'd heard Bea talking with Wendall and recalled there had been an altercation at his reception. "At the reception she said, 'You should be ashamed of yourself.' At the time, I assumed she was referring to his marriage to Flora. And Wendall said, 'No hard feelings.'"

"No hard feelings, I got your building, makes sense."

"Bea said something about how Wendall was going to be sorry. I wasn't sure exactly what she meant, but she may have decided the only way to get the building was to get him out of the way."

"Didn't she want her work in the gallery?"

"I think she wanted the building more. After all, if she had the building, she could display her artwork along with the jewelry."

"So, she's mad at Wendall for stealing away her building, and she's mad at Larissa for ripping up her pictures, so she kills Wendall and hopes to pin the murder on Larissa because everyone in town knows how much Larissa hates Wendall. Pretty slick. But exactly how did she do it?"

"With any luck, that's what I'm going to find out tonight."

"The Farmer and the Cowman" song included just about the entire cast. Everyone assembled on stage to go through the song before Evan blocked the scene. I sat in the orchestra pit with Jerry and two musicians who had decided to play for the rehearsal. Technically, the other members of the orchestra didn't have to be there until a week or two before the show opened, but sometimes they liked to get a head start. I recognized the drummer from *The Music Man*, and the clarinet player was a woman from the garden club.

Evan called for attention. "I'd like everyone to sing the song twice, and then I'll show you your places. We'll work the dance later."

While the actors were singing, I looked for Bea. I didn't have the best angle from the pit, so I stood up in one corner. There she was, singing along as if she hadn't a care in the world. Maybe she didn't. After the singing and the blocking, Evan told everyone to take a short break while he worked with the dancers. Bea headed for the side door.

"Be right back," I told Jerry and hurried out of the pit.

I almost missed her. Bea had already gotten into her Honda and zoomed out of the theater parking lot. I hopped into the Mazda and followed her. To my surprise, she headed toward the gallery. She parked in the back parking lot. I went around the block and parked on the street. Then I cautiously made my way to the gallery's back door. It was open. I went inside and slipped into the children's room. I could hear Bea in the main gallery. She was talking on her cell phone.

"I'm at the gallery. Yes, I'll meet you here. Around back. It's unlocked."

I stepped behind the door as she came down the hall. I could see her waiting by the door. She turned off her phone and took something out of her purse. Not a piece of wood, but another brick.

Someone was going to get a nasty surprise.

I looked around the room for a weapon. One of the little easels was my best choice. I folded it and waited. I didn't have to wait long. From the back windows I could see Larissa coming up to the back door. I knew Bea planned to barrel out and hit her with the brick. Before Larissa had her hand on the door, I stepped out into the hall behind Bea, swung the easel like a baseball bat, and clipped her in the knees. She yowled and fell. The brick landed with a clunk. At the same time, Larissa opened the door and jumped back, startled.

"Bea! What happened? What's going on?"

Bea started up, but I pointed the easel like a sword. "Stay right there."

Larissa took in the scene, confused. "Madeline what is all this? Bea told me to come. She said she knew who had killed Wendall."

"She knows who killed Wendall because she did, and she planned to do the same to you."

Bea growled and attempted to get up. "You're crazy!"

I poked her in the chest with the easel to keep her on the floor. "Then explain the brick."

She tried to push the easel aside. "What do you want?"

"I think it's more a case of what you want. Let's start with Building 2604."

"What do you know about that?"

"I know you wanted it. I know you put in an offer, and Wendall Clarke beat you to it. I know you were here Wednesday night when Larissa destroyed your pictures. You overheard Pamela call Wendall, so all you had to do was wait for him here. You took him by surprise, and when he was down, you hit him on the head."

Larissa stared at her. "My God, Bea! I never knew you hated Wendall so much."

Bea transferred her angry glare to Larissa. "Not as much as I hated you. How dare you destroy my pictures? You know nothing about art, nothing!"

Oh, there was so much more to it than that, I thought, as Larissa sputtered for a reply. "Larissa," I said, "Bea didn't hate Wendall. She loved him, didn't you, Bea? Wasn't he your first real love in high school? When you married someone else and then found out you were pregnant, you really hoped it was Wendall's child, didn't you? That's what you really wanted."

Bea could hardly contain herself. "Ferris is his son!"

"As much as you want that to be true, I don't think it is. And when Wendall refused to acknowledge Ferris and then bought the building out from under you, you felt doubly betrayed."

Her voice shook with emotion. "Well, of course I did!"

Larissa looked as if she couldn't believe what she was hearing. "Wendall betrayed me, too, Bea, but I never would've killed him. You're insane."

"Oh, listen to you, Miss High and Mighty Captain of the soccer team! I was just as good as you were!"

I'd heard enough of this. "No more high school! Larissa, do me a favor and call the police."

I expected Bea to put up a fight, but she stayed seated on the floor, scowling, until Chief Brenner and another officer arrived. I told the chief what I'd found out. Bea didn't say anything until the officer hauled her up. Then she said, "I want my lawyer."

Larissa watched as Bea was escorted out and into a squad car. "She was going to kill me. That's why she said to come alone."

"I think she planned to knock you over, just like she did Wendall, hit you with the brick, and then hurry back to the theater. The whole cast is there tonight. It would be easy to slip back in and have everyone think she was there the whole time."

For a long moment, Larissa said nothing. Her mouth trembled as if she were holding back her emotions. "Thank you, Madeline."

"You're welcome."

"My apologies if I said anything ugly about you or your husband. If there's anything I can do to make it up to you."

"Well," I said, "maybe you can be a little less critical about other peoples' artwork in the future."

Chapter Twenty-three

When I returned to the orchestra pit, Jerry and the others were playing "The Farmer and the Cowman" for the dancers. He lifted his eyebrows inquiringly, and I gave him an okay sign. He had to wait until the end of the number to ask what had happened.

I leaned over the edge of the orchestra pit to give him the short version. "Bea tried to kill Larissa, but I struck first. Tell you all about it when we get home."

Jerry couldn't wait until we got home. As soon as rehearsal was over and we were in the car, he wanted to hear the whole story.

When I'd finished, he said, "So the main problem Bea had with Larissa was Larissa ripping up her art."

"I think that's what sent Bea over the edge. I have to say I sympathize. I know how I'd feel if someone ripped up *Blue Moon Garden*."

"Yeah, but you wouldn't take revenge in such a roundabout way, would you? Why didn't Bea go after Larissa first?"

"She was still angry with Wendall for stealing her building and for not being the father of Ferris. She saw a way to get rid of both of them, and when setting Larissa up for Wendall's murder didn't work, she went to plan B."

"But all that great jewelry. If it was selling well, she could soon afford any building she wanted."

"But she wanted building 2064. Nothing else was going to suit her."

As I drove up the drive, our house looked inviting in the deep October twilight, porch lights gleaming. A breeze sent stray leaves dancing across the yard. Far off in the woods, owls hooted, practicing for Halloween, and two little bats fluttered erratically in the purple sky.

Jerry pointed to them. "Look. Uncle Val's pets."

"As long as they stay up there. The attic's off limits." Now's the time, I told myself. "Let's sit outside for a while."

We went up on the porch, and Jerry pulled his rocking chair over so he could sit close. "I was thinking. You know, we need another car, and Bea's not going to be using that blue Honda—"

I didn't know whether to laugh or not. "Jerry."

"She can't drive it if she's in jail, and her son's got his VW. Why should the Honda sit in the driveway? I can keep it in good running order until she gets out in...what...never?"

"I think we'd have to ask Ferris about that."

"And what about all that jewelry? I know how to get into the house."

"Please tell me you're kidding."

"I'm kidding. I have a real job now."

"For which I am grateful." We rocked for a few moments until I thought of something. "There are a couple of things still up in the air about this case."

"Such as?"

"It really bugs me that Honor got to keep a pink sapphire that she does not deserve."

Jerry laughed. "Oh, that."

"What?"

"It's a fake. I can't wait till she tries to pawn it."

"A fake? How do you know?"

"Big Mike told me. She doesn't get a reward for all that bad behavior."

"Well, good."

"What's the other thing?"

I leaned forward so I could look him straight in the eye. "The night of Honor's séance, I know you were Aunt Gloria. How did you do it?"

He had on his neutral face. "A good con man never reveals his secrets."

"But you aren't a con man, anymore."

"I'm still a man of mystery."

I sat back. "You're not going to tell me, are you?"

He looked pleased with himself. "Nope. Was Honor really scared?"

"Yes. You win. And here's your prize. You and I have something very important we need to do."

"Which is?"

"We need to decide on a name for our baby."

This took him so completely by surprise he just looked at me as if trying to process what I'd said. When it finally sunk in, he stammered, "But you're not—you told me you weren't—are you pregnant or not?"

"I'm not," I said. "But I could be."

He grabbed me and gave me a long, satisfying kiss. Then he and I spent the rest of the evening trying to make it happen.

Pamela called the next morning. She was all aflutter, having heard the news of Bea's arrest.

"I simply could not believe it! I mean, I couldn't even believe she broke the gallery window, much less murdered Wendall! She must be crazier than anyone thought. And to think she was hiding in the gallery at the same time I was there! I might have been next!"

I really didn't think Pamela had ever been on Bea's hit list, but I didn't say so. "I hope that's the last of the gallery's problems."

"Oh, it is! You haven't heard the news. Flora Clarke has graciously offered to sell the gallery to the Art Guild. That's the main reason I called. We really want it to work. Would you consider helping us?"

"I'll do what I can." My doorbell rang. "Someone's at the door, Pamela. I'll call you back."

I was surprised to find Flora Clarke at the door.

"I wanted to come thank you in person, Madeline."

She had on her black suit, her makeup perfect but subdued. She could easily play The Widow Game, I thought, if that's what she plans to do. "You're welcome. So you're off to Florida?"

"Yes. There's no need for me to stay around here anymore."

"I hear you plan to sell the gallery to the Art Guild."

"I'll give them a good deal. It seems the right thing to do."

"How about doing another right thing and stop scamming people?"

"I don't know." Her hand went up to tug her curl, but this time she caught herself. "It's hard to give up a life you've always known. But I don't think I'll ever find another man like Wendall. I really loved him. You have to believe me."

"I believe you."

"I appreciate that." She smiled a slight smile. "I'll try to reform."

I believed she had loved Wendall. I wasn't sure I believed she was going to change. Maybe if Wendall hadn't been killed, he could've had a positive influence on her. Then again, if she was also in love with flirting and scheming, he might've been just another conquest.

Or maybe, like so many deluded beauty queens, she thought her self-worth was determined by her looks, that her only talent was being beautiful, and she'd better make the most of it while she could. I wished I could've had this conversation with her. I'd had it with myself many times. I'd conned people, too. With my fake hair and my fake smile, I'd tried my best to convince judges I was the prettiest, because that's all that mattered.

But I wasn't just a pretty face in an overly sequined gown. That wasn't me.

I'd caught Wendall Clarke's murderer. And that mattered a hell of lot more.

Jerry came to the door as Flora drove away. "Baby Flo's left all alone, huh?"

"But not freezing to death. She's heading to Palm Beach."

"I have an idea she'll be okay." He patted my stomach. "So what do you think? Did it take? Do we have a little Hortensia or a little Jackson growing in there?"

I put my hand over his. "Don't get too excited yet. I have to see the doctor."

"Well, sit down and put your feet up just in case."

We sat down on the sofa. Jerry put his arm around me, picked up the remote, and clicked on the CD player. Once again the glorious soprano voice of *The Ballad of Baby Doe* filled the room.

"Last aria," Jerry said. "'Always through the changing.' That's us, Mac."

Always through the changing, I thought. I've untangled another knot of Celosia's never-ending relationships. Jerry may not be completely reformed, but he's severed another tie to his disreputable past and has a new career. Maybe it's time. Maybe I'm really ready to start a family.

I was going to let go and let it happen.

To receive a free catalog of Poisoned Pen Press titles, please contact us in one of the following ways:

Phone: 1-800-421-3976
Facsimile: 1-480-949-1707
Email: info@poisonedpenpress.com
Website: www.poisonedpenpress.com

Poisoned Pen Press
6962 E. First Ave. Ste 103
Scottsdale, AZ 85251